The Last Wish

Amy Iketani

Published by Amy Iketani, 2023.

This is a work of fiction. Similarities to real people, places, or events are entirely coincidental.

THE LAST WISH

First edition. November 19, 2023.

Copyright © 2023 Amy Iketani.

ISBN: 979-8223879558

Written by Amy Iketani.

Also by Amy Iketani

Coming Home
The Last Wish

Watch for more at instagram.com/amyiketaniwrites.

For Mom

You are loved and missed

Chapter 1

Today was not going to be a good day. Russell could already feel it. It was mid May and already hot in Atlanta, Georgia. It seemed to him that they skipped spring this year and went straight into summer. He was used to the heat and humidity, since he was originally from Florida, but not so soon. Russell drove his normal commute downtown and pulled into the parking lot on Peachtree Street.

He grabbed the blueprints from the trunk of his car and went inside. The architectural firm he worked for was on the tenth floor. Russell pulled at the collar of his button down shirt and tie as the elevator ascended. He was already perspiring and hoped his boss wouldn't make it any worse.

Stepping out onto the tenth floor, Russell managed to pour himself a cup of coffee and escape into his office without anyone seeing him, yet. The plaque on his door read: RUSSELL REED. He was an architect here for ten years and was good at his job.

His boss, Stanley Causgrove, owned the firm and they usually got along great. They played golf and tennis together on occasion and their wives socialized at times. Well, the wives don't anymore. Russell was getting settled at this desk when Vonn, his assistant, knocked on his door. Vonn always had a smile for him when he arrived in the morning. Today, though, she had a look of concern.

"Mr. Reed, Mr. Causgrove would like to see you now," said Vonn. "They are waiting in the conference room."

Russell simply nodded. He sipped his coffee and looked at the family portrait that was on his desk. It showed a happy time, many summers ago, of Russ, Lynn and their son, Adam. It was taken at their beach house on Jekyll Island. Before she got sick. Before she died. Russell found himself smiling as he looked at each face. Summers on the island were his best memories and Russell allowed himself to stay in the moment a bit too long.

"Russell!"

It was Stanley yelling from down the hall. Russell nearly spilled his coffee on his clean white shirt, something he didn't need today. He abandoned his coffee and picked up his blueprints. Stanley had already warned him that the client wasn't happy with the proposed changes to the plan that Russell suggested. All F.G. Homes saw was the money they needed to spend to move the location of the amenities of their new luxury apartments.

It was up to Russell to explain that this would actually give them room for another apartment building in the complex. Money spent would equal money earned. He was prepared for his presentation, just didn't appreciate being called out on his day off.

Russell walked into the conference room and greeted the six people already seated at the table. Three men were from F.G. Homes and the other three were Stanley, Vonn and Walter, a team member who usually only rooted for Team Walter. Russell was calm on the outside, but inside he was still anxious about this meeting. Why didn't the blueprints speak for themselves? This seemed like a waste of time to him, but he placed his papers in the middle of the table and began his talk.

He showed the executives from F.G. Homes how rearranging some items would give them more income potential. Russell explained that the original plan was for seven housing units, which would have been fine, but he was the one who discovered room for more. The men talked and nodded, it seemed to Russell that this meeting was taking longer than it should. They talked amongst themselves for several minutes and then looked up at Russell.

The three visitors stood up and smiled. They reached over to shake Russell's hand and congratulate him on his vision. Stanley and Vonn stood and smiled, too. Walter remained unchanged. While everyone walked out of the conference room in happy conversations about the new blueprints, Russell escaped to his office.

He had been confident that they would like the changes and they did. Now if he could just leave and end this day on a high note he would be satisfied, but he knew that wasn't going to happen. When Stanley returned from escorting the visitors to the elevators, he knocked on Russell's door.

"Come in," Russell said.

"Hey Russ," Stanley started. "Now there's the matter of the Barnett building."

Russell already knew where this was going. Stanley had called him last week. The Barnett building was an office building downtown that had gone through several revisions over the past few weeks. It was up to him to satisfy them and he couldn't.

"I'm giving it to Walter," Stanley said.

Russell's head shot up and he looked at Stanley. He couldn't say anything. He had tried and failed. The clients deserved someone who could give then what they wanted.

"You hit it out of the park with the F.G. Homes project, but other than that, you've been batting zero," Stanley said. He loved the Braves and seemed to manage inserting baseball references into every conversation. "I know things haven't been easy for you Russ. We all miss Lynn." Stanley looked over at the family of smiling faces on Russ's desk. "It's been a year. Maybe you need to talk to someone or take some time off."

Russell simply looked from the family portrait to Stanley, who was sitting on the other side of his desk. "I miss her," he finally said.

"I am trying to keep going like normal, like Lynn would want, but it's so hard."

Stanley waited for Russell to say more but he didn't. "I'm not going to pretend I know how you feel because I don't," Stanley said. "I do know that your world was just turned upside down and one year is not enough time to adjust. You're not giving yourself time to grieve."

Russell knew he was right. Stanley was older and wiser. He knew that the longer he tried to ignore the grief, his work would suffer more that it already was. Maybe he could manage some time off, even work from home.

Stanley stood up. "School's almost out. Summer is right around the corner. How old is little Adam now?"

"Seventeen," Russell answered.

"Wow, how time flies!" Stanley replied. "Take the boy to the beach house. I don't think you even stayed last summer. You both need time away to refresh."

Russell felt his eyes start to water but held it back as best he could. "Yes, sir. You might be right," he answered. "But, I still want to work. Send me clients, I can still work from the beach."

Stanley laughed and nodded his head. He agreed to pass on some clients that he thought he could handle. Jobs that he didn't think would require the four hour drive back to Atlanta from Jekyll Island. Stanley stood up, patted Russell's shoulder and wished him well.

Russell was relieved when he was finally left alone in his office. He looked around. He had awards on his walls, awards sitting on his shelves and probably a bonus coming after this morning's meeting. He loved what he did but did it still bring him joy? He knew he was going home to an empty house. Well, Adam was still at home, but he was a junior. One more year and he would be away at college.

Russell just wasn't sure he could keep going on like this. Empty. Russell collected items from his office that he thought he might need over the summer. He never took this much time off before. Every summer they went to the beach house, but Russell could only come for a few days at a time. Usually it was Adam and Lynn who spent the whole summer there.

Russell walked through the firm and announced he was leaving for the summer. Any messages could be forwarded to him there. They all knew he wasn't the same since Lynn died. Her cancer made her sick for years and slowly drained Russ, too. Vonn gave him a hug and she wished him a wonderful summer. Walter even shook his hand and wished him well. Secretly, he was probably glad to be rid of him. Russell wasn't going to worry about that right now. He needed to heal himself and Adam.

As Russ drove south on I-75 towards home, he wasn't actually sure how Adam would react to their going to the beach house this summer. He knew Adam loved his time there, but since Lynn died, they haven't been back. Not staying last summer was hard, it felt unnatural. It wouldn't be the same without Lynn, but Russ hoped that they could make some new memories. At the very least, he hoped that going this summer wouldn't be a huge mistake and cause them major depression until they returned home.

Since Russell wasn't confident whether Adam would love the idea or hate it, he decided to stop and get Adam's favorite meal. He went to Zaxby's and got two chicken tender plates and headed home. Time heals all wounds, isn't that the saying? But how much time? No one talks about how much time it will take for the ache in your heart to go away. When the need to feel them beside you fades. When the prospect of living the rest of your life without love and laughter doesn't seem so bleak and imminent.

Russell pulled into the driveway and parked in the garage. He unloaded his things from his office and put them in his study. He placed the food on the kitchen island and went upstairs to change.

It was still early, Adam wasn't home from school, yet. He only had a few days left of junior year which probably meant he had finals soon.

He put on shorts and a t-shirt and grabbed socks from the drawer. Russell would go for a run. He sat on the bench by the back door and put on his sneakers. He liked running and it would help him clear his head. A few miles would also give him time to prepare for his speech to Adam. Russell hoped his most important client would be agreeable to his blueprint for their summer. He really hoped that they wouldn't argue about this. Russell knew Adam had football camp, but that wasn't until later in the summer. They could come back for that.

The summer was really in Adam's hands. Neither one of them even wanted to stay last year. Lynn died on June first, so it was really a miracle they even got through the summer. One day had rolled into the next until. All of a sudden, it was time for school again. Russell had been pretty hands off when it came to Adam and school. He passed, that's all he cared about. He also knew that senior year would be different. Russ would have to pay more attention and keep on him if he was to get into college, especially with a football scholarship. He promised himself that he wouldn't let Adam down, or Lynn.

This was their summer to reconnect and focus on their future. Adam never took his dad up on his offers of listening or talking if he needed it. Russell would have to create time to listen and talk this summer. Adam needed him. They needed each other.

Chapter 2

Adam Reed was very thankful that the end of his junior year was right around the corner. He knew his grades had slipped. How was he expected to stay on the honor roll when he just buried his mother? Adam dreaded going to school each day and also dreaded going home. There was no safe place anymore. His best friends, Carter and Nathan, even treated him differently. He thought he was acting normal, but maybe he wasn't the best judge of normal. He had just watched his mother fade away the last several years.

School came easy to Adam. When he dropped off the honor roll, the school counselor got involved. She checked on him regularly and called his dad. Adam didn't even mind, he knew he needed help. Another classmate, Gail, lost her dad this year. The counselor set up a counseling session for them, thinking that they might want to talk to each other but that didn't help. Adam just didn't want to be reminded of his loss. Even though he knew it was affecting every aspect of his life, he was fooling himself into believing that it wasn't.

Football was different. When Adam was on the field, nothing else even mattered. He was quarterback and loved it. Football was his saving grace and so was his coach. Coach Booker was kept in the loop with his other teachers and the school counselor. Coach did what he could with the time he had Adam on the field. Unfortunately, Adam had to want to help himself. No one else could do the work. He had to pull himself out and want to do it before it was too late. Senior year was coming fast and then college. Coach Booker hoped that Adam would find something to hold onto before the quicksand swallowed him up.

Adam had a girlfriend last year. He and Sherry dated most of sophomore year. Adam was cute, nice, and athletic. Lots of girls wanted to date Adam, but he and Sherry were together until junior year. After that everything changed. Even Sherry couldn't get close to him. She had hoped he would ask her to the homecoming dance and when he didn't, she knew there would be no prom. Prom was the furthest thing from Adam's mind.

Adam hated feeling like this. He knew he was pushing people away, people who loved him and cared about him. It was just hard to think about algebra, The Scarlet Letter, French, or a tuxedo. His mom was gone, dead. He was going home to a dad who was a workaholic. There were no more fresh baked cookies, a warm hug or someone to watch a late movie with. Adam never talked about his mom and neither did his dad. Maybe that's what he missed. The fact that she was here one day and gone the next left Adam always searching.

It was during Algebra that Adam had a meltdown. He realized he did the wrong homework. He tried to explain to the teacher that at least he did homework. He apologized for not having done the work, but she wasn't going to accept his homework. Adam walked back to his desk, slammed his book closed, grabbed his backpack and walked out the door. He walked down the hallway and out the main entrance. He knew the news of this act of rebellion would quickly get back to his dad, but he didn't care. At this moment, Adam didn't care about anything.

He realized how freeing that was to say to himself. He didn't care about anything. Adam went to his jeep and drove out of the parking lot. He didn't have a destination. He took I-75 south and just drove. When he saw Indian Springs Park, he pulled over. He used to come here all the time with his mom. He pulled into the parking lot and turned off the engine.

Adam didn't even realize he was crying until he looked up and his vision was blurred. He wiped his eyes on his shirt and got out of the jeep. We walked over to the rippling water that trickled down the rocks and took his shoes off. He sat on the edge and put his feet in the water. Adam cried for the little boy who had no idea how cruel his future would be to him.

Adam was glad it was Friday. Next week were finals and then they were done. He wasn't sure what that meant for their summer, exactly. Last year they didn't stay at the beach house after his mom died. That was okay with him, but it felt strange and wrong. Maybe he should talk to his dad about trying to go out to Jekyll Island this summer, even if only for a month or so. Adam missed it. He loved the beach house and maybe he would feel closer to his mom. Lynn loved the beach house. She had been coming there ever since her parents bought it when she was a baby. Lynn was happy to be bringing her own son there, too. It was tradition.

Adam was enjoying his time outside. He was walking from rock to rock as the water rushed past his feet. He nearly lost his footing when his phone rang and startled him.

"Hi Carter," Adam said.

"Hey man, you left school?" Carter asked.

"Yes, I had to get out of there."

"Everything okay?"

"I'm fine. Just went for a drive," Adam replied.

"Well, I'm having a party this weekend. Are you coming?" Carter asked.

Adam hesitated. He usually avoided parties that required interaction with large groups of people. Maybe this is what he needed. "Sure, I'll be there," Adam finally replied. He hoped he was making the right decision.

"Hey, great! See you tomorrow night!" Carter said, then hung up.

Adam knew the kind of parties Carter threw. It would be massive. Their friendship went back to elementary school when he, Carter and Nathan were inseparable. They did everything together and their parents knew each other. Those were the days of carefree laughter and hanging out at the mall. Now, they were all hoping for a football scholarship. Nathan's backup plan was the Marines. Carter would go to work in his dad's car dealership. Adam didn't have one.

His phone rang again. This time it was his dad. Adam let it go to voicemail. He had a good idea what the call would be about. He never walked out of school before. He was a rule follower, something his mother instilled in him. Adam didn't drink, either. He thought it was stupid to get so wasted and then do things you wouldn't normally do and then regret them. He would rather skip that whole step and just avoid the temptation. He still went to parties, he was usually the designated driver. His dad knew this about him and that helped build a solid foundation of trust with Adam.

Adam thought about his dad and wondered if he would be open to going to the beach house this summer. Yes, there were pros and cons to going, it would be very emotional, but it has also been sitting for two years. There would be things they needed to do to maintain it and it might be good to focus on something else for a change. He tried formulating his speech in his head.

Adam remembered the Covingtons who lived next door. They had a son, Trey, who was his age. They would play outside from sunrise to sunset. Some of his best memories out on Jekyll Island involved Trey. His little sister, Mandy, was such a brat. She always wanted to tag along, but they were doing boy things, no girls allowed. The neighbor on the other side of their house was old Mrs. Fern Davidson. Her husband, Gene, died a few years before Adam's mother.

When Adam was little, Mrs. Davidson was hard for him to say, so his mom let him call her Mrs. Fern, so that stuck. Even after all these years, Adam calls her Mrs. Fern. He always thought it was funny that she had hanging ferns all around her front porch and back porch. In his little boy brain he figured she was supposed to choose ferns over any other plant.

The beach house was magic. Lynn made sure of it. It was usually just Adam and his mother most of the summer. His dad would come and go for work. That was okay with them. They always got up for the sunrise. Lynn would make breakfast after they walked on the beach. Adam didn't mind getting up early at the beach house because he knew each day would be worth it. His mom made the effort, even the years when she was sick. Even when she didn't want to go in the water, she would sit on the back porch swing and watch Adam. He loved waving to her from the ocean and seeing her wave back. That was his safety net. And it was gone.

Adam remembered conversations on that porch swing with his mom. They would watch the waves and she would talk about traveling the world. He knew she had been to Paris, but he couldn't recall where else she had visited. Lynn had talked about places she hadn't been to, yet, but planned to go to someday. Places that had interesting cultures, food, clothes or music. Young Adam had tried to picture those places she described but probably never got them right.

"Someday, mom," Adam said out loud.

Adam realized that he was recalling memories of his mother and he wasn't feeling sad. It actually felt good to remember her, especially sitting here with his feet in the water at Indian Springs Park. They shared the same brown hair and brown eyes. People used to say they looked alike, but Adam knew he looked just like his dad. It wasn't a bad thing to look like his dad, he just secretly wished he looked like his mother. Her smile was so warm and welcoming. You couldn't help but love Lynn.

Adam looked at the time and knew he had been there long enough. By the time he drove back home, his dad would probably already be there. He decided to walk on the rocks one more time before going back. He wanted to walk up the slight incline to where the water flattens out. Adam watched his feet and was careful about where he stepped, but not careful enough. His right foot was no match for the green algae on the rock and he fell on his side. His right arm braced his fall, so he didn't get hurt, just wet. After the initial shock of falling wore off, Adam started laughing. The laughing slowly turned to tears. In Adam's memories, his mother was always by his side to catch him, not anymore.

After carefully standing up and getting his footing, Adam walked back to his jeep. His shorts would dry, his tears may not. He was broken and he wasn't sure how to fix it. This wasn't it. Would the beach house fix his broken heart? It was worth a try. After laying his forehead on the steering wheel, he got up the courage to head home.

His dad had left another voicemail. Adam never listened to them, he would wait to hear it all in person. His dad was very predictable. Adam knew he would be mad and wasn't going to keep taking his mother's death as an excuse to throw his life away. It was always words to those effect every time he got a call from school. Adam tried, he really did. His mind kept going to the big picture or the grand scheme of things and homework and prom didn't fit into those. His mother was gone and not coming back. That was never on any test question or in his text book.

The thirty minute drive home gave Adam time to calm down. He wasn't going to go in and argue. This would take finesse and strategy. He needed to get his workaholic father to go to the beach for the summer. Adam pulled into his driveway and put his face in his hands.

"Mom, help me, please!" Adam said inside his car. After a few deep breaths, he walked in the side door. He put his backpack on a chair at the kitchen island and pulled out another to sit on. His dad was drinking a beer and tapping at the keys on his laptop.

Russell looked up at his son and wasn't sure where to start. "We need to talk," Russell said.

"I know," Adam said.

"The school called me."

"I know."

Russell paused. The look on his son's face made him change course. "How would you like to spend the summer at the beach house on Jekyll Island?"

Chapter 3

Adam looked at his father. Surely he had heard him wrong. Adam had this whole speech prepared about why they should go to the beach house this summer. During his drive home, he had worked out points and counter points to any objection his dad could have come up with. What Adam didn't prepare for was his father suggesting it first. Adam was at a loss for words.

"Well, do you like the idea?" Russell asked. "I know it might be hard, but it may be just what we need. We didn't stay last year, so I know there's going to be plenty of things for us to do to keep our hands and minds busy."

Adam considered bringing up the whole walking out of school thing, the party, or the counselor, but in the end he simply said, "Yes."

"Great," Russell said, visibly relieved that he didn't have to push too hard at all. He finished his beer, closed his laptop and went over and patted his son on the shoulder. "I think we'll have a great summer." Russell disappeared upstairs leaving Adam alone in the kitchen.

Adam still wasn't sure how to process what just happened, but felt happy to be going to Jekyll this summer. He hadn't had much to look forward to before, at least nothing that mattered to him. He would get to see Trey soon, and Mrs. Fern. Adam allowed himself to smile, there was hope and that was enough for now.

Upstairs, Russell called his younger brother, Ted. Ted was single and still lived in Orlando. Russ wanted to let him know that they would be out at the beach house this summer. Ted didn't often pop in unannounced, but he wanted to let him know just in case. The brothers talked for a little while. They caught up on their parents, jobs and Adam. Ted thought going to the beach would be good for both of them.

Downstairs, Adam called Carter. He explained that he and his dad were going to Jekyll Island for the summer. Carter reminded him about the party tomorrow and said it would be epic.

"You say that about every party, Car," Adam said.

"And they are!"Carter replied.

Adam locked the doors and shut off the lights. Upstairs, he paused in front of his dad's door.

"Goodnight, dad."

"Goodnight, son. I'm glad you agreed to go the beach this summer."

Adam half smiled and nodded his head. "Dad, about school today," Adam started.

Russell put his hand up, "No, don't worry about it. I was mad, but I get it. Just focus on your finals and let's get outta here."

Adam felt thankful that there would be no arguing and nodded again. "Thanks, dad," he said and then went to bed.

The next day, they both stayed busy. Russell mowed the yard and trimmed the bushes. He would have someone do it while they were away. He also started making a list of the things he wanted to take to the beach house. He was confident he would need his power tools and paint supplies. Russell kept in touch with the Covingtons who lived next door and would let him know if anything was out of place. The latest update was that the back porch would need some attention when he came next time.

In the attempt at finding the power drill, Russell had managed to pull everything out of the garage and onto the driveway. It looked like they were having a yard sale. Adam came out to the garage to get a bottle of water when he noticed the mess his dad had made.

"I think we need to keep some of that stuff," Adam joked.

"Well, actually I'm finding that most of this is stuff we don't use anymore. Maybe a yard sale is a good idea," Russell said as he straightened up.

"Mom usually just donated it." As soon as Adam said it he looked at his dad. It was not a topic that they usually brought up to each other. He wasn't sure how his dad would react.

"Well, maybe we should," Russell replied.

Unsure of what to say next, they both went back to what they were doing. Russ went through more boxes and shelves. Adam went back to his room and studied. Was this how awkward the summer was going to be? Adam tried to focus. He went over to his bedroom window that faced the front yard. He looked down and could see his father wiping at his eyes with his shirt sleeve. How would they both heal when their words hurt so much?

Even with Adam's occasional snack breaks, he really did study most of the day. He deserved to go to Carter's party tonight. He was confident that he would pass his junior year. He just needed to get his head in the game for senior year. That was where the scrutinizing eyes of the counselor, teachers and his father would be. Hopefully a few football recruiters, too.

Adam's stomach growled at the smell of steak being cooked on the grill. He went downstairs to see his dad bringing the freshly cooked steaks in the kitchen.

"Hungry?" Russell asked.

"Actually, Carter is having a party tonight and I told him I'd go. Kind of an end of year party," Adam said.

"Isn't it a bit early for an end of year party when you still have finals next week?"

"Well, no one said Carter was the sharpest pencil in the case," Adam said with a smile. "Anyway, it has something to do with them going away the following weekend, so it's now or never."

"It's fine. I'll just leave your steak here for when you get home. I'm sure you'll be hungry by then," Russell said.

"Okay, thanks." Adam looked at his father. "Also, thanks, again, for not yelling about the school thing yesterday."

Russell had already started eating his steak. "Son, would it have done any good to yell at you for walking out of school? No, it just would have made things worse. I want to make things better and the only way I see that happening is to get out of here for a while," Russell said. "Also, I took a leave of absence at work."

Adam, who was putting on his hoodie, stopped and looked up at this dad. "You what?"

Russell put down his fork and knife. "I've been struggling the last few months at work. My head hasn't been in it lately. I know F.G. Homes loved my blueprints I did for them but the rest, well, I could have done better."

Adam looked at his father as if he grew a second head. He never expressed any of this to him before. Adam never suspected that his father's work had suffered. He worked so hard everyday. Russell's wife of twenty years was gone, not coming back. Of course it would affect his work.

"I'm sorry, dad," Adam said. "I didn't know. Maybe we should talk about these things with each other more often." He looked down at this feet. "Sometimes I feel so alone."

Russell came over and hugged his son. "Me, too." When Russ released his son he said, "Let's make time to talk more. Remember your mom, more."

Adam nodded. This was a start. In fact, this felt like a life preserver to a drowning man. "Thanks, dad," he said as he left the house. He sat in his jeep for a few minutes to collect his thoughts.

Maybe things were starting to turn around in his life. He was starting to feel hopeful again. Adam started the engine and actually had a half smile on his face. He picked up Nathan on the way to Carter's house. He was now responsible for getting him back home in one piece.

At the party, Adam walked around and then grabbed a soda. Carter had a deejay and enough alcohol to supply the local bars. Adam just shook his head and walked out to the backyard. He watched kids try to swim in the pool yet keep their cups above the water. It was a skill that apparently not everyone possessed.

Nathan came out to sit next to Adam on a lounge chair. "We're seniors now, man!" Nathan said.

"Technically, not yet," Adam replied.

Nathan just looked at him. "Come on, don't be like that Adam. This is the end of the year party!"

Adam stood up, "Just don't forget to show up Monday for finals." Adam left Nathan sitting on the lounge chair. He was very ready to get out of town. Too bad there were still a few days left of school.

There was a group of girls who kept looking over at Adam. They would look, laugh and then turn back around. He knew the girls, especially the one who never looked away, Sherry. Adam just shook his head and went out the front door to sit on the porch. He was sitting on the first step when a girl sat down next to him. He knew instantly it would be Sherry.

"Hi Adam, you don't look like you're having any fun," Sherry said.

"I'm fine," Adam replied. He looked at her bottle of beer and said, "Looks like you are."

Sherry took a sip, "Yes, it's almost over. We will be seniors next week."

"I'm glad," Adam replied. "Junior year sucked."

"I wish you would have talked to me more. You know you can come to me whenever you need someone to talk to," Sherry said.

Adam took a sip of his soda and ran a hand through his hair. He knew he hurt Sherry by not being there, but he was too broken to care. "I'm sorry, about everything."

"I know this last year has been hard for you. I didn't want to make it any harder so I backed away. But I hope you know I still care about you and want to help in any way I can," Sherry said.

"This last year is a blur. I was going through the motions and not caring about anything. Except football. I can be on the field and think only about football. It was my only escape," said Adam.

"I always loved watching you play. I still do," Sherry said.

Adam looked over at Sherry and smiled. It was the first smile she had seen on him in months. She leaned over and kissed him on the lips. It didn't last long and he wasn't expecting it. She wasn't even expecting to do it, but it felt right. It wasn't a passionate kiss like they used to do in his jeep, it was friendly.

"Well, I'd better go see what the girls are up to inside," Sherry said as she stood up and left.

Adam stayed sitting on the step a bit longer. He hated that he had to wait for Nathan in order to go home. Maybe he could convince him that it was later then it really was and time to leave. Adam went inside to find Nathan. He laughed when he found him asleep on the couch. He called to Carter to help carry him to his jeep. Just as they buckled him in to the passenger's seat, he woke up and wondered where they were going next.

"Home!" Adam and Carter said together. They both laughed and gave each other a high five.

"Later, man. Good party," Adam said as he put the jeep into reverse.

"Love ya, man," yelled Carter as they drove down the street.

The last couple of days had Adam's head spinning. Nothing was turning out how he thought it would. Things were actually going better than expected. Now if he could just figure out how to keep the momentum going, he would be fine.

Chapter 4

Finals. The word, itself, was so ominous. Adam was never afraid of tests or finals, but now that he was coming out of his junior year fog, he felt his senses heightened. It was like he was hearing and seeing things for the first time clearly and it was a bit frightening. Adam only had one more to take and he would be done. He would officially be a senior. Now there was another ominous word.

Adam walked into the classroom and took his seat for the last time this year. First row, last seat. Sherry was in the desk next to him. They smiled at each other and cleared their desk. Did she sit there all year? How did Adam not notice before? The junior year fog must have blinded him in ways he will never fully understand. The teacher passed out the final test and everyone got to work.

He stared at the test for a minute and he realized he was struggling with writing his name on the paper. Focus, he told himself. He did. The old Adam who could pass tests without hardly studying was back. For good measure, Adam went over each question and checked his work. Confident in his answers, he picked up his backpack, turned in his test and exited the school for the last time as a junior.

There were some kids meeting up at Chick-fil-a for lunch and he was invited to go along. The football team was going to Waffle House. Adam didn't really feel like hanging out with anyone right now. He drove out of the parking lot with no real destination in mind. It wasn't until a few minutes later he realized he was heading back towards Indian Springs State Park.

Adam went right to the water and walked in. It was cold to his feet and felt good. He sat down on the rocks along the edge but kept his feet in. He pulled out his phone to make a call then hesitated. He looked at the screen and wondered who he would call. He didn't want to talk to any of his friends right now or his dad. It took a second to register that the person he yearned to talk to the most was his mom.

There were so many things he wanted to say to her. He wanted to tell her that he was glad junior year was done, that there was a good chance he would be team captain next year and that Sherry kissed him. He knew it was a pity kiss, but it made him feel normal again. It made him feel again.

Most of all, he wanted to say that he missed her. He missed seeing her at his games, hearing her voice as she talked on the phone, her hugs when he came home from school, her singing him to sleep when he had a bad dream. Mom. He missed her.

Adam knew his dad wanted to leave for Jekyll Island as soon as possible. Maybe even tomorrow or the next day. Adam had to be back home in July for football camp, so they were lucky if they got six weeks at the beach. That was enough. He was excited to see Trey. There were times throughout the years when Adam wished for a brother. He had Trey in the summer and Uncle Teddy when he came up from Orlando, but that was it.

AT HOME, RUSSELL WAS going through his list again to make sure he remembered everything. He was an architect so he like to be precise and exact. They were taking Adam's jeep, since it had more storage space. Plus, how cool was it to drive around the island in a jeep. Usually Russell's responsibilities ended with tools and ocean gear. Lynn's job was the food and bedding. Russ did his best with the grocery shopping. If he forgot anything, they could buy it there.

As for bedding, he didn't even know what size beds they had at the beach house. Again, that was something he would have to play by ear.

Russell had bought Adam some new snorkel gear. He was sure that anything left at the house would be too small now. Adam was fifteen the last time he was there and has grown at least a foot since then. He wondered how big Trey and Amanda would be now.

Russell pulled out his work laptop and decided to get some things done before they left. He checked his emails and followed up on others. He made some calls to Stanley and Vonn to make sure they were all on track to let him work on some things remotely. He appreciated their compromise and hoped it would work. He knew there may be one or two times he might need to come into the office. But that was only if things weren't working out via email. That was acceptable to Russell.

Adam was just pulling into the driveway when his dad was checking the school's parent portal for the final grades.

"Good job, son," Russell said as Adam came into the kitchen. "You managed to finish junior year pretty solid."

Adam came around to look over his dad's shoulder. Yes, his grades were good. Thankfully the fog did not rob him of his academic career. Senior year should be even better.

"Thanks, dad. I'm going to go pack now," Adam said.

"Okay, now that your jeep is back, I'll start loading things in and we can leave tomorrow morning. How does that sound?"

"Sounds good," Adam replied. He went up to his room and laid down on the bed. The day he had been dreading and now suddenly yearned for was here. They were going to the beach house. He didn't know how he would feel when he first walked in, but he was certain it would be emotional. Everything would be where it was left from last time. Mom's things would still be there, too. But not mom.

Adam looked around his room. He didn't plan what he would take to the beach house this summer. He didn't even think he was going until a few days ago. His PS5 and skateboard were a must have. Clothes, swim trunks, toothbrush, no problem. He was packed. He was carrying some things downstairs to go into the jeep when he saw his dad carrying the urn.

"Dad, what are you doing?"

"Your mother wanted her ashes scattered in the ocean at the beach house," Russell replied.

"But," Adam didn't know what to say. The urn was on the mantel for a year, he supposed it would always be there. The idea of coming back to this house and his mother's urn not being there never occurred to him.

"I'm sorry I didn't discuss it with you first. This is what your mom wanted. If you're not okay with it, we can do it another time," Russell said.

"It's okay," Adam said softly as he took his things to the jeep. What was one more shock? He was somewhat comforted by the urn always there. His mom's ashes. Was this ever going to get easier?

"Spaghetti or roasted chicken?" Russell asked when Adam came back inside. "We are cleaning out the refrigerator," he explained.

"Spaghetti," Adam replied.

The whirl of the microwave was the only sound as the two guys passed each other getting silverware, plates and drinks. They both sat down at the kitchen island after their dinners were properly heated. They ate in silence, each in their own thoughts. It was Russell who spoke first.

"Hey, I'm sorry about earlier. I shouldn't have taken down the urn without talking to you about it first. We can keep her here as long as you want," Russell said.

"It's fine. It's whatever," Adam replied.

The clink of forks hitting dishes and glasses being raised and set down on the marble countertop was the only sounds for the rest of the dinner. Adam was starting to feel that knot in his stomach again and stood up to put his dish in the sink. He started to wash the dish and glass with a little too much force and his dad was afraid he would break it and cut himself.

"Just leave it, son. I'll clean up."

Adam simply dropped the sponge and walked back upstairs to his room. He knew he was acting irrational. Why didn't he just tell his father what he really felt? He wanted to talk to someone. He couldn't call Carter or Nathan, they wouldn't understand. There really was only one other person who came to mind.

"Hello, Sherry?"

"Hi Adam. How are you doing?"

Adam could feel the tears coming. "Not so good."

"I'm here, Adam. Just breath," Sherry said.

"We're going to Jekyll tomorrow for most of the summer," Adam said.

"I know you're conflicted about it. But think of it this way, you won't know if it'll help or not until you get there. It just might help to be at the last place your mom was really happy and alive."

Adam grabbed a tissue from his bedside table. He blew his nose.

"Adam, I'm here for you if you ever need to talk. We're friends, remember that."

"Thanks, Sherry, that means a lot. Goodnight."

Adam got up and took a shower. He felt calmer. The tightness was still there, but better. Sherry always had a way of settling your soul. She was a good friend. They tried to be boyfriend and girlfriend, but in the end, he knew he wasn't good enough for her. Today was exhausting. Adam laid down on his bed and turned on tv. He watched the first Marvel movie he landed on. It really didn't matter, though, because he fell asleep ten minutes later.

Russell was finishing up the dishes and cleaning out the fridge. He took a bag of trash out to the street and then started loading up the jeep. He thought about Adam's response tonight. Was he moving too fast with Lynn's ashes? It had only been one year. He didn't want to upset Adam, but he also didn't know if they were going to keep going to the beach house. If this went badly and both of them wanted to come back, there wouldn't be another opportunity to spread her ashes like she wanted to. He would take them and decide later. They could always bring them back.

Russell rolled his eyes as Adam loaded in the PS5. He doubted Adam would be spending much time inside playing video games, but he didn't want another argument. He packed it in and would say nothing. He made sure all of the tools and water toys were put in first. The food went in next. Russell made space for his work bags and then their personal bags. He closed the doors and locked the jeep.

Inside, Russ made sure things were cleaned up and put away. The goal was to stay for about six weeks. Adam had to be back for football camp in the middle of July. He prayed they could handle six weeks at the beach house. It would be emotional. It was where Lynn was happiest. It was where Lynn died. The one year anniversary is next week.

Russell was eager to see their neighbor, Fern. She lost her husband a few years ago and it will be nice to get some advice from her. Russ would be looking for any wisdom he could get. He tried not to burden Adam with his own struggles and sadness. He thought he was protecting his son from the grief he was experiencing, but maybe he was making it worse. Maybe if they both vocalized their grief, they could get through it together. He promised to work on it this summer.

"Lynn, we're going to need your help," Russell said out loud before returning into the house for the night.

Chapter 5

"Wake up!" Russell yelled.

Adam was awake. He just didn't want to get out of bed. Leaving the comfort of his bed was venturing out into the unknown. Adam was never afraid of trying new things. It was just that usually there was no threat of ripping his heart out. Here, now, this house was safe. The beach house was the unknown, at least this year it was.

"I'm up!" Adam yelled downstairs. He sat at the edge of his bed. He thought about what Sherry had said to him, that it might just help him. Then he thought about what his Coach had said before their playoff game.

"I know you might be scared," Coach Booker had said. "But so are they! You've trained for this. You know what to do! Win! Now go and kick some butt!"

They lost the playoff game. The team was pretty upset about it for a while. They had a good season, too, only lost a couple of games. Adam focused on Coach's words. He knew deep down they were all scared. Scared or not, they still had to keep going. Now kick some butt.

When Adam finally arrived downstairs with his backpack, Russell was finishing his coffee and toast. "You want some?" Russ asked, holding up the last bite of toast.

"No thanks." Adam just walked out the back door towards the jeep.

A few minutes later, Russell followed him. He made sure the door was locked and then started the engine. Adam already had his head phones on, so there would be no need for awkward chatting. Russell put the jeep in gear and headed towards Jekyll Island.

It was a drive that he could do without even looking. They lived south of Atlanta, so there wasn't any big city to go through. From the Stockbridge area to Jekyll Island would take approximately four hours. The obvious variables would be hunger and traffic. It was an easy route, south on 75, east on 16 and then south on 95.

Russell had to admit that the butterflies were there. He didn't know if this was the right thing to do, he just knew they needed a change. Stanley gave him a job to work on and even though it was relatively small in comparison to a luxury apartment complex, it could still be difficult. This was a repeat client that worked with Walter in the past. This time he requested to not work with Walter. Whether that meant Walter upset him, or Walter passed on the project, he didn't know. Russell just accepted the job and got out of town.

He didn't tell Adam that this job most certainly would require him to return to Atlanta at least once. He was going to mention it to the Covingtons next door and see if they couldn't keep an eye on Adam for a few days. Adam would be angry and call it babysitting, but it wasn't really. Adam would soon be eighteen and he already did trust him. Russ was more afraid of Adam feeling alone when he had to leave, rather than someone who might get into trouble.

They were making the turn east at Macon. Adam was getting hungry but knew it was too early to stop. He saw a granola bar between the seats and opened it. Adam tried to focus on the road. He knew his dad had driven this route longer than Adam was alive. He tried hard to not let his thoughts go to his mom. That was still a dangerous place for his heart.

After driving a couple more hours, Russell asked Adam if he wanted to stop and eat. Adam nodded and they pulled into a McDonald's after filling up their gas. It was good to stretch their legs and walk around. Russell and Adam were both so wrapped up in their own thoughts that neither one of them talked. They would look out the window or down at their food in silence.

It was okay. Russell didn't want to push him. He was still surprised and thankful that he agreed to come at all. He would let Adam process it all in his own way. All hell could break loose once they got to the actual beach house, but for now he would treat him like a wounded puppy.

Adam couldn't help it. His thoughts kept going to his mom. He was remembering times at Jekyll when he was a kid. Trey had thought he saw a shark and started yelling and screaming, which made Adam do the same. Little Mandy, who loved sharks, wanted to go out and see it. It was Adam's mom who yelled at the boys and grabbed Mandy before she went out further than allowed to look for a shark. Lynn was pretty sure that Trey made it up, but she stayed on the beach with us everyday for a week while we played in the water.

Adam knew his mom had other things to do while at the beach house than watch a couple of boys in the water. For Lynn, it was more than a second home. It was home. Lynn had been coming there since she was a baby. She knew Fern and Gene next door and their kids, Iris and Forrest. The other neighbors had changed a few times. There was no one she really got to know until the Covingtons moved in. Their boys were the same age and that was perfect for Adam. Little Mandy tried to tag along, but the boys didn't want anything to do with her. It was up to Lynn and Mandy's mom, Julie, to keep her entertained. They would tell little Mandy that someday the boys will let her join in, they were sure of it.

Russell and Adam got back on the road and back to their own thoughts. Russell remembered the first time Lynn brought him to the beach house. They were in their early twenties and had been dating a few months. They drove up in the fall. The tourists were gone, the temperature and humidity dropped and there wasn't any traffic. Russell wasn't really impressed until they drove over the large bridge that crossed the causeway. Driving from Brunswick to Jekyll Island was magical. There was marsh lands, terrapin crossing, marinas and large houses. Lynn drove through the quaint streets and villages that looked like a scene from a movie. She drove into a private driveway and pulled up in front of this massive white house on the beach. It was two stories but wide enough to be two houses.

Lynn had taken Russell's hand and led him in the front door. She took out her key and opened the door to let Russell in first. His eyes stayed looking forward as the architect no doubt wanted. There was a direct line of sight from the front entryway to the back where sliding glass doors led you to the wrap around back porch which then led you to the sand and ocean. It was a brilliant design. Russell, being a new architect himself, was impressed. Lynn led him through the house and out to the back deck.

Since it was fall, outside was windy and chilly. They decided to stay inside and put a log in the fireplace. Lynn had brought wine and sandwiches and they had a picnic in front of the flames. Russell loved Lynn. Even though they had only dated a few months, they knew each other for a couple of years.

Russell put his hand up to Lynn's face. "Lynn, will you marry me?"

Lynn's face went through a series of emotions in those few seconds it took her to say, "Yes!" At first she was surprised, then happy, then the tears came. She secretly hoped this would get him to propose, but if it didn't, at least it might put the idea in his head for later.

They made love in front of the fireplace. It felt oddly forbidden to Lynn. Although it was her house, her parents did not know she was here. For Russell, it was exciting. It was a side of Lynn he hadn't seen yet and loved getting to know. It was the first time they made love to each other and it would always be a special memory for them both.

Even after life's challenges threw them curve balls, they never forgot that night. After they got married and had Adam, they still brought up that night. Even after Lynn's parents died tragically in a car accident, their move to Georgia, or Lynn got sick, they still brought up that night. It was the one constant that brought their lives into focus.

Now, Russell was standing in that same spot from nearly twenty years ago. He had gotten out of the jeep and was now glued to the spot at the front door. Was he waiting for Lynn to take his hand? Russell could feel his eyes watering and wiped at them with his sleeve. The slam of the car door brought him back to the present. Adam came around with bags in his hands and looked at his dad.

"Are you just going to stand there?" Adam asked.

Russell simply smiled at his son and jiggled the keys in his hand to find the right one. "Let's go in, shall we?" He asked.

Both were slightly hesitant. They laid their bags down by the staircase and walked straight through to the back sliding glass doors. Russell gave quick glances right and left to the other rooms. Everything was dark and covered with dust cloths. Momentum carried them forward. Adam slowly opened the sliding door and stepped out. Bob Covington had already warned Russell that the back porch needed work, so Russell didn't mind the creaks and cracks. Adam and Russell stared at the ocean.

Russell put a hand on his son's shoulder. "Well, we made it here and walked through the house. I would call that a win."

Adam wasn't so sure. Winning wasn't everything. Coach Booker taught him that. It was giving it your all and then finding more to give. Adam just wasn't sure he had that much left.

"Right, dad," Adam replied and turned to get the rest of their things unloaded.

Russell turned to follow his son but was frozen when he saw the fireplace. He was suddenly back at that moment that he proposed to Lynn. He could smell the fire, feel her skin and smell her perfume. He remembered making a promise to her to always come back to the beach house every summer. Even when they had six children, they would still come.

Russell found himself laughing but also on the verge of tears. God, how was he going to get through this? Adam came back through and put a hand on his dad's shoulder.

"You okay?" Adam asked.

Russell sniffled and wiped at his eyes. "Yes, just ran into a memory."

Adam simply patted his shoulder a couple of times. "Well, I unloaded everything from the jeep."

"Thanks, son," Russell replied. "I'll put the food away."

Adam followed his dad into the kitchen. Russ looked at him a few times while filling the refrigerator. "Everything okay?" Russell asked.

"It's just that I can still feel her here," Adam replied. "Is that weird?" Adam walked around the kitchen and saw the calendar on the wall with Lynn's handwriting on it. Notes by the phone that gave the numbers to pizza delivery and a taxi company. "I feel like she could be sitting in the next room."

Adam's voice trailed off and Russell came over to hug his son. He didn't need to say anything, Adam was comforted by his dad's embrace. They stayed like that for a little bit longer, until Adam raised his arm to wipe at his eyes.

"The memories will come, Adam. We can either fight them or embrace them."

Chapter 6

Russell heard Adam walking around upstairs. He decided to start removing dust covers downstairs and open some windows. Russ took his time going from room to room. He saw the pictures and knick knacks that filled every room. It was difficult, but Russell tried to focus on the mundane task of folding the white sheets that covered all the furniture. It was monotonous and endless. The perfect task for such a turbulent wave of emotions that Russ knew would be coming.

He saw that Adam had brought in the urn but left it sitting in the entryway. Russell wasn't exactly sure where it should go but knew he didn't want it on the floor. He laid down the sheet he was folding and went to the urn. He picked it up as if he was holding a newborn baby. Without really thinking about it, he carried it to the mantel above the fireplace, their fireplace.

"Welcome home, sweetheart," Russell said out loud.

A knock on the back door brought Russell out of his melancholy.

"Hi, Bob. Good to see you," Russell said to his neighbor.

"Welcome back," Bob replied. "I just wanted to say that if you need anything, don't hesitate to ask. Julie is taking Mandy out to get her braces removed, but Trey and I are here all day."

"Thanks, Bob. I see the porch and agree with you that it needs some work. I brought a few tools, but obviously couldn't bring everything," Russell said.

"Oh sure, I probably have what you need, no problem," Bob said. He looked like he still had something else to say. "And I, uh, just want to say again how sorry we are, about Lynn. So, if there's anything you need.."

"Thanks, Bob. I know. I'll call you," Russell replied.

Russell was left standing on the porch alone. He looked at it more critically now and saw how the sea air had damaged it. Some parts just needed a new coat of paint while others needed new wood. The swing would need to be painted, too. They would deal with this project later.

Russell went back inside and continued removing dust covers. Unfortunately, Bob's visit disrupted his focus. Now Russell was seeing every photo, every picture Adam drew for her and the seashell collection Lynn added to every year. He sat down on the couch and picked up the framed photo of him, Lynn and Adam. They were sitting on the porch swing. Adam was about seven. Even the frame was decorated with tiny shells that a seven year old found on the beach that year.

The ringing of his phone brought Russell out of his thoughts. He put the picture back on the table and pulled his phone out of his pocket. It was work. More specifically, it was another client he was working with this summer. He had been trying to get ahold of him and decided to take it outside. Russell answered the call and walked out the front door.

Upstairs, Adam had walked slowly down the hall. His room was one of the bedrooms that faced the front of the house. He went in his room first. Adam laid his bags on the floor. He removed the dust covers in his room and folded them neatly in the corner. He lifted his backpack to the bed and started unpacking. First, he had to open all his drawers and look at his clothes. He knew most of them would be at least a size too small for him now. He decided to tackle that job later. Instead, he walked around his room and touched the various things on his desk, shelves and dresser. His mom loved collecting shells. Whenever she and Adam found a new, interesting one they washed it and found a place to display it.

Adam loved those times with his mom. The days when he had her all to himself. He always hoped and prayed for a sibling, but it never happened. It would have meant giving up some of his time with his mom, but he would have done that for a brother or sister. Adam walked to the other rooms. There was a spare room next to his. This is where Uncle Teddy stayed or if a friend from home came to visit. Again, he folded the dust covers and placed them in the corner.

At the back of the house was another guest room, bathroom and then the master bedroom. Adam stood in the doorway before slowly entering this room. This room had the best view of the beach and the ocean. The king sized bed faced the windows that gave a panoramic view of the ocean. Adam opened the curtains and started folding the dust covers.

He froze when he lifted the cover and spotted the green stuffed turtle tucked into his mom's side of the bed. Adam let the sheet fall to the floor as he sat on the bed and reached for the turtle. At first, he just pet the soft animal then he hugged it. He hugged it as if his life depended on it. Adam felt the tears come to his eyes as he opened them. His mom's bedside table still had bottles of pills and medication. The stuffed turtle was a gift from him to his mom when she got sick for the last time.

Her sickness came in waves over the last several years, but they all knew that the last time would finally take her. That's why she asked to come to the beach house at the end of May and finally saw her last sunrise on June first. She had three days here. Adam didn't need a calendar to tell him that date was only a few days away. One year.

It was Memorial Day weekend, which usually meant a cookout, party and games. Adam thought the Covingtons might have something planned, but didn't know for sure. Usually it was the Reeds who planned the festivities. He was not really excited about mingling but he was ready for a distraction. Adam placed the turtle back where he found it and went back to his room.

Adam set up his PS5 and laid down on his bed. He wasn't in the mood to play video games and he wasn't tired. Instead, he put on his running clothes and went down to the beach. Each house on this street had sand dunes and brush between the houses so Adam couldn't see either neighbor from where he stood. He did, though, see his dad standing at the water's edge.

"Hey dad," Adam yelled. "I'm going for a run on the beach."

Russell turned and waved at this son. He watched as he ran on the wet sand as the sun got lower in the sky. Adam would be gone over an hour. They usually ran in the mornings, at sunrise, when they were on Jekyll Island. Russ would run tomorrow. He figured Adam had some things to work through and watched him until his figure grew too small to see.

Russell considered going for a swim, but the effort of going upstairs to change did not appeal to him. He decided to do the next best thing. He walked back up to where their grass met the sand. They had several adirondack chairs lined up and he sat down. He closed his eyes and listened to the waves. Memories rolled in with each wave, too. Russ remembered sitting here, holding hands with Lynn or sipping wine. They would watch Adam play in the sand or teach himself how to surf.

The tear rolling down the corner of his eye betrayed the smile on his face. Even though it hurt, it was nice to remember the good times. He didn't want to think of the years they came here after Lynn did her chemo treatments or getting the news that her cancer had come back, again. It was almost like every good memory was tinged with a little bit of sadness. Almost.

Russell thought he could hear Lynn's laughter. This sound made him sit up and open his eyes. A figure on the beach to his left drew his attention. It was Fern, the old widow who lived next door. There was no mistaking who it was. He watched as she walked down to the water's edge. She was barefoot and wearing a housecoat. She looked older and more frail that the last time he saw her.

Russell had meant to go check on her as soon as they arrived, but he wasn't ready to talk to anyone about Lynn, yet. He knew Fern would want to. Fern had watched Lynn grow up here. She watched Lynn run on the beach with her own kids, Iris and Forrest. Russell had never met Fern's kids. They never came around once they went off to school and got jobs. He had heard that they did during holidays, but knew she always thought of Lynn as another daughter.

It took Russell a minute to realize that Fern wasn't just watching the ocean, she was talking to it. She talked with her hands and even laughed as if having a whole conversation. Well, he would definitely stop in to see her tomorrow. If she was in the beginning stages of Alzheimer's or dementia, he would have to let her kids know. For now, he watched her talk to the waves. She was happy and animated. Russell leaned back and relaxed. He let the waves lull him to sleep.

Russell woke up when Adam tapped on his arm. He had finished his run. Russell noticed that the sun was ready to set behind the house. He stood up and walked back inside with Adam. Adam asked about Mrs. Fern out near the water. Russ explained that he would go and talk to her tomorrow. Neither one of them were in the mood to cook dinner.

"You go shower and I'll order pizza," Russell said.

Adam grabbed a bottle of water out of the fridge and took a long drink. "Extra pepperoni," he said.

"Fine. Just please go shower," his dad joked.

As Adam went upstairs, Russell went to the number hanging by the phone. It was Lynn's handwriting. Written under the phone number was a small notation 'extra pepperoni'. Russell took a deep breath and dialed the number.

A shirtless Adam came downstairs when the pizza was delivered. Russell knew Adam worked out a lot for football but had never really appreciated how defined he had become. He was no longer a boy. It wouldn't be long until he left for college and met someone. His old man had better get in shape, too.

"Do you want to run on the beach at sunrise?" Russ asked.

"Yes, just like old times," Adam answered.

They ate their pizza and cleaned up the kitchen. "Who's doing the cookout this year?" Adam asked.

"I'll get with Bob tomorrow and ask. I don't mind helping, but I don't think I'm prepared to host. Not this year," Russell replied.

Adam nodded his head. "Well, I can help. I'm an expert burger flipper."

Russell laughed. "Oh are you? Why is this talent not used back home?"

"It's a limited time offer. A Memorial Day weekend exclusive. You should be honored," Adam joked.

"I am. I'll be sure to let Bob know he can take the day off. Our burger flipper has arrived," Russell replied.

The two guys laughed. It was a moment of lightness that they both needed. "Well, I'm going to head up to bed. Lock up when you come up," Russell said.

Adam promised he would. He thought about going back outside and sitting on the beach, but he was tired, too. He locked up the house and followed his dad upstairs. Adam thought that maybe he could play a few games of Madden before he fell asleep.

Chapter 7

Russell and Adam woke up at sunrise. They both got dressed and went out into the cool air. They ran on the beach for about an hour and a half. Back at home, they each took their shoes and shirts off and jumped in the ocean. Adam enjoyed doing things with his dad that didn't involve talking about the past. The past would always be there, he wanted to focus on the future.

Russell enjoyed these mornings with his son, swimming, laughing and talking about the little things. These were the moments that made it all worth it the last few days. He spotted Bob coming out of his house and started to get out of the water.

"I'm going to talk to Bob about the cookout. I'll see if there even is one," Russell said.

"Okay, I'm going to grab some breakfast," replied Adam.

Adam walked in the house as Russell called to Bob.

"Hey Russ," Bob said. "Are you all settled in?"

"Getting there," Russ replied. "I was wondering if there were any plans for a cookout this year? I'd be happy to help or contribute."

"Hey Russ, don't worry about it, I've got it covered. We didn't really know when you guys would be coming, so no pressure. I invited our other neighbors and some friends, so just bring any drinks you might like and join us," Bob said.

"I know Adam is eager to see the kids, maybe go surfing with Trey," Russ said.

"Oh that's all Trey has been talking about!" Bob replied. "Mandy is spending the weekend with friends in Savannah. Julie is actually going to drive up there tomorrow and get her. I guess we aren't cool anymore," Bob joked.

"Trust me, I know the feeling," Russ answered. "If Trey wasn't here to hang out with, I'm not sure I would have gotten Adam to come. We both needed a distraction and hopefully this summer is just enough to keep us going."

Bob encouraged them to come anytime, but most guests will arrive around three. Russ promised to bring drinks and snacks. It would be good to see some more people. Russell was actually smiling when he passed Adam in the hallway. He was finished with his shower and going downstairs to eat. Russell went into the shower and felt encouraged that today would be a good day.

He joined his son in the kitchen for breakfast. He filled Adam in on the plans for the cookout. They were to bring some side dishes or snacks along with drinks. Russell thought they probably needed to stock up on a few things for themselves, too, but he also needed to get some work done before the party.

"I'll go to the store. Just make me a list," Adam said. They were sharing a car this summer and he wanted to pick up some things of his own.

"Okay, that will work out great," his dad said. Russell wrote down everything he needed and gave him his credit card. "If there's anything you forgot, add it to the list. I know I forgot shaving cream so it's on there."

Adam finished his cereal and took the list and card. "Thanks, dad. I'll be back before you know it."

Actually, Russell knew that he probably wouldn't see him for a few hours. That was fine, it actually worked out great for him. Before Russell started working, he wanted to go next door and visit Fern. As Adam went out the front door with the car keys, Russell went out the back door towards the beach. He suspected Fern would be on her back porch.

She was. Russell could tell she wasn't sure who was approaching her at first, but then recognition lit up her face.

"Russell, how good of you to visit," Fern said.

"Hello Mrs. Fern, how are you doing?"

"Oh just fine, I can't complain," Fern answered. "So you're here for the summer, are you?"

"For most of it. Adam will have to go back for football camp at the end of July, but until then, we will be next door," Russ said.

Russell asked about Fern's children. Iris, still single, is down in Jacksonville. She's the one Fern sees the most, which usually amounts to three times a year. Forrest and his family are in Macon, GA. He stays so busy with work, family and the twins, he doesn't get away much. They call her once in a while and talk, so she's thankful for that. Fern liked her privacy and independence, though. Not having to rely on anyone to do things for her.

"Well, I'm here if there's something you need done, just let me know. I'd be happy to fix something for you," Russell offered.

"Now that you mention it, my dryer has been acting up lately. If you don't mind, maybe you could take a look at it," Fern said.

"I will tomorrow. I'll bring Adam and my tools," Russell replied.

Fern talked about the weather and the storms that they had gotten over the last year or so. She hoped that this hurricane season wasn't going to be as bad as last year. She brought up memories of Iris and Forrest running on the beach and then of little Lynn always bringing her seashells.

At the mention of Lynn, Fern turned to Russell. "I'm very sorry about Lynn. She was an angel with that lovely blond hair. She loved it here. It was fitting that this be her last memory." Fern looked back out to the ocean. "My Gene, too. We never wanted to live anywhere else, so it was natural for him to die here. I will too, when my time comes," Fern said.

"I've seen you out at the water, talking," Russell started.

"Oh yes, I talk to Gene everyday," Fern confirmed. "I tell him about my day and if I hear from the kids. I'll tell him about your visit, too."

Fern saw Russ looking at her. "I'm not crazy Russell. You can stop worrying about me." Fern laughed. "I know his spirit is still here, I feel him. What am I supposed to do, ignore him?" Fern asked. Then, looking at Russell, "You still feel Lynn, don't you? In your house."

Russell looked down at this hands and cleared his throat. "Yes. Yes, I do."

"Exactly. Nothing wrong with that, it's natural. Their spirit is still here with us," Fern said. "Talk to her. It helps me to talk to Gene." Fern paused. "It would be better if he could answer me, too, but I'll take what I can get. It's comforting."

Russell thought about everything Fern said as he walked back to his house. Maybe talking to Lynn would help, he wasn't sure. Adam wasn't home, yet, so Russell opened up his laptop. He was able to get a good amount of work done before he heard the jeep pull up. Russell went to go help his son unload the groceries. There was a small bag that Adam tucked behind the door and his dad didn't question him about it.

"Where's my card?" Russell asked with his hand outstretched.

Adam was eating grapes when he looked up, confused. "What card? What are you talking about, dad?"

Russell kept his hand out and looked at him like he was ready to yell. Actually, Russ was smiling and so was Adam when he handed over his dad's credit card.

"Thanks, dad," Adam said. "I hope you don't mind, I got a couple things for me."

"No, that's fine," his dad assured him. "Hey, party starts at three so we want to be on time. I was also thinking to take a plate over to Mrs. Fern, too."

Adam promised him that he'd be ready on time. He grabbed the bag he set aside and went up to his room. He emptied the contents on the bed. There was gum, skittles and snickers for him. There was a copy of the latest manga for Trey and then a shark keychain. He hoped Trey was still interested in Japanese anime. Adam picked up the shark key chain and held it in his hands. He bought it for Mandy. He knew she would be driving soon and she liked sharks. Adam instantly thought of her when he saw it.

Adam came downstairs and they walked out the back door. They carried everything they were bringing to the party and walked along the beach to the Covington's back door. They could smell the hamburgers already being cooked on the grill. Russell and Adam walked in from the beach and laid everything on the table by the back deck. Julie came out and greeted them, offered condolences and then told them to help themselves.

Trey came running out the back door when he spotted Adam. They hugged and went inside the house. Trey took him up to his room to show him the latest video game he got. Adam gave him the manga he bought.

"Oh wow! I didn't know this was out yet," Trey said. "Thanks, man."

"You're welcome," Adam replied. He looked around Trey's room. It had been a couple of years since he was here last, but not a lot has changed. Maybe some new posters or video games, but Trey was still the same. They started playing video games and it felt like old times.

"Where's Mandy?" Adam asked.

"She's spending a couple nights at her friend's house. She'll be back tomorrow," Trey replied. "There's finally peace and quiet," he joked.

Adam just laughed with him. He didn't really know what it was like to have a sibling. He guessed having a girl around all the time would be terrible, maybe. They seemed to have picked up right where they left off. Before his mother died. They made plans to take the boat out, go fishing and surfing.

"I just have to help my dad fix our back porch, but other than that I'm free," Adam said.

"Excellent," Trey replied. Then they did their funny handshake that they both still remembered.

Russell was doing his best to mingle and make small talk with the other neighbors who were invited. It wasn't easy and he hated every minute but he knew that's what was expected of him. Everyone wanted to express their condolences to him and Adam. He wished he could just get on top of the table and yell out 'thank you everyone, I'm fine' and be done with it. He noticed that Adam escaped inside the house. He wished he could do the same.

Russell had a hamburger and plenty of sides on his plate. He ate and even went back for a cupcake. Around six, he asked Bob if he minded him taking a plate of food over to Fern. Bob said he could take as much as he liked. So, Russell made a plate, covered it and excused himself. He walked along the beach until he was in front of Fern's house.

She was sitting on her back porch swing. Russell waved and she waved back. He came up the stairs and showed her the plate of food.

"Oh my goodness, that's three days worth of food!" Fern exclaimed.

"Well, shall I take it inside for you?" Russell offered.

"That would be great, thank you."

Russell walked in the back door and made his way to the kitchen. The house was dark and dusty, but otherwise pretty clean. He opened the refrigerator and saw that it was pretty empty. She had the essentials, but not much else. She saw the phone numbers for Iris and Forrest written by the telephone and decided to take a picture of them, just in case. Russell went back outside to sit with Fern.

"How do you get your groceries, Fern?"

"Oh, there's a nice lady from church who shops for me once a week. I give her a list and then pay her when she comes," Fern replied.

Satisfied with this, for now, Russell dropped the subject. He sat a while longer and told her about the party at the Covington's. She said they do stop by once in a while to check on her. Fern said their little Mandy reminded her of Lynn. Russell took that as his cue to leave. He said goodnight to Fern and returned home.

Chapter 8

Russell walked back to the party. He had nothing else to do. If he sat alone now he just might start getting sad, again. He needed more people for a distraction. He walked along the sand until he came up to the Covington's back yard. It was getting late, almost nine. Most of the guest had gone home. There were still a few neighbors sitting around and laughing so Russell joined them.

"Where are Trey and Adam?" Russell asked.

"They went out on the water. Waves are pretty decent but I suspect they'll be back soon," Bob replied.

Russell hadn't looked out on the ocean. Now he turned and scanned the water and saw two figures sitting on top of surf boards. Not many waves. Russell was glad Adam had Trey. He needed someone to talk to and confide in, a peer that could help give him advice and perspective. Something a father might not be able to relate to. He also needed the distraction, the fun and excitement of a summer on the beach.

A burst of laughter made Russell turned back around to the circle of guys.

"What's so funny?" Russell asked.

"Last year's Memorial Day party," Bob started. "It rained so hard just as we were cooking the burgers and Carl thought he could still do it and grabbed a beach umbrella and held it over the barbecue." All the men laughed. "It was a disaster."

Russell looked at Carl, Bob's other neighbor and smiled.

"I guess you had to be there," Carl added.

Realizing what Carl had just said, the men looked from one to another and stopped laughing. They all looked at Russell. The one person who wasn't there last summer.

"I'm so sorry, Russ," Carl said.

"It's okay. Really, you don't need to stop laughing just because of me," Russell replied. "But now that you said rain, you jinxed it."

Everyone looked up at the sky and saw the same big, dark cloud coming over the water. The men all laughed, but it was more a nervous laugh compared to before. Russell didn't care. He did it, he mingled for the first time in a long time. He walked down to the water's edge and called for the boys to come in. They probably didn't see the cloud looming behind them.

As they paddled in towards shore, the boys looked around and saw the cloud just as it started to rain. Trey and Adam were laughing and paddling with equal enthusiasm. Adam had a great day. He missed his time with Trey and was sad to think that his summer would be cut short this year. His friend hadn't been touched by much sadness. All his grandparents were still living, his parents were healthy and he had a sibling.

On some level, Trey was the perfect person to be around right now. He knew Adam needed time to grieve, but he also knew the importance of living. Trey didn't understand how sitting in your bedroom listening to music was going to make you feel better or keep you moving forward. To Trey it was dying a little, too.

If Adam would get quiet or hesitate when asked if he wanted to do something, Trey would ask, 'What would your mom say?' Adam knew exactly what she would say when he was in a mood. She would tell him to suck it up and get out there. So, when Trey asked Adam to go surfing, he wasn't really sure he was in the mood. Trey just started pulling the boards out of the garage.

As the boys carried their surf boards back to Trey's house, Adam realized he had fun.

"Thanks, man, for this," Adam said. "I had a good time."

"I knew you would!" Trey replied. Trey slapped his friend on the back and they both laughed. "What about tomorrow? More surfing?"

"Well, I promised my dad we would help Mrs. Fern and then work on our deck," Adam said. "It's supposed to be our summer project."

"Okay, well, when you are ready for a break, just wave at me in the water," Trey said. "I'll be the one on top of the big wave."

The boys laughed again and grabbed some cookies and a soda. They went back inside to change. The Covingtons thanked Adam for coming over and said he was welcome anytime.

"Thanks," replied Adam.

"And Mandy will be home tomorrow," Julie added. "I'm sorry you haven't gotten chance to see each other, yet. She can't wait to see you, Adam."

"Me, too," Adam replied. He thought about the last time he saw her. She was fourteen and had braces. His dad said she had gotten the braces off the other day, that was good.

Adam walked back towards home in the rain. It wasn't far and he didn't mind. Rain on the beach was beautiful but it was too dark to see right now. His father was sitting on their back porch when Adam approached. He was on the swing with a beer in his hand.

"Did you have a good time today?" Russ asked his son.

"I guess so. Did you?"

Russell thought about it. "I think I did, a little. I went to see Fern and gave her a plate of food."

"Oh, so you escaped is what you're saying," Adam joked.

Russell laughed as his son sat on the swing beside him. They watched the rain and the distant lightning. They both sat with their own thoughts about the day. Their goal for coming to the island was for a distraction from their regular lives. Today was exactly that, a break from reality. Russell was the first to get up and claim he was tired. Adam followed shortly after. In their own bedrooms, they remained awake.

The next morning, Russell was the first one downstairs with his running clothes on. He knew Adam was awake and waited for him. They both knew what today was. June first. One year. There was no need to say it out loud and they both told themselves they would not be sad today.

Russ and Adam did their morning run on the beach and then breakfast after. It was becoming their routine and they both enjoyed it. Afterwards, they would go to Mrs. Fern's and see what was wrong with her dryer.

Russell brought his tool box and a vent cleaning tool. He suspected it was a lint problem, but wouldn't know for sure until they pulled it out. This would be good for Adam to see, too. He wished for an easy fix because Russell really wanted to get started on their back deck. If they finished the dryer early enough, they could maybe start the deck today.

Fern was sitting on her back deck as usual. She waved at them and showed them the laundry room. It was small but tidy. The guys got to work. First they turned it on to see what happened. Fern said it just didn't dry her clothes, it shut off too soon.

Adam helped pull it out and Russell inspected the vent. Sure enough it was full of lint. It was a simple solution but a complex problem. Russell had to clean the entire vent from the dryer to the outside and it took much longer than anticipated.

Fern saw their struggle and felt bad. Often coming to check on them and offering to call someone. Russell assured her they could finish the job. It was messy, hard and complicated, but they did finish. Fern had sandwiches and lemonade made for them in the kitchen. The three sat down at her kitchen table and ate.

"Thank you so much," Fern said between bites. "I don't know what I would have done without a dryer much longer."

"We're happy to help," Russell replied. "Do you ever call your kids to come see to things around here?"

"Oh Iris will come, but she's not much help. And Forrest, well, he's just much too busy."

"Do you mind if I call Iris and just talk to her about how things are around here?" Russell asked. He had wanted to call Iris and find out why she doesn't check up on her elderly mother more often. The last thing he wanted was for Fern to find out he called Iris without asking permission first.

"Well, you can try," Fern said. "You would have better luck finding an elephant in the ocean than getting Iris to come here for no reason. I don't need her."

"Oh I know you don't," Russell said. "But perhaps I can just get her to come visit. Wouldn't you like that?"

Fern looked at him and nodded ever so slightly. It was hard for her to admit she was lonely. She missed the sound of laughter around the house.

"Okay, I'll call and ask if she could spare time for a visit." Russell and Adam helped clean up their lunch dishes and gave Mrs. Fern a hug good bye. Russ made her promise that if there was anything else she needed fixed, to wave him down immediately. Adam carried the tool box home this time.

On the walk back to their house, Russell thanked his son for his help and asked what his plans were for the rest of the day. Adam and Trey had plans to ride bikes and maybe surf.

"I thought that you and I could do something to remember mom," Russell started.

"Dad, no. Not now," Adam said strongly. "I know what you want to do and I'm not ready. I can't spread her ashes yet." He dropped the tool box on the sand and ran towards Trey's house.

Russell let him go. He wasn't ready to let go of Lynn, yet, either. It could wait. Russell went inside and put his tools away. He thought about working a little but decided not to. It was time for some fun. He was hot and sweaty from working on Fern's dryer so he was going to hit the ocean.

He went to find his surf board in the garage and carried it to the beach. He took off his shirt and laid it on the adirondack chairs. Russell was still in great shape. He worked out when he could but mostly he ran. Russ was muscular and for a man who could almost be considered middle aged, had a full head of thick brown hair that he kept cut short. Sometimes his hair would fall down onto his forehead, like now when the wind was blowing. The hair on his chest and head was starting to turn gray but he didn't mind.

Russell let the surf board float until he couldn't touch the ground. He hopped on and started paddling out. It was a beautiful sunny day. The waves were getting stronger the further out he went and he felt like a kid again. He missed this. Russ even caught a few waves but mostly he fell off the board. He felt free and happy. Feelings he hadn't felt in a long time and wasn't sure he even remembered how.

Russell floated on his surf board, feet dangling on either side. He raised his hands high in the air and yelled 'Thanks Lynn' as loud as he could. This was the feeling he wanted everyday. He knew Adam was feeling happy here, maybe he could, too. The beach house was magic. There was no other explanation.

Chapter 9

Russell told Adam that today was the day they were starting to work on the back deck. They had put it off long enough. After their daily routine of running, breakfast and shower, they headed to the home improvement store in the jeep. They had already been at the beach house a week and they were both starting to relax and find a new normal.

Stopped at a red light, Russell looked over at his son. He had his head phones on, eyes closed and was mouthing the words to the song. Russ smiled. He hadn't seen this kind of light hearted mood in Adam for years. Russ suspected that coming here was a good decision, but this confirmed it. He continued driving with a smile of his own.

Russell had spent the evening before measuring boards, listing supplies needed and drawing up a plan for the back deck. They walked into the store knowing exactly what they required. The question was would it all fit in the jeep, probably not. Russell decided to focus on what they could reasonably get done in the first day or two.

Adam went and got the big flat bed cart to start putting all the lumber and supplies on. The paint could wait, that was the last step anyway. After finding all the nails and screws they needed, they added this to the cart and checked out. Adam let his dad load it all into the jeep. It took a bit of skill, but his dad got it all to fit except for a few inches that hung over the back of the jeep. Russell tied a red flag on the end and they drove back to the beach house.

As Russell pulled up to the front of the house he realized the easiest way to the back deck was to go through the house. Russell and Adam took turns carrying items and holding doors until the jeep was completely unloaded. Russell pulled out his blue prints and showed his son what needed to be done.

The rotten wood was removed first, then Russell got out his circular saw. They worked as a team measuring and cutting wood to fit the newly emptied spot. It was tedious and time consuming but they were having fun. Russell laughed the first time Adam used the saw because he scared himself with the noise of it up close. His dad let him take the lead when they needed to measure the next piece, cut it and then screw it back into place.

They took a break for lunch and went inside. They sat around the kitchen island and ate hungrily. It was well past noon and they were starving. Progress was made on the porch, but it would probably need another week's worth of work until it was done completely. After lunch, Russell decided to call it a day. They could now go have fun. Adam said he was actually going to go to his room and take a nap. Russell nodded and contemplated doing the same. However, work won out.

Russell pulled out his laptop and checked his emails. Being a workaholic, Russell usually checked his emails multiple times a day. Here, at the beach, he checked them every couple of days. He was shocked when he saw he had eighty-seven unread messages. Was it always this many and he never realized the volume of mail he read each day? He sat back in his recliner and read through each one. Things were progressing nicely on the clients he was working with. He thought he was doing a great job of balancing work and beach life.

Confident that he replied to the necessary ones and deleted the junk, he decided to call Fern's daughter. What harm could there be in letting her know that her mother is in need of more care. She's elderly and alone, that by itself should be enough. He wasn't sure how this call was going to go. He never had to call any of Fern's kids before. Russell hoped that she would be open to the idea of her mother's neighbor calling her and asking her to come.

Iris picked up on the second ring. "Hello?"

"Hello, this is Russell Reed," he said hesitantly. "I own the beach house next to your mother." There was a slight pause.

"Yes? Is she okay?" Iris asked.

"Yes, she's okay. It's just that I've been over to see her each day and noticed some things that I wanted you to be aware of," Russell answered.

"Like what?" Iris asked.

He was a bit surprised by her short questions and her business tone. "Well, first, she walks to the water each night and talks to your father," Russell paused wondering if she might respond to this fact. No response. "And, she doesn't have much food in the house. She claims someone shops for her but I haven't seen her. Then, yesterday my son and I cleaned out her dryer vent and pulled out a decade's worth of lint. It could have been a fire hazard."

Russell waited for Iris to respond. "Well, I'm busy at work but I could come out this weekend. Is that okay?" Iris asked.

"That sounds great," Russel answered. "I'll see you Saturday."

After they hung up Russell tried to replay the conversation in his head. She didn't sound concerned but she must have been to commit to coming out this weekend. He was going to be sure to meet Iris and finally be able to talk to someone in Fern's family and about their mother's care.

Russell didn't want to think about Iris any longer. He got up and went to the back porch. An afternoon rain shower was passing through. He loved sitting and watching the rain. Careful not to step on any nails or screws that might be lying around, Russel sat on the porch swing. He even closed his eyes and listened to the rain. It was calming and relaxing. He could feel the tension leave his body as he swung on the porch.

The rain lasted about an hour. Russell suspected that he actually fell asleep but wouldn't know for sure unless he looked at the time. His phone was inside and he made no attempt to go get it. What Russell didn't know was that when Adam went upstairs, he didn't take a nap.

Adam felt too emotional when his father mentioned his mother's ashes. He ran to his room and grabbed the pink Jekyll Island sweatshirt from his chair. It was his mother's. He sat on his bed, hugged the sweatshirt and cried. He missed her so much.

Adam was enjoying his time here at the beach, but his happiness was on the surface. He still had the knot in his stomach. The emptiness was still there and he feared it would never go away. Even riding bikes and surfing with Trey didn't fill the void. He tried texting his friends back home. Carter was on a cruise. Nathan was working. He even tried Sherry but she was in Europe somewhere and needed wifi to text. He never felt so alone.

Adam heard the rain. He loved the rain on the beach. He didn't know how long it had been raining, but got up to see it. He went downstairs and saw his dad on the porch swing. Just as Adam stepped out onto the deck the most beautiful double rainbow appeared over the ocean. It was complete, you could see from one end to the other.

Russell heard Adam come out onto the deck, but neither one of them could take their eyes off of the rainbow. Adam reached into his pocket and took a picture of it. It was Adam who first made the suggestion.

"Dad, let's go down to the water, for mom."

Russell simply nodded and stood up. They walked together down to the beach. Adam went over to the dune and picked a few wild flowers that grew there and caught back up with his dad. They slowly walked down to the water's edge and stood there. They felt the water washing over their bare feet. They heard the sound of the waves breaking as they came to shore. The rainbow was still visible in front of them. It was Adam who spoke first through his tears.

"I miss you, mom, all the time."

Russell put his arm around his son's shoulders. "I miss you, Lynn, all the time," Russell echoed.

They both stood there, deep in their own thoughts. Adam gave his father a few flowers that he had picked and they both through them into the ocean. They watched as the flowers turned and twisted in the waves. Eventually, they got carried out further. Adam watched one particular flower that stayed above the water, its white petals facing the sky. He waited until he couldn't see it any longer and whispered 'goodbye mom' and wiped at his eyes.

Russell pretended he didn't hear Adam's final good bye to his mother. He didn't want to intrude on his son's personal prayer. Instead, Russell was looking around. He thought he heard talking and looked to his left for Fern. He didn't see her out and thought that was a good thing. He looked to his right. Out in the distance he thought he saw some kids in the water. They were laughing and jumping in the waves.

The more Russell focused he realized it was just two kids. They had surfboards and were trying, unsuccessfully, to catch some waves. The ocean had actually gotten eerily calm and quiet. At first, Russell thought it was two boys in the water. He now saw that it was actually Trey and a girl. He didn't recognize the girl he was with.

Russell saw how the two interacted. This was someone he felt comfortable playing around with and trying to knock down from her surfboard.

"Hey," Russell said. "Does Trey have a girlfriend?"

Adam looked at his father. "Not one he's mentioned to me. Why?"

Adam followed his father's gaze and looked to his right. He saw two teenagers playing in the ocean on surf boards. At first, Adam came to his father's first conclusion that they were two boys. Maybe Trey invited another neighborhood friend over.

Adam saw his dad turn to go back towards the house and he turned to follow. Then the person with Trey flipped their hair. It was a girl. He now made out the red bikini she was wearing. They were laughing and falling in the water. Obviously Trey never told him he had a girlfriend. He was sure this detail would have come up as they planned their summer around video games, biking, hiking, surfing and swimming. How did a girl not come up?

Just then it clicked. This girl who was playing so easily with Trey, the long brown hair and the bikini was not a girlfriend. She looked different now. Adam tried to picture her how he last saw her. She had pony tails, braces and had barely hit puberty. She had worn sundresses and hair bands. She would follow them around, well mostly him, everywhere they went. Adam had been here over a week but still hadn't seen her. She was either at her friends or out with her mother.

Russell had put it together quicker than Adam did. As soon as Adam said Trey did not have a girlfriend, the only other logical conclusion was that it was his sister. Russell could see she had grown up a lot since they were last here. Russ turned back around to check on his son. He finally saw the recognition on his face.

"Mandy," Adam said softly to himself.

Chapter 10

Russell and Adam worked on the back porch again after their morning routine. It felt good to Russell to have something physical to do. He still ran and surfed each day, but manual labor on your own house was a step above. He could start seeing the results of all their labor and it was very satisfying. They were not only making the necessary repairs to the deck and swing, he was teaching Adam how to do it for the future.

Russell had already updated his will. As soon as Lynn died, he went to his lawyer and changed everything to Adam as beneficiary. This house would be his someday. It was good practice for him to learn how to take care of it. Losing Lynn made Russell feel vulnerable but he would never show it in front of Adam. He was almost eighteen, but still a boy in his eyes.

Adam was glad they were done cutting all the pieces of wood. The porch was looking good. They had made another trip to the home improvement store for more supplies and it was fun watching his dad try to get it all to fit. Every time he seemed to managed it somehow. The drive into town was nice once in a while. He didn't miss the crowds, stores and traffic. Once they went over the bridge and onto Jekyll Island he was happy again.

Now they were sanding the back porch. Russell had borrowed one from Bob, so they both were using one. This was more work because every surface needed sanded whether it was replaced or not. It was a dusty job, too.

They soon learned that the easiest way, and the most fun way, was to sand shirtless and then run into the ocean to wash off. So every once in a while, one or both of then would lay down their sander and start running to the water. They would laugh, swim and play for a minute then back to work.

This was precious time for Russell and his son. He secretly wished they wouldn't be done with the porch in a few days. He was ready to use the porch again, though. They had it all ripped up the last few days. Now it was finally coming together. A fresh coat of white paint and it would look like new.

They ate lunch outside today because they were too dirty. Russell pronounced them done for the day and they cleaned up the tools. Russell told Adam how proud he was of him. He had done a great job of following directions and then taking the lead. Russell never asked his son what he wanted to be when he applied for colleges. Secretly he hoped he would want to follow in his footsteps, but he would never say it out loud. Too much pressure. Adam would figure his future out on his own.

"I'm going to take these tools back to Bob," Russell said. "We won't be needing these anymore. The rest is all paint brushes and our wrists."

Adam rolled his eyes. "I'm going to go surfing."

Russell walked down towards the Covingtons while Adam went to get his surf board. There were some good sized waves this afternoon. He was sure he could actually get up on some of them. Adam walked with his board down the beach and into the ocean. He was still shirtless and covered in white dust. He dove into the water and came up on his board. He shook out his hair and wiped his face. His brown hair had a slight wave to it when it was wet. This was from his mother.

Adam was enjoying the cool water and letting the sun warm his skin. He was starting to get tan. He managed to catch a few waves, but mostly he was either sitting on his board or laying on it. The roll of the waves was calming to him. His eyes were actually closed when he heard someone calling to him.

At first, Adam thought it was Trey. When he looked closer he could make out the same red bikini from yesterday. Mandy. Adam couldn't take his eyes off of her. He watcher her approach the water and paddle out to him. She didn't dive in like he did and her long brown hair blew in the breeze. It came down to the middle of her back and she was smiling. When Mandy came within six feet of Adam she sat up on her board and faced him.

Adam was suddenly speechless and shy. This was definitely Mandy, Trey's little sister. But it also wasn't. She was beautiful. Mandy had a great figure that filled out her bikini, this he noticed right away. But her smile was so big and welcoming, he couldn't help but smile back.

"Hi," Mandy said.

"Hi," Adam replied.

There was a few awkward seconds as the two realized they didn't know what to say. Mandy brushed her hair out of her face and tucked it behind her ears. Adam suddenly felt self conscious and crossed his arms in front of him.

Mandy laughed. "You look good," she said trying not to stare at his abs.

"So do you," he replied, thinking that was the stupidest thing he could have said. "I, uh, haven't seen you around much."

"I was staying with some friends up in Savannah for a few days. Then mom took me shopping and she lets me drive, so I don't mind going every chance I get," Mandy said. "I'm sorry about your mom, Adam."

Adam couldn't stop staring at her eyes, they were so green. At this moment they were the same green as the darkened ocean. "Thank you," Adam replied. "We were only here for a few days last year. This was her favorite place in the world." He paused and looked down at his hands. "It was where she wanted to spend her last days."

"I get it," Mandy said. "This is how I imagine heaven to be. I don't ever want to leave."

Adam believed her. And in that moment, he felt the same way.

"You know, I still have the stuffed shark you gave me," Mandy confessed. She didn't know why she just said that. She never wanted to admit to Adam the huge crush she has had on him her whole life. That was private and she didn't want anyone to know.

Adam smiled. He knew about the crush she had on him. Trey told him years ago. He thought it was cute at the time. Now, he felt like she just confirmed that it was still there. Maybe he was starting to crush right back. "That was a long time ago."

"It was my tenth birthday," Mandy said.

"How old are you now?" Adam asked.

"Sixteen," Mandy replied. "I just got my license." She turned her gaze to the horizon. "You'll be a senior. I bet you're happy about that, I know Trey is."

Adam watched her movements while she looked away. She was graceful and poised on the surf board. "Yes, I guess. Junior year went by in a fog. I need to focus more because senior year is so important, you know?" He couldn't believe how honest he was in his answer. Mandy felt familiar and new all at the same time.

"There is a lot of pressure put on seniors, for sure," Mandy agreed. "They actually want you to choose what you want to do with the rest of your life as a teenager! How is that possible?" Mandy pushed her hair out of her face and continued. "Of course I always knew what I wanted to be, but not everyone is so lucky."

Adam looked up at her and she was smiling. He smiled back. "Marine biologist," Adam said.

Mandy looked as if she had just won the lottery. "Yes! You remembered."

"Of course," Adam replied, feeling shy again.

Their boards had drifted closer together. Their knees were nearly touching. The waves were bringing them even closer together. They both became silent, aware that their knees just touched.

"Oh look," Mandy said, pointing at an approaching wave. "This one looks big enough to get."

Thankful for the distraction, they both faced the shore and watched over their shoulders. They laid down on their boards and started paddling. They gave each other plenty of space in case one of them got up. As the wave came under them and carried them towards shore, they both got up on their boards and stayed up. With their arms outstretched for balance, they rode the wave towards the beach.

Mandy fell in first, then Adam. They swam to each other and laughed. They got back on their boards and headed back out. They were able to catch quite a few waves and get up on their boards. Sometimes it was Adam who fell in first, other times it was Mandy. Either way, they were having fun. Whenever they would accidentally bump into each other, they immediately apologized and separated.

Russell was watching their interaction from the back porch. He knew they didn't see him, they only had eyes for each other. It was plain as day to see on their faces. It was great to see him having fun, but they were leaving in a few weeks. How was this going to end? He didn't want to see Adam hurting anymore. Russell wasn't sure if he should encourage this new budding relationship or not.

Tired from the surfing, Adam asked if she wanted to go in. She nodded her head and they went to shore. They placed their boards on the sand and sat in the adirondack chairs. They sat back, relaxed and looked out to the horizon. The things Adam took out of his pockets before he got in the water where still beside the chair. Adam reached over and found the shark key chain he had bought her last week at the store. He always had it on him.

"Here," Adam said. "I got this for you." He put the key chain in her open hand.

Mandy turned the metal key chain over in her hands. It was cut out in the shape of a shark. She felt her heart beat faster and turned to look at Adam. "Thank you, I love it."

"I'm glad," Adam said. "I wasn't sure if you still liked sharks but I took a chance."

Mandy was so touched by this gesture from Adam. She knew he only did it to be nice and that it meant more to her than it did to him. She hated that the world had been so cruel to Adam. "I love sharks," Mandy said. "They are so misunderstood. Without them, the food chain in the ocean would be so unbalanced."

Adam just nodded. This was the Mandy he remembered. Always ready to spout shark trivia at a moments's notice. But the Mandy sitting next to him was not the same little girl. She could be any other girl back home that he dated, only she wasn't.

"I'm sure the sharks will have nothing to worry about once you're in charge," Adam said.

There was an awkward silence. Mandy was looking down at the key chain.

"Well, I'm going to go in and see if my dad needs help with anything," Adam said.

"Okay, me too," Mandy replied.

They both stood up and faced each other.

"Thank you for the key chain," Mandy said and reached up to give him a hug. Adam was a foot taller than her and she was on her tip toes.

Adam leaned down and gave her a hug and said, "You're welcome."

They each grabbed their surf board and headed home. It wasn't until Adam was nearly on the back porch that he noticed his father smiling on the swing.

"What are you smiling about?" Adam asked his father.

"What? I'm just smiling the same way you are," Russell replied.

Adam didn't even realize he was smiling. He just shook his head and went up to his room. He laid down on his bed and ran his hand through his hair. Adam knew that nothing from today on would be the same. Mandy just made the beach house more magical.

Chapter 11

Today, after their run, Adam asked his dad if they could take a day off working on the back deck. Trey and his family were going to spend the day on St. Simon's Island and had asked if he wanted to come along. Russell let him go. He needed time with his friends. He wasn't going to push a relationship with Mandy. That was up to them to work out. Bob and Julie were there, they wouldn't let anything happen between them, anyway.

Russell hoped Adam would feel comfortable confiding in his dad. He didn't even know if they liked each other, it just seemed that way. They grew up together. Maybe Lynn had her suspicions, but she never relayed any of that to him.

Russell checked his emails and did some work. Then he remembered that today was Saturday and closed his laptop. Fern's daughter was supposed to come up today. He would go over there to meet her and fill her in on what's been happening since he's been here.

Fern still liked walking down to the water and talking to Gene. He didn't think she was losing her mental capacity, it was more for comfort. He wanted to convey that to Iris so that they didn't lock their mother up in some home. She really just needed someone to check on her everyday. Russell had been doing that while they were here, but they would be leaving in a few weeks.

Russell walked up to Fern's backyard and saw her sitting in her chair like always. She waved and he waved back.

"Hello Russell," Fern said. "How are you today?"

"I'm doing well, Fern," Russell replied. "How about you?"

He heard noise coming from inside the house and turned to look.

"Hurricane Iris is in there. You're gonna want to keep your distance," Fern replied.

Russell stood up and looked in the door. He went in.

"Well, I warned you," said Fern quietly.

Russell saw bags of trash lined up in the hallway. A woman with curly blond hair was going through kitchen cabinets, reading labels and then throwing them in another trash bag. Russell watched her go from cabinet to refrigerator. He cleared his throat and she turned her attention to him.

"Hi, I'm Russell Reed," he said.

Iris Davidson stood up tall and looked at the man in her mother's kitchen. "So, you're the one who called me," Iris said. It wasn't a question.

"Yes, you must be Iris."

"Yes, sorry," Iris said. "I'm just completely shocked that mom has so much old and expired food in here. I try to come when I can and I tell Forrest to come, but I guess it's not enough."

"Well, you're here now," Russell said.

"Thank you for calling me," Iris replied.

"Can I help?" Russell asked.

Iris handed him a trash bag. They laughed and he helped go through Fern's cabinets. Russell asked about her job. Iris was a realtor in the Jacksonville, Florida, area and has a nice life down there. She never married. Iris knows that now that her mother is getting older, she can't really take care of herself and she's going to have to make some decisions.

"Do you want some coffee?" Iris asked.

"Sure," Russell replied.

Russell noticed that she had already brewed a fresh pot. She poured three cups, put them on a tray and carried it out to the back porch. She handed one to Fern and another one to Russell. They all sat and sipped their coffee.

"So how long are you staying here, Iris?" Russell asked.

"Well, I have the weekend off," Iris replied. "I may come back next weekend, too."

Fern just nodded her head. She had heard this all before. She would come for a weekend and then disappear for months. She missed having her kids and grandkids around, but she knew it was always up to them when they came and went.

"How long are you staying, Russ?" Iris asked. "I know there isn't usually anyone there except for the summer months."

"Yes, well we will probably go home in a few weeks, the middle of July. I'm here with my son and he has football camp to go to," Russ explained.

"And where's your wife?" Iris asked.

Fern and Russell both looked up at Iris. "She passed away a year ago. Cancer," Russell answered.

"I'm so sorry. I didn't know."

"I know," Russell said. "It's okay."

There was silence as everyone drank their coffee. Iris was a curious woman and it was obvious that she loved her mother, but rarely made time for her. She was less than two hours away and didn't come very often. Russell makes time to see his brother and parents, although now he is questioning whether he is doing enough.

Iris stood up and collected the cups. Russell followed her inside. He helped her carry the bags full of trash outside to the curb. He explained that if she needed any help with anything else that all she needed to do was call him. Iris's cold exterior was melting. He thanked her for the coffee and went out to say good bye to Fern. He gave her a hug and went out towards his house.

Russell didn't know what kind of relationship Iris and Fern had. They seemed to get along, even though he knew Fern wanted more time with her daughter and son. He just hoped they could come to an agreement that would make everyone happy.

Russell walked up to a dark house. Adam wasn't home, yet. He decided to go for a swim. It was dusk and the water was calm. Russell let the water wash over him. He dove to the bottom and came up for air. It was refreshing and healing. He could see other swimmers down the beach, but no one he knew. He had solitude and privacy.

Russell kept trying to make everyone else happy. It felt natural but was also draining. He was a caregiver to his dying wife for years, he raised a son and now wanted to focus on himself. Was that selfish? He didn't think so. Russell wasn't looking for another wife, he just wanted to be happy again.

"Hey dad!" Adam yelled from shore.

Russell had just come up for air and waved back. He swam towards shore to hear all about Adam's day with the Covingtons. Just as he was coming up on the shore Russell stepped on something hard. When he bent down to get it, he saw that he had stepped on the most perfect spiral seashell he had ever seen. He held it up as he got closer to Adam.

"Wow, that's a nice one," Adam said.

"Tell me about your day," Russell said.

Adam told his father all about the day on St. Simon's Island on their walk back to the house. Bob had taken his boat and they went out fishing and snorkeling. He said that he and Trey had a lot of fun. Russell inquired whether Mandy had gone on this outing as well and Adam said she had. Russell smiled as Adam told him about the fish they caught and how many.

He said how Mandy thought she saw a shark, but it was really just a dolphin. Bob had let him drive the boat, but only for a few minutes.

"We need to get a boat, dad," Adam said. "You would love it."

"I'm sure I would," replied Russell.

Adam was still talking as his dad heated up microwave dinners for the two of them.

"Oh, and the Covingtons are having a big fourth of July party," Adam said, "with fireworks and everything."

Russell was washing up their dishes when Adam finally took a breath and finished telling about his day. Russell suggested they watch a movie tonight. Adam agreed. They both enjoyed action and horror movies but opted for an action one tonight. Adam made popcorn and sat next to his dad on the couch.

"Mrs. Fern's daughter came today," Russell said before the movie started.

"How is she?"

"She seems nice," Russell said. "I think she'll come more often now that she knows her mom needs help."

Adam gave his dad a sideways look and grabbed a handful of popcorn. He was glad to see his dad relaxing more. He couldn't remember the last time the two of them sat, ate popcorn and watched a movie together. Adam did it all the time with his mom, but rarely just his dad, at least not since middle school. This felt good.

Adam didn't tell his dad that he and Mandy exchanged numbers. Or that they held hands underwater. She was so excited to see the dolphins, even though she really wanted them to be sharks. He was on his best behavior today. He wasn't sure how Trey would react if he knew he wanted to spend more time with his sister. Trey was his best friend here and he didn't want to hurt him or mess things up.

Trey would always come first, at least that's how he hoped it would be. They were friends first. Trey had mentioned something about a party tomorrow night. It was the weekend before fourth of

July and it was tradition to party at the lighthouse. Adam had never been able to go before. He would bring it up with his dad tomorrow.

After the movie ended, they both went upstairs. Adam called Carter, he was home from his cruise. He said how it was dead without Adam there and then paused. Carter apologized, poor word choice. Coach Booker asked about him. Adam wanted him to know he was okay. The beach house was a great idea. He was actually having fun. Carter teased that there must be a girl and Adam denied it. Friends knew but also didn't push. Adam would tell him when he got home.

He laid on his bed and thought about his day. He picked up the seashell his dad gave him and put it on his shelf. It was one more for his continuing collection.

"Goodnight, mom," Adam said quietly and went to take a shower.

Russell was thinking about his own day and decided to call his younger brother.

"Hi Teddy," Russ said. "I hope it's not too late."

"No," Ted replied. "What's up?"

"How often do you visit mom and dad?"

"I guess a couple times a year. Why?" Ted asked.

"I guess I do, too. Is that enough?"

"What's wrong, Russ? Why are you suddenly worried about mom and dad? Did something happen?"

"No," Russ replied. "It's just this elderly neighbor of mine. She's all alone and walks to the water and talks to her dead husband. Her house is a mess, no food and she sits outside all day."

"Sounds like she needs to go to a home," Ted suggested.

"No, it sounds like home needs to come to her," Russ replied.

"What are you talking about?"

"I called her daughter and she came, but she's only staying for the weekend. When she leaves, her mother will go right back to what she was doing before," Russ said.

"Russ, stop. You can't solve everyone's problems," Ted said. "They will work it out. All you can do is inform the family of the situation and it's up to them. Ball is out of your court."

"You think mom and dad are good?" Russ asked.

"Russ, they are in a golf community out west. They are fine. Better than me," Ted said and laughed. "Don't beat yourself up about this."

"Okay," Russ said.

"Promise?"

"Yes," Russ replied. "Thanks, Teddy."

Russell did feel better after talking to his brother. Ted was right. It was out of his hands, especially once they left. He was not going to keep calling and checking on Fern, that was Iris's job. He would talk with Iris again, tomorrow, before she left. Russell was getting worked up for nothing. He just needed sleep.

Chapter 12

Russell and Adam were enjoying their morning routine. Running on the beach at sunrise was not only good for their physical health, it was good for their mental health. Everything looked different in the morning. A new day gave a new perspective.

Adam welcomed the opportunity to clear his head each morning. He was conflicted in his feelings for Mandy. She was Trey's little sister, but she wasn't little anymore. He was afraid to cross the line and ruin everything. He told himself he wouldn't do anything to ruin his friendship.

Fern was always on Russell's mind. He tried to remind himself that she wasn't his responsibility. He would talk with Iris before she left. He would feel better knowing she had a plan to look out for her mother.

Russell thought they could finally finish the back porch today. After breakfast they put on old painting clothes and got to work. Adam brought the gallons of white paint outside along with various sizes of brushes. Russell explained the basics of painting and they got to work.

Adam enjoyed the feeling of seeing the whole project come to a close. He was actually proud of the work they had done and to finally be working on the last part was rewarding. He initially hated the idea that his dad would monopolize so much of his summer doing something he knew nothing about, but in the end he was glad they did it.

He felt closer to his dad than he ever felt before. Adam knew this summer was either going to be their best or worst and he was pleasantly surprised it was their best. They only had each other now and it was working out fine.

"Hey dad," Adam said. "There's a party down by the lighthouse tonight. I was wondering if I could go."

Russell stopped painting to look at his son. "A party? Don't you think you're a bit young for that kind of party?"

Adam kept painting. "I don't know, I've never been to a lighthouse party before. If it's bad, I'll leave," Adam replied. "You know I don't drink. I just want to check it out and see what all the talk is about."

Russell relented. Adam was a good kid. "Okay, but you call me if there's any trouble and I'll come get you."

Adam rolled his eyes. "Okay, dad."

Russell smiled and went back to painting. The rest of the time they didn't talk. They didn't need to. The sound of their brushes mixed with the ocean waves was enough background noise to keep them in their own thoughts. It was a gorgeous day. The sun was high and air was warm, letting them know that June was almost over.

It had been a good month for them on the island. Russell realized there was more to life than just work. Although, he still worked occasionally, it was not the ten hour days he thought he needed to be successful. The thought of even opening his own firm or just being a consultant crossed his mind. It would give him more time with Adam until he went away to college and it would allow him the freedom to travel. Maybe even spend time with his parents. It was definitely on his mind lately.

Trey came over to check on their progress. Russell thought he really wanted to see if they were done yet so they could go surfing. Trey was impressed with the porch and even joked that maybe Adam finally found his calling. A quarterback who paints could be in high demand, Trey taunted. Adam threw his paint brush at him. Luckily it missed but it almost caused an all out paint war.

Russell suggested that Adam go have fun with Trey. He didn't want to leave, yet. They were almost done and Adam let Trey know he would be out in a little bit. Russell was impressed and they continued working until it was indeed finished. They both stepped back and admired the completed porch. It looked beautiful and new.

Adam went off to join Trey with his surfboard and since the porch couldn't be walked on, yet, Russell grabbed his own board. He was far enough from the boys that they wouldn't mind his old man surfing, too.

It felt good in the water after a day of painting. Russell managed to get up on the wave a few times, but mostly he was sitting on his board. He was facing the horizon and thinking of Lynn. He imagined what it would have been like to actually grow up here. He was experiencing it and he was envious. How wonderful this life must have been for her!

Russell decided to paddle into shore. As he did this, he noticed a figure sitting on the beach. When he got to the sand, he laid his board down and joined the woman on the towel.

Iris smiled as he came closer. Russell shook his hair out and grabbed his own towel on the chair. They sat next to each other and watched the waves roll in.

"Looked like you were having fun," Iris said.

"I was," Russell confirmed. "But it's also a great place to think."

"Yes, I always liked sitting right here and solving life's problems," Iris said.

Russel smiled and looked at Iris. "Wow, that's some serious thinking! What did you come up with?"

"Well, first of all," Iris started. "I'm having someone come and help mom three times a week. If I need to make further adjustments to that, I will."

Russell nodded his head. Her plan actually put his mind at ease, too. "That sounds like a solid plan."

Iris explained how stubborn her mother could be. Russell suspected that she was just like her mother, but didn't dare say so. She had called her brother asking him to come visit. Forrest said he would try. Russell understood that it was on her shoulders. He offered to help by looking in on her until he left next month and she was grateful.

Russell admitted it would be hard to leave this place. He never spent this much time here before. When Lynn brought Adam he would always have to drive back and forth to Atlanta for work. He was lucky if he had five days in a row here. Even those days were filled with phone calls and emails. He never just relaxed.

Iris said it was the same for her. If she stayed longer than a few days, it usually ended in her and her mother arguing. It was easier to just leave and stay away than deal with their issues. Iris said she always felt that Forrest was her parent's favorite. He was successful, married, and had children. Iris had been in and out of so many relationships she stopped even bringing them to meet her parents. It was easier to start her own life in a new city.

"You know," Russell started, "you really should go swimming. For old time's sake, I mean."

Iris looked at him and smiled. "Maybe later." Iris stood up and brushed the sand off her shorts.

"Well, If I don't see you before you go, I wish you well. Call me if you need anything," Russell said.

"I may try to come back one more time, you know, to check on mom," Iris replied.

"That would be nice," Russell said with a smile.

They waved good bye and they both went home. Russell showered, changed and looked for something to eat. He made instant ramen, sat at the kitchen island and pulled out his phone.

There were only a few texts and emails, they could wait. Russell finished his dinner and went into the living room to watch the news. He was content in the quiet house until Adam came running in, grabbed and apple and said he was going to change before the party. Russ heard him as he moved from room to room getting ready for his night out. He didn't know much about the lighthouse party, but he trusted Adam to make good decisions.

Russell waited until his son came back downstairs to ask him for more details. Trey was driving there, but he would drive home if Trey was not able to. There wasn't much more that his dad could say other than he had too much cologne on. As quickly as Adam had come in, he was gone. Russ remembered being seventeen, almost eighteen. He got into his own share of trouble that his parents had to ground him for. Adam was never like that.

The sun was setting and Russell was getting restless. He was tired of watching tv and with Adam out at a party, he wanted to go out, too. He decided to put his swim trunks on and go back into the ocean. He just wanted to feel the weightlessness of the water.

It was dark and the stars were bright. The moon was enough illumination to find his way to the water. Russell walked in slowly. Just his feet at first, then up to his waist. It was easy to get carried away in the melancholy of being alone. He missed the companionship of having someone there with him, of human touch.

Russell went out deeper and dove to the bottom. He stayed close enough to shore to see his house. There were a few lights on downstairs but upstairs was dark. Another reminder that no one was waiting for him.

Movement on the beach caught his eye. It was a figure coming closer to the water. Iris. Did she see him, he wondered? Iris waved at Russ and he waved back. She was more hesitant entering the water. She only put her feet in. He observed her movements as he waited for her to come closer. She was still only knee deep, but he could see her more clearly. She had a two piece bathing suit on that showed off her trim figure. Her blond, curly hair was shoulder length and it was blowing in the slight evening breeze. Russell had to admit she was pretty.

Iris was now waist deep and making noises that made him think she was scared of the waves coming into shore. Russ walked closer to her and held out his hand. Iris looked at him and took it. He gently led her deeper into the water. They were up to their shoulders now. Iris was giddy and nervous.

"I haven't been in the ocean in years," Iris said. "The big waves always scared me."

"Well, they aren't big now," Russ replied. "Plus, I'm here to save you."

Iris laughed again but kept her gaze on Russ. "I never asked what you do, Russ," Iris said after a few minutes of silence.

"I'm an architect," Russ answered. He explained about his job and how he was a workaholic only one month ago. His perspective on work changed dramatically after coming here.

"The beach sure has a way of clearing your mind," Iris agreed.

They stayed floating, drifting and standing in the water. They didn't need to speak, it was nice just having someone there. They would glance at each other when they thought the other wasn't looking. They were acting like shy teenagers and it felt good to both of them. Russ didn't know what Iris was thinking, but he wanted to get to know her better. He hoped he would see her again.

Iris didn't tell Russ that the only reason she came out to night swim was because she was sitting on her porch and saw him go in the water. He was handsome with his salt and pepper hair and toned body. She quickly changed into her swimsuit and followed him. She even decided right then that she would make another trip to Jekyll Island before they moved back to Atlanta.

"Well, I enjoyed this," Iris said. "I am getting tired and I think I'll go inside now." She hated to leave but it was late and she was exhausted.

"Okay, I'll help you out," Russ offered.

They walked towards shore and Iris stumbled as they came out onto the sand. Russ reached out with his hand and Iris took it, again. They looked into each other's eyes.

"Thank you," Iris said and leaned in to kiss him.

Russ, surprised, kissed her back. "Good night," he said and watched her walk away.

Chapter 13

Today was July fourth. The biggest party day of the summer. Russell and Adam had spent the last few days driving around and hanging out. They went fishing, swimming at Driftwood Beach and then into Brunswick and did some shopping for the party. The Covingtons were hosting again but this one would be bigger and better than Memorial Day. Everyone along the beach had bought fireworks and would set them off tonight.

Adam couldn't wait. He had met a girl at the lighthouse party and even invited her tonight. Trey did, too. That was a fun night. There was a bonfire, drinks and lots of kids. Adam had never seen anything like it. Trey did drink too much and Adam drove them home. At least tonight, they were within walking distance.

Adam helped Russell take all the food and drinks over to the Covington's backyard. Bob was already cooking on the grill and Julie had food displayed so appetizingly on the porch. Trey had his speakers on the floor with his music blasting. Neighbors came from next door and across the street. Someone even brought a second grill. Russ and Adam brought their own chairs, made a plate and sat down. Russ saw kids playing corn hole, others using the volleyball net and even more people were in the water. It was such a relaxed atmosphere that time seemed to stand still.

Russ talked to Bob about his banking job and realized he enjoyed the conversation today. When they first arrived, Russell was still pretty uptight and didn't think he could ever relax enough to sit around, have a beer and discuss the interest rates. Today he could.

He even met some new people who lived in the neighborhood that he never met before. Russell was actually enjoying himself at a Covington party.

Adam and Trey went out on their surf boards. There were a lot more kids here than last time and they all seemed to be having fun together. Except for Mandy. Russell saw her in the doorway looking out at the kids in the water. There weren't many girls at the party, he noticed.

"Mandy, do you want to come help me take a plate of food over to Mrs. Fern?" Russell asked.

"Sure," Mandy said with as much enthusiasm as she could muster.

Russell just smiled and filled one plate with a hamburger, potato salad, baked beans, cole slaw and chips. The other one that he handed to Mandy had cookies, a cupcake and a brownie. They walked out to the beach and down towards Fern's house. Russell noticed Mandy watching the boys play on the surfboards.

"Do you have a lot of friends here, Mandy?" Russell asked.

"Yes, but they always go away for July fourth," Mandy said. "When you live here year round, families tend to leave for holidays rather than stay."

Russell supposed that was true. They had reached Fern's back porch and Mandy set her plate down on the table. Russell thanked her for her help and said she could get back to the party. She did. Russell laid out all the food in front of Fern and handed her a fork. Fern smiled and tasted some of everything. They sat watching the water. Even from here they could hear the kids laughing in the ocean two doors down.

Russell asked Fern how the helper Iris hired was working out. She said it was going fine. When Russell asked why it was only fine, Fern replied that the girl kept moving things. Russell laughed and asked her to elaborate. Fern didn't want to and left it at that. Russ just smiled and hoped the girl wouldn't quit.

Russell got up the courage to ask about Iris. Fern said she was fine, they talked just this morning.

"Did she say when she would be visiting again?" Russell asked.

"No," Fern said. "But she did say she had some vitamins she wanted me to start taking, so it sounded like she might come soon."

Russell simply nodded his head. He couldn't stop thinking about their kiss. It was only a single kiss, but he still thought about it. It had stirred feelings in him that he hadn't felt in a long time. Fern was enjoying the food and the company. She said she would miss him when they finally left. Having them next door was like having her children around again.

He hated to leave her, but Russell excused himself and went back to the party. It made him sad to think about leaving this place. It was getting dark now, sunset was fading behind the houses. The orange glow on the water showed a few kids still on their surf boards. Russell noted that Adam and Trey were not part of the group in the water.

As he came into the Covington's back yard, he saw the boys sitting and eating another plate of food. "You're going to get a cramp if you swim after eating all that," Russell teased.

"It's fine, dad, we're sitting out until the fireworks," Adam replied.

"Sitting out or pigging out?" Russell asked. He turned around when he heard a girl laughing. It was Mandy.

"Mandy, do you want something to eat before these two eat it all?" Russell asked.

Mandy laughed. "No, sir, I'm okay for now."

Russell noticed that she watched Adam the whole time. She definitely had a crush and hoped that Adam didn't break her heart. Trey's mother called him into the house. Adam went to sit on a blanket on the beach. Mandy followed Adam.

Adam moved over to give Mandy room on the towel. She looked at him and then out at the water. He looked at her then noticed the scar on her right foot.

"I remember when you got that," Adam said, touching the scar.

Adam's touch surprised Mandy and she looked at the scar. "Driftwood Beach. You and Trey were chasing me and I tripped over a branch poking out of the sand."

Adam put his hands back on his lap. "I'm sorry about that."

"It wasn't so bad," Mandy said. " You gave me a piggy back ride to the car."

The memory of that day many years ago made them both look at each other. Mandy had changed so much. She was beautiful. It was still strange for Adam to think of her that way, but here, sitting inches apart, it was hard not to.

Mandy saw so much maturity in Adam's face and eyes. He was older and more confident. She noticed that he even shaved now because stubble was starting to show. His hair blew into his eyes and she reached up to move it away. At first Adam flinched and almost backed away until he realized what she was doing. It was sweet and intimate. They each had touched each other with only one finger but it sent ripples of current through them. If it was any other girl he would have made the first move to kiss her, but not here and not Mandy.

Mandy was breathing hard and hoped Adam didn't notice. She didn't know why she reached out and moved his hair. It was just something she had wanted to do and did it. She watched his reaction and he seemed okay with it. Then why didn't he make a move? It was his turn. Instead, he just stared at her. He looked at her eyes, her hair and her lips. When Adam didn't kiss her, she felt so disappointed. She wanted to touch him again, but knew there were people watching them.

It had gotten dark. Dark enough to start the fireworks. Trey came up behind Adam and slapped him on the back.

"It's fireworks time!" Trey yelled.

Adam and Mandy both turned, he was thankful for the distraction and stood up. Mandy did, too.

"And the girls are here," Trey said.

"Girls?" Mandy asked.

"Yes, me and Adam's girls from the other night," Trey replied. "They wanted to party and see the fireworks, too."

Adam looked from Trey to Mandy. All he could do was shrug his shoulders and look apologetically at Mandy. She just shook her head and walked towards the house. Adam watched her until she went inside, she never looked back. He didn't mean to hurt her but he knew he did. These girls didn't even mean anything to Adam and inviting them wasn't his idea, it was Trey's. Adam started to go in the house and look for Mandy when he heard the first fireworks exploding. Adam turned around and went back on the beach.

Up and down the beach they could see fireworks shooting up to the sky. It was so beautiful. There were fireworks of every size, style and color imaginable. Trey came up beside Adam. He had two girls with him. Adam didn't even remember which girl he made out with last week. Maybe that made him a jerk, but he could only imagine kissing one girl tonight and it wasn't one of these.

Adam looked back towards the house and thought he saw a figure in an upstairs window but it was too dark to know for sure. Russell came up beside his son and asked if everything was okay.

"Yeah, sure," Adam replied. "No, I don't know."

His dad just looked at him and smiled. "I understand," Russell said. "It's about a girl, isn't it?" Adam nodded his head. "Just talk to her. Tell her how you really feel."

Adam gave a half smile and watched as more fireworks went up into the air. Russell put an arm around his son. "Relationships aren't always easy, but they are worth it when you find the right one."

Russell left him so Adam could be with his friends. He walked back up to the house. Russell saw Bob and Julie sitting arm in arm on their porch swing watching the fireworks. It was a lovely sight and he hated to interrupt them.

"Bob and Julie, good night," Russell said. "It was a great party as always. Thank you."

"Hey anytime, Russ!" Bob called out. "Have a good night, careful getting home."

Russell heard Bob laugh at his own joke. He had to smile, himself. It was a fun night and maybe next year, he could host it. He wasn't sure why he was thinking ahead to next year. Russell needed to actually sit down and run the numbers to see if they could even afford to keep the beach house. Adam would not want to sell it, but on one income, it would drain them to maintain two houses. He would worry about that later.

Right now, Russell stood at the water's edge and felt the water wash over his feet. At this moment he couldn't think of anywhere else in the world he would rather be. Fireworks exploded above him and lit up the water. The colors danced on the surface and then disappeared only to be replaced by a more brilliant display. Yes, the beach house was magic.

"Good night, Lynn," Russell said out loud before turning towards home.

Chapter 14

Adam woke up the next morning tired and restless. He hated how he had hurt Mandy last night and wanted to make it up to her. He went for his run, not even waiting for his dad. He ran longer and harder than he did this whole time on the beach. Adam showered, ate and then texted Mandy.

He didn't know what to say or even how to start it. "Good morning," Adam texted. Then he added, "I'm sorry about last night." He anxiously watched his phone for a reply. He even started to wonder if she was awake, then he saw that she was typing.

"Good morning," Mandy texted back. That was it.

Adam thought again about how he could get her to talk to him. "Do you want to go get breakfast?"

Another pause and then, "Sure," Mandy texted back.

He was so relieved that she agreed to meet him. "Meet me at my jeep in ten," he typed.

Adam went downstairs, grabbed the keys and wrote his dad a note. He was already in the jeep when Mandy got in. They both awkwardly greeted each other and then Adam drove them to the diner down the road. He held the door open for Mandy as they entered the diner, chose a booth and sat down.

"I'm glad you agreed to come with me. I think we need to talk," Adam said nervously.

The waitress came with menus and asked for their drink orders. When they were alone he continued. "I'm sorry about last night and those girls."

Mandy looked at Adam. "It's okay. You don't owe me any explanation. You are free to do whatever with whomever you want."

Adam looked down at his hands. The waitress came with their orange juices and took their orders. "But I do," Adam said. "I like you." He rubbed his hands together when he felt the perspiration on his palms. "I felt a connection the minute I arrived here and I'm sorry I ruined it."

The waitress brought their orders. Mandy got pancakes and scrambled eggs. Adam got eggs, bacon and toast. Neither one of them made a move to start eating.

"I like you, too. I always have," Mandy said. "And you didn't ruin it." Mandy smiled at Adam and he smiled back.

That was all he needed to know. It wasn't ruined. They were free to eat their breakfast, talk and laugh. Adam pointed out that she had something on the corner of her mouth and wiped it away. She laughed when he dripped orange juice on his shirt. Luckily it was a dark shirt, but it was still a cause for more laughter. Mandy liked the familiarity of hanging out with Adam. She imagined in her head it was their first date. Adam paid the bill and they went out into the sunshine.

He was starting to head for his jeep when Mandy said, "Let's go in here." It was a store devoted to ocean animals with their images on everything from shirts and hats to beach towels and tote bags. Adam watched Mandy's eyes light up at all the marine animals she loved. She walked around the store with one hand extended so that her fingertips could lightly brush everything in the store.

She stopped in front of a plate with an image of a hammerhead shark on it. "You know, hammerheads are the most sensitive shark when it comes to being caught and tagged," Mandy said. "They don't handle stress well and can die easily."

"I did not know that," Adam answered. He watched her in her element. "So where will you go to school?"

"Probably College of Coastal Georgia," Mandy said. "It's small, close by and I can commute. I would hate to study ocean animals and not be near the ocean."

Adam nodded. The logic made sense to him. "I know you would be good at it," Adam said.

"Thanks," Mandy replied. "What about you? You still don't know where you want to go?"

"I don't even know what I want to do," said Adam.

They walked around the rest of the store and Adam watched her admiring a book of sharks. She looked at every page and then put it down. She said she was ready to go and they returned to the jeep.

They didn't drive straight home, though. He drove around Jekyll Island without any destination in mind. It was nice to just have the companionship without any of the judgement or sorrow. He and Mandy were friends but he was really having feelings for her. Adam looked straight ahead as they drove down narrow roads.

Mandy would steal glances of Adam as he drove. To her, this was a dream come true. How many times had she fantasized about being alone with Adam? She couldn't even count. He was never interested in her, although he would always make room for her when he played with Trey.

"I like that you are actually laughing and having a good time," Mandy said. "Smiles look good on you."

Adam looked over at Mandy and, right on cue, he smiled. This made Mandy laugh. They were riding with the top of the jeep off. The wind was blowing their hair and it was perfect.

"Turn here," Mandy said.

Adam followed her orders and turned. It was a small sandy road that was shaded with tree branches. "Is this a road?" Adam asked.

"Yes, it opens up at the other end. It's my favorite place on the island."

Adam continued driving until it widened to a small parking area. It was level and sandy, only big enough for a couple of cars. They got out and walked straight down a more narrow path. When they emerged from the trees, Adam saw that it had a view of St. Simon's Island, all the way down Jekyll Island and even a smaller island off to the side. It was a place on the island he didn't even know existed.

Adam turned to Mandy, "This is beautiful."

"I'm glad you like it," Mandy replied. "I come here when I really want to get away."

"Thank you for showing me this," Adam said.

He took Mandy's hand and stood there looking at almost a full three sixty view. It was a special moment and Adam suddenly felt emotional. He was overwhelmed with the need to show his mother this spot. Maybe she had already discovered it herself years ago.

Mandy wasn't expecting him to be so emotional but it didn't frighten her. She reached in her purse and handed him a tissue. Adam wiped at his eyes and smiled at her.

"I'm sorry," he said. "I don't know where that came from."

"You don't have to apologize," she said. "You can be yourself with me."

Adam suddenly felt vulnerable and uncomfortable. "We'd better get back."

Mandy simply nodded and followed him back down the narrow walkway to the jeep. The ride home was different. There was no more laughter, side glances or smiles. Adam's mood had changed and she didn't know how to get him back.

"Maybe later we can go surfing?" She asked.

Adam half smiled and said, "Sure."

RUSSELL WOKE UP TO a very quiet house. Downstairs he found a note in the kitchen that just said, 'Gone out'. Russell didn't really know what that meant but he trusted Adam. He went for his run without his son. It was another gorgeous morning, the sun had come up and casted a red and orange glow over the water.

Everyday Russell and Adam pushed themselves to run longer each morning. Now, they were running nearly two and a half hours each morning. It felt good and he wanted to continue doing it even when they went back home. Home. Russell hadn't thought about home in a while. Just as he was nearing their beach house, he heard yelling.

Russell was passing the Covington's place and he slowed down to hear if they needed help. Instead, he overheard Julie yelling that she didn't want Mandy hanging out with a boy. It was inappropriate and he was going to be leaving soon. Then Bob said that Adam was a good kid and wouldn't hurt their Mandy.

Russell couldn't believe what he was hearing. Were they arguing about Adam? Adam and Mandy? They barely spent any time together. Then Julie said that Adam's father wasn't exactly keeping a very good eye on his son. That they shouldn't be out there alone right now. Russell's thoughts went back to the note in the kitchen. There was no mention of where, with whom or why he went anywhere. Shit.

He ran back to his house and tried to call his son. It just went to voicemail which probably meant they had no signal. What were you doing, Adam? Russell knew his son wouldn't be stupid, but everyone makes mistakes. All he could do now was wait.

Russell showered, tried to eat and then turned on the tv. Maybe it was all his fault. He wasn't exactly putting any limits or restraints on Adam's actions. Russell just felt like his son had been through enough. He deserved to have a summer that was carefree and fun.

He heard the front door open, keys thrown on the entryway table and foot steps approach the living room. Russell stood up.

"Where did you go?"

"Breakfast and a walk."

"With who?"

"Mandy."

"What else did you do?" Russell hated to ask for a play by play of his son's day, but he was pretty sure the Covingtons were doing the exact same thing next door. He needed to know.

"What's this all about?" Adam demanded. "I felt like I treated Mandy badly yesterday, or at the very least, ignored her, and I wanted to make up for it. I texted her asking if she wanted to go to breakfast and she said yes."

Russell looked at his son. "You said something about going for a walk?"

Adam shifted on his feet and rolled his eyes. "Yes, we went for a drive and she showed me her favorite spot at the top of the island. We talked and then came home." Adam was getting impatient. "What's wrong with going out for breakfast?"

Russell released a breath he didn't even know he was holding. "Nothing, really, it's just that when I went for my run this morning, I overheard the Covingtons arguing."

"About what?"

"You."

"Me?"

"Yes, they seem to think you shouldn't be alone with Mandy, that, in their words, it is 'inappropriate.'"

Adam let his shoulders sag. Russell thought he looked like a guy who just got the wind knocked out of him. His expression was pure sadness.

"I'm sorry, son. I'm just letting you know their thinking on the subject," Russell said. "They don't know I overheard, so it's best to continue as you were. If they want to say anything to us, let them say it."

Adam's expression and demeanor didn't change. "I like her, dad."

"I know."

Adam finally turned and went to his room. He threw himself on his bed and pulled out his phone. There were no new messages from Mandy. Was she getting yelled at like he was? They didn't do anything wrong. It was a big mess, blown completely out of proportion.

He decided to text her, assuming she was still allowed to have her phone. Adam simply texted 'hey'. He turned on his side and hugged the teddy bear.

His phone made a sound and he quickly read the message, 'hi'. He asked if she was okay and she texted, 'yes, but my parents weren't happy.'

Adam told her he was sorry about that but he had a good time. Mandy said she did, too. He promised that next time they would let their parents know exactly where they were going. She agreed, but secretly wondered if they would let her go out alone with him, again. They said goodbye and Adam rolled over on his back.

He could see the sun was setting and he didn't want to stay inside. Adam called Trey and asked if he wanted to go surfing. He could always count on Trey for a distraction. He was the kind of friend that didn't care if he was sad or happy, he would make sure he had fun.

"Yes!" Trey answered, "See you there."

Chapter 15

Most mornings Russell and Adam went swimming in the ocean after their run. They would sit on the adirondack chairs, take off their shoes, socks and shirts and race to the water. Cheating was allowed. Russell realized the only way he could win against the youth of his son was to either push him down or knock him over as they sprinted to the ocean. Adam was not above cheating, either, but usually he didn't need to in order to win.

This was the time Russell cherished with his son. The carefree mornings before real life took over. They both knew their time here was quickly coming to an end, but neither one wanted to talk about it. Russell had called Coach Booker and they were still expecting him in two weeks.

They slowly walked out of the water and was returning to the house when Russell spotted a figure laying on Fern's backyard. He called to Adam and they both went over to check it out. What they saw made Russell turn to his son and tell him to call 911.

It was Fern. She must have fallen down the steps. She was conscious but in pain. Adam came back with their phones and said they were on their way. Russell took his phone and called Iris. He explained that they just found her laying on the ground and that an ambulance was coming. Iris said she would be there in two hours.

Fern was talking but couldn't move. That was probably for the best since she most likely broke something. Maybe a leg or a hip, they didn't know. Russell and Adam both knelt by her side and held her hands. They talked to her but noticed she would go in and out of consciousness. They kept her company until the paramedics took her.

Russell and Adam returned home to wait for Iris. This wouldn't have happened if Iris had found proper care for her mother. Russell was angry at her nonchalant care of Fern. Fern had been through enough in her life, she didn't deserve to be ignored by her own children.

When Iris arrived, she knocked on Russell's back door. She wanted to know which hospital they took Fern. Russell told her but only after saying that someone should have been with her. She should have been with her. Iris yelled right back saying this wasn't her fault. Whether she or anyone was there or not, it wouldn't have been prevented.

"Maybe it could have," Russell said as Iris slammed the door on her way out. He was angry at her, but the few moments that Iris had stood in his kitchen made him realize that he also missed her. He missed the talking, interaction and even the yelling with someone. Maybe this time Iris would stick around.

Russell decided to go and tell the Covingtons about Fern. He was not sure how their reaction would be to him. They hadn't seen each other since Russell overheard them arguing about Adam spending time with Mandy. At least he knew about it and couldn't get blindsided. He slowly went up the beach, across their yard and knocked on their backdoor.

Julie answered. Russell explained what happened to Fern and how he and Adam found her laying at the bottom of her back steps. She expressed her shock and sympathy and said that if there was anything they could do just let them know. Russell explained that her daughter, Iris, is here now.

"Oh yes," Julie said. "She was here earlier, wasn't she? She's nice."

Russell confirmed that she was here a couple of weeks ago and that she was, indeed, nice. He asked where Trey and Mandy were, he hadn't seen them all morning. She said they were inside doing chores.

"Can't waste everyday running around and going out," Julie said.

Russell knew this was a direct stab at Adam. "Well, the kids need time to play, too. We are leaving soon and it would be a shame to waste precious time. They're good kids, no need to punish them."

"It's not punishment, Russ, it's called supervision." Julie closed the door.

Russell walked back towards his house. Adam had been inside playing Madden, but saw now that he was on his surfboard in the water. Russell was going to lay down and take a nap but decided, instead, to join his son. He went inside, changed and brought his board to the water.

"How are you doing?" Russell asked.

"I'm okay," Adam answered. "Trey and Mandy said they can't come out right now, so I thought I'd just wait."

"Wait for what?"

"Anything or anyone." Adam answered. "Sometimes I feel like I'm missing out on things but I don't know how to prevent it. I make a move and nothing happens. I do what I'm told, I'm nice to people and I even hang out with my dad," Adam looked up and smiled at Russell. "I just feel like I'm not moving forward, I'm stuck in the same place." He paused before adding, "I don't know if that makes any sense."

"It does," his father confirmed. "It just means that it's not the right time."

They paddled out further and caught some waves. Russell was hoping the activity would help get Adam out of his head. No good comes from overthinking. They were enjoying their time together until Adam saw Trey and Mandy come into the water. Adam went over to join them, sure that they were all under the watchful eye of Julie.

Russell was going to stay out a little longer until he saw Iris coming home next door. He came in and dried off before going over to see how Fern was.

Iris confirmed that she did have a broken leg. She was also dehydrated. They were keeping her another day or so because they could not be sure if she hit her head or not. Iris had gone grocery shopping on her way back and Russell asked if she needed any help.

"Sure," Iris said. "I'll never turn down help unloading the car."

Russell helped with putting the groceries away, too. Iris told him that she had planned to come up at the end of the week anyway. Her mother's little accident just pushed it up a few days. She had a contract on her place in Jacksonville and was now just waiting on a date to sign the final papers. Iris was moving in with Fern.

He wasn't sure how to react. He was very happy that she would be here, but he was leaving soon. Russell would love the opportunity of getting to know her better, but was it even worth it? He was falling for this woman and hardly even knew her. The advice he gave his son was to tell a girl how you feel. He would, but not now.

Iris said the stress of today was getting to her. Russell said the best thing that he has found to relieve the stress is swimming. She smiled.

"Only if you come with me."

Russ nodded his head. He still had his swim trunks on from earlier. A fact that was not lost on Iris. She had been trying not to stare at this bare chest the whole time he was in her house. He waited until Iris changed into her two piece swimsuit, grabbed a float and then walked with her to the water.

Iris sat on the float so that she didn't have to tread water, that was too tiring. Russell stayed where he could still touch the ground. He asked her about moving to Jekyll Island. He wondered how this would impact her real estate career. She said she was already in the process of getting licensed in Georgia, then there really would be no difference. She just had to deal with living with her mother.

Russell laughed at that. He knew that couldn't be easy. Iris was starting to relax. She would let her head fall back and her curly hair get wet.

"I'm sorry about what I said earlier, that someone should have been there for your mother," Russ said. "It probably wouldn't have made a difference."

"It's okay," Iris replied. "I know you just care about her and want what's best for her. That's what makes you such a good neighbor."

"I care about you, too," Russ admitted.

"I care about you," Iris said. "But you are leaving soon. It wouldn't work."

Russell remained silent. He dove to the bottom because he didn't want to have to admit it out loud. He knew it wouldn't work but yet here he was swimming with Iris. They stayed together in the water until the sun started setting over the houses.

As they made their way onto the beach, Iris asked Russell if he'd like to come over for dinner. He said he love to, but not tonight. He asked for a rain check and she agreed. Russell wanted to make sure his son was okay. He was watching them from afar and even though the three of them were swimming and surfing together, Adam still managed to find a way to get close to Mandy.

Was it subconscious, biological or chemical that always brought Adam and Mandy together? Adam was aware of it. He tried focusing his attention on Trey. He listened to him talk about the girl he was now dating or his football team that was undefeated last year. Even then, he moved closer to Mandy.

Mandy felt it too. She liked being included like old times, but she knew this was nothing like old times. It was new and exciting. She watched Adam. The way he ran his fingers through his wet hair, the way his eyes wrinkled when he smiled or the way he always sneezed when salt water went up his nose. These were the things she loved about him.

Julie called Trey and Mandy in for dinner. "Do you want to join us, Adam?"

As much as Adam would have loved to, he shook his head, "Thank you, Mrs. Julie, but I'm having dinner with my dad."

Trey and Adam did their silly hand shake that they've been doing since elementary school and Mandy just rolled her eyes. Adam came up behind her, "I saw that!" Adam said.

They were all laughing as they went different directions to their own houses for dinner. Russell was just setting the table for a spaghetti dinner when he looked up to see Adam still so happy.

"Looks like someone had a good day," Russell said to his son.

"I could say the same thing about you," Adam teased. "I saw you late night swimming with a lady."

Russell felt his face blush. They joked and teased each other. The camaraderie was something that made coming to the beach house worth it. They sat down to eat and talked about their days. Russell told him about what Iris said about Fern's injuries. They were just glad they found her when they did.

Adam said Mrs. Julie had invited him to eat dinner with them but he declined. He didn't want to feel like they were watching every move he made. Russell was sorry he felt like that, but it was probably true.

Adam helped his dad clean up the dishes. "Is it another movie night?" Adam asked.

"It sure is," his dad answered, "your choice tonight."

"Okay," Adam started while drying a dish, "I'm in the mood for a romantic comedy."

Russell turned to him to make sure he was joking. "No, I veto that choice."

Adam smiled while following his dad into the living room listing every single romantic comedy he could think of. Finally, Russ had enough. "No, I'll choose." They finally settled on another action movie and ate more popcorn. These were the memories that would stick with Russ forever. He looked over at the fireplace. That, too.

Chapter 16

Rain in the morning interrupted Russell and Adam's plans. They stayed inside and waited until it ended. Russell continued to work while Adam continued getting restless in the house all morning.

"I'm going to Trey's," Adam said. Russell waved him off.

Adam knocked on Trey's back door but it was Mandy who answered. She said her parents had to take him into town for some football thing. It was going to take a while and she didn't want to go.

"Actually, I was going to ride my bike to get ice cream. Do you want to come?" Mandy asked.

Adam did not want a repeat of last time, so he called his dad. Russell said it was fine as long as she asked her parents, too. Mandy called her mom but it only went to voicemail. She must have her phone turned off or silent. Instead, Mandy left a detailed note. They hoped that would be enough.

The rain stopped long enough for them to ride bikes to the ice cream parlor down the road. They parked their bikes and went in. They each got a double scoop of their favorites. Mandy got mint chocolate chip and Adam got chocolate. They left their bikes and walked onto the beach. The rain apparently kept most people inside because they had the beach to themselves.

There were still dark clouds but they didn't care. They sat on the sand and started eating their ice cream. They each offered the other a taste of theirs. It was sweet and intimate. Just as they finished their ice cream, they felt the first drops of rain. The rain drops got bigger fast.

Adam and Mandy looked around for cover and saw a large oak tree with low hanging branches. They ran to it and found that it could keep them dry. Their hair was already dripping and their clothes were wet. They huddled together to stay warm.

Mandy reached up to push a lock of Adam's hair out of his eyes. It was a gesture she had done before, but this time no one was looking. He reached up and did the same to her. He moved her hair from her face and tucked it behind her ear. Their eyes never veered from each other.

When they kissed, it was soft and uncertain. Their hands remained cupped on each other's cheeks. Neither one backed away and Mandy leaned in to kiss Adam again. This time it was not so timid.

Again, they stopped to look at each other. They were uncertain about what to do next and then Adam put his other arm around her waist. Mandy's other arm was touching his chest. She had always dreamed her first kiss would be with Adam, but after his mother died and they didn't stay, she gave up hope. Until last month.

Adam leaned down and kissed her again. This time not only did their mouths and tongues search for more, their hands did, too. It wasn't until a crack of thunder startled them that they finally broke away.

Adam, finally realizing what he had just done turned away from Mandy and touched his own mouth. Mandy, confused watched him as he ran the other hand through is hair.

"Is everything okay?" Mandy asked. "Was, uh, I okay?"

Adam figured out that she was really asking if she was a good kisser, turned to her. "Yes, it's not that. I don't think your parents would approve of us being together, not like this."

Mandy knew he was right. "But I don't care about that. I love you, Adam."

Looking at Mandy, Adam couldn't lie. "I love you, too. But I don't think we can be together."

Mandy wiped at the tears that were forming in the corners of her eyes. The rain had stopped. She realized the intimacy of the moment had passed, she was ready to get out of there before she embarrassed herself any further. "We'd better go."

Mandy turned and headed back towards their bikes. Adam, feeling horribly, followed.

RUSSELL WENT OUTSIDE to sit on the beach. It had rained earlier, but the clouds were moving on. He loved watching the rain move across the water. It danced in different directions and the sky could be completely covered in clouds and look so ominous, then minutes later rays of sunshine would break through the clouds. If you took your eyes away from it, you missed a critical piece in the theatrical display.

Russell heard voices off his left shoulder. He turned to look towards Fern's house and didn't see anyone outside. If voices were being carried as far as his chair, Fern and Iris must be yelling. He got up to see if he could help the situation.

As he got closer to Fern's house, he could make out bits of conversation.

"I'm not going anywhere!"

"Mom, it was only a suggestion!"

"You can't make me leave!"

Just as Russell was on the porch, he heard a crash. Worried that someone had fallen, again, he let himself in. All eyes went from person to person and then to a broken coffee mug on the floor.

Russell's sudden appearance in their kitchen instantly silenced their yelling.

"What happened?" Russell inquired.

Fern and Iris immediately started talking at once. Russell closed his eyes and put his hands up. They stopped.

"I can only hear one of you at a time," Russell said. "Mrs. Fern, you start, please."

Fern gave her daughter a quick side eye and said, "She wants me to move into a home for old people. I'm not old and I don't want to move." Fern sat down and crossed her arms.

Russell looked at Iris, "I merely suggested that this is a big house, too big to take care of. I can find her a cute little place with people her age that she could actually do things with."

"But I thought you were moving back here?" Russell asked, confused.

"I am, but that doesn't mean we have to live here," Iris explained.

Russell, now feeling like he had a firmer grasp on the argument, decided to ask one more question. "Why is there a broken coffee mug on the floor? Mrs. Fern, you didn't try to throw this at your daughter, did you?" He was half smiling and half joking, but when Fern hesitated he grew more concerned.

"No, I just threw it, Russell. I was so frustrated. She's not listening to what I want," Fern said, pointing at Iris. "I don't want to move!"

Russell looked at Iris. "Can I talk to you outside, please?"

Iris followed him outside and onto the beach. He didn't want Fern to overhear their conversation. They sat on the sand and Russell stared straight into the ocean.

"I know you haven't come back here often, me either, really. I used to only stay a couple of weeks each summer then go back home to work. But being here everyday for nearly six weeks has changed my perspective on this place. And Fern has lived here her whole life,"

Russell looked over at Iris. "To remove Fern from her home would be like ripping out her heart. She wouldn't survive."

Iris looked at Russell, "I was just going over options."

"Well, may I suggest you look at options that include your moving in with her."

Their shoulders were touching and they both knew it. "Why do you always seem to appear when I need you?" Iris asked softly.

"Just lucky, I guess," replied Russell.

They both leaned in and kissed. There was a yearning that they both had and wanted desperately to fulfill. But for now, Iris excused herself saying she wanted to check on her mother.

MANDY RODE HER BIKE straight home. None of the detours or side roads she had planned to take Adam. This date started great in her head, but ended badly. She was humiliated and wanted nothing more than to be in her bedroom, crying. She could hear Adam peddling just as fast behind her.

Did he know he broke her heart? Was he capable of seeing it or not? Right now, Mandy just wanted to get as far away from Adam as possible. She could see the turn for their driveway up ahead. As she turned in, so did he. Mandy got off her bike and scowled at him.

"Go home!" Mandy yelled.

Adam, taken aback by her tone and words, stopped what he was doing. He didn't realize she was so upset. He put his kickstand down on his bike and explained.

"I just want to talk to your parents and assure them that we only went for ice cream and then home," Adam replied.

"Oh, so you think you were such a gentleman?" Mandy asked, coldly.

"I'm trying," Adam replied quietly.

"Well, try harder. Gentlemen don't go around saying they love you and then say they don't want to be with you!"

"I didn't say I didn't want to be with you. I said I don't think we can be together. There's a difference."

Mandy was crying now, tears running down her cheeks. "Just words, that's the only difference because either way, in the end, we aren't together. Why do you get to make that decision?"

Adam tried walking closer to her but she backed away. "Because I know it's what your parents want, too."

Mandy stopped crying. How did he know she had that argument with her parents? Unless they talked to him, too. Mandy started to feel embarrassed that her parents were trying to decide who she could see and who she couldn't. Her anger was now shifting from Adam to her parents.

She wiped her tears away and took one step closer to Adam. "I'm sorry," Mandy said. "I don't think they're home, yet, so they won't even know about today." She tried a faint smile.

"You have to believe me when I say I don't want to hurt you. Your parent's wishes mean a lot because if I make them mad, they won't let me see you ever." Adam walked up to Mandy, they were within arms reach. "I couldn't bear not seeing you again. You are all I think about."

Adam leaned down and kissed Mandy. They were acutely aware that her parents and brother could pull into the driveway at any moment but they didn't care. Maybe that's what made it more special. They hugged and kissed until they heard a car. It was a false alarm, but they realized they were taking a big, unnecessary risk.

Mandy turned to go in her front door. Adam got on his bike and prepared to ride to his house. "I'll call you later," Adam yelled back and rode away.

Adam was smiling when he walked in his front door. He looked straight out onto the beach and saw two figures kissing. Then he saw one figure stand up and walk away. Adam went out onto the beach to sit with his father.

"Well, I see you've been very welcoming to Mrs. Fern's daughter," Adam teased.

Russell smiled. "Yes," he replied. "Actually, I'd like for us all to have lunch or dinner together. I'd like for you to get to know her a little better."

"So this is serious?" Adam asked.

"Maybe, I feel butterflies, again." Russell turned to his son. "How did things go with Mandy? Did her parents say anything?"

"Things went well," Adam's smile gave it away. "I told her I loved her. And her parents never came home, so they don't even know we went out."

Russell put his arm around his son. "Well, I'm happy for you, son."

"I'm happy for both of us, dad."

It was true. They were both happy. Only a couple of months ago they were as miserable and depressed as two guys could be. Who would have thought how quickly things would turn around on the island? Well, maybe one person. As Russell and Adam stood up to go inside, they both whispered something to the ocean.

"Thanks, Lynn."

"Thanks, mom."

Chapter 17

Trey called Adam and invited him on the boat. Adam was excited about hanging out with his family on the water, again. "Who all is going?"

"Just my family, and you," Trey answered.

Adam said he would be over in twenty minutes. It also meant that in twenty minutes he was going to hang out with Mandy for the day, discretely, of course. Perhaps if Adam could build up their trust in him, they wouldn't be so against their being together. He really didn't know what they didn't like about him, but he would always try to make a good impression.

Adam told his dad that he would be gone for the day, another invite on the Covington's boat. Russell was happy that he was still being included and it would give him some peace and quiet at home. There were some issues with his latest client and he feared he may have to go back to Atlanta in the next couple of days.

"Have fun," Russell said as Adam went out the back door.

Russell called his client and tried to figure out exactly what he didn't like about the new blueprints. The client wanted a restaurant in a space too small for enough parking. Russell suggested raising the restaurant and provide parking underneath. Revision after revision and he was still not satisfied. He didn't want to lose the client, but he was running out of options. A trip to Atlanta was inevitable.

Russell also spent a lot of his day answering emails. He had to admit that he was slacking. He would check them every couple of days instead of everyday. There were so many today that required his attention, we went to make a fresh pot of coffee. He was pouring himself a cup of coffee when there was a knock on the back door.

Russell opened the door and let Iris into his kitchen. He watched her look around and wipe her hands on her shorts.

"I wanted to apologize for yesterday. I'm embarrassed that you heard us yelling and even the reason we were arguing is another level of embarrassment for me."

Russell offered her a cup of coffee. "No, thank you. I'm taking mom out to have her hair done and then grocery shopping. She doesn't like to go out, so this is a huge accomplishment."

"Well, congratulations, then," Russell said. "And you don't need to apologize. How about you come over for dinner tonight, instead? We did have a rain check on dinner, if I remember correctly."

Before leaving, Iris smiled and agreed to come for dinner. Russell felt the butterflies, again, when he thought about his date. It was a proper date, too. He'd better get back to work. He would think about dinner later.

Russell went back to his laptop and worked some more before finally giving up. He was too distracted by his date tonight. He closed his computer, grabbed the keys to the jeep and went to the store.

Almost two hours later, Russell was unloading all the packages into the kitchen. He had fresh cut flowers and filled a vase with water. He placed the flowers in the middle of the dining table. Next, he put the lobsters in a cooler until it was time to cook them. He arranged the rest of the food so that he wouldn't forget anything. Baked potatoes and rolls were in the oven, corn was ready to boil and shrimp would be sautéd. Salad was ready to be mixed and he had classical music playing in the background.

Russell was nervous and excited, just like a teenager again. Even more so when there was a knock at the back door. Russell opened the door for Iris. Her hair was curly but pinned up on one side. She was wearing a yellow sundress that showed off her golden tan. As she walked past him, he caught the flowery scent of her perfume.

First, he offered her a glass of white wine. He had it chilling in the refrigerator and opened the cork. They sipped their wine and talked about their days. Russell asked how her mom was getting around in the cast? Fern was doing fine. The doctors didn't want her to put much pressure on it, yet, so she found a used wheelchair and that's how she is able to take her places. Mostly she sits on the back porch.

Russell explained a little bit about his issues with his client in Atlanta. He explained that he may have to go back in a day or two and would be gone a few days. He didn't say that this would be a good chance to see if they really missed each other or if the feelings faded with distance.

They were enjoying their conversation. Russell couldn't keep his eyes off her as she spoke about her plans for moving in and taking care of her mother. Only the beeping of the timer took his attention away from Iris. He took the food out of the oven and said that it was time to cook the lobster. They only took a few minutes, so he saved them for last.

"Have you every cooked a lobster, Iris?"

"No," she replied.

"Well, you will today," Russ announced. "Come over here and I'll show you what to do."

There was a big, tall pot that had been boiling since Iris arrived. Russell took the lid off with a pot holder and then grabbed a cold, wet lobster from the cooler. It was still alive and wiggling. Iris immediately jumped back and started laughing.

"I'm not touching that!" She yelled.

"I'll do one and show you how it's done," Russell explained. "Then you can do yours."

"I don't think I can," Iris replied.

"Then I guess you don't eat," Russell teased.

Iris came closer to the pot and watched what Russel did. She was curious. He explained that you put their tail in first and then close the lid. Iris watched as he did this. Next it was her turn. Russell showed her where to grab the lobster. He removed the lid of the pot as she cautiously dropped the lobster in tail first.

Iris was laughing as she went to wash her hands. She also felt proud, she had never done anything like that before. They sat down to eat the shrimp, potatoes and corn as the lobster cooked. When Russell pronounced them done, he used tongs to pull them out and plate them. He showed Iris how to remove the meat from the legs and claws. They dipped them in melted butter and savored the flavor of fresh lobster.

Iris had never experienced anything like this before. Next, he showed her how to disconnect the tail from the body, extract the meat and dip it into melted butter. They didn't talk while they ate the lobster. They were too busy eating and watching each other. Russell poured them more wine and brought more rolls to the table.

When they finished their dinner, Russell quickly cleaned up the mess and took Iris to the back porch. She commented on how great it looked, their hard work had paid off. They both relaxed on the swing and looked out at the ocean. The sun was setting behind them, so the orange and red glow covered the water.

"Thank you for dinner," Iris said. "It was delicious and educational."

"I'm glad you enjoyed it."

They sat sipping their wine, both silent in their own thoughts.

"So how are you doing?" Iris asked. "You mentioned that you didn't stay here last year because it was too hard. How is it now?"

Russell paused. "It's better. Last year it was too fresh, you know?" Russell looked at her. "But Adam and I have made so many new memories that it has a different feel now. It is definitely better."

"I know what you mean," Iris said. "When dad died, I didn't ever want to come back. It was too hard. But then I thought about how hard it was for mom and came a few times a year."

"It's never easy, losing someone, we just have to keep pushing. It's like when a big thunderstorm comes and drenches everything. You know it won't last, but while you're in it, it feels like it will never end. And then the sun comes out. I'm starting to see the rays of the sun."

Iris nodded her head. "I'm glad it's better for you."

"To be honest, you are a big reason why it feels better," Russ said.

Iris took Russell's hand and held it in her own. They sat swinging and holding hands. "This feels good," Iris said. Russell agreed. They listened to the music coming through the windows and Russell felt like he could stay here forever.

Adam came running up the beach and stomped onto the back porch. Everyone jumped as they startled each other. Adam wasn't expecting anyone to be sitting on the porch, let along his dad with a date. Russell and Iris weren't prepared for someone to be jumping onto the porch this evening.

Introductions were made and Iris stood up to leave. Adam asked his father if they could go into town tomorrow. His dad had to pick some things up, also, so he agreed. Adam, obviously happy at the prospect of going into Brunswick the next day, went inside and left them alone.

"You don't have to go, Iris," Russell said.

"It's fine," she said. "I had a really nice time. Thank you."

"Do you want to go into town with us tomorrow. Our errands won't take long and I know this great little restaurant, Indigo Coastal Shanty, that serves the most delicious fish sandwich you've ever tasted."

"Well, how can I say no to that?"

"Great! Come by around eleven," Russel said.

Iris left and Russ stayed on the porch. It was a great date, especially for someone who hadn't dated in decades. He heard dishes moving around inside and figured Adam was finishing all of the left over food. After a while, Adam came back out to the porch.

"How was your date?"

"Good," Russell replied. "How was yours?"

Adam sat down and rolled his eyes. He talked about how much fun a boat is. Now Russell rolled his eyes. Anyway, Adam said they all caught fish again, snorkeled and saw more dolphins. Today, though, they also got to use their new jet ski.

He didn't tell his father that Mandy was too afraid to ride it herself, so Julie actually let her ride it with him. It was the best feeling in the world to have her holding on to him from behind. He could hear her laugh and scream as they hit waves and jumped in the air. He wanted more of that, maybe next time.

Adam said good night and went up to shower. It was late and he was tired. He sat up in bed when he heard a text come through. It was from Mandy. She wanted to say she had a nice time today. She especially liked riding the jet ski with him. Adam said he did, too. He could still feel her arms around him.

"I really wanted to kiss you, again," Adam said.

"I did, too," Mandy replied. "I want to see you again tomorrow."

"I'm going into town with my dad and Ms. Iris," Adam said. "Maybe when I get back."

"Okay, text me," Mandy said.

"I will."

Adam felt wide awake now. He turned on his PS5 and played Madden. It was so hard to be so close to someone he couldn't be with openly. He just wanted to hold her and kiss her. Someday, he promised himself. Someday she would be his, that was for sure.

Chapter 18

After their morning run, Russell and Adam got ready to go into town. Russell was glad that Adam and Iris will have this time to get to know each other. He really wanted them to get along and like each other. Iris arrived at their back door right on time. They walked through the house and out to the jeep. Adam let Iris sit up front with his dad.

Adam first asked to stop at the souvenir shops on the island. He went in and purchased the shark book that Mandy had been looking at earlier. Maybe he could give it to her tonight. Back in the jeep, they crossed the bridge that connected Jekyll Island to the mainland. Adam loved looking out at the marsh lands. It was so beautiful here.

In Brunswick, Russell needed to purchase a phone charger. He wasn't sure what happened to his and guessed that he threw it away by accident. Adam went into the cute little store next door and Iris followed him. They looked around at all the beach themed items. Iris picked up a couple pillows with seahorses on them.

Adam kept looking and came to the jewelry counter. He spotted a hammerhead shark necklace and bought it.

"Who's that for?" Iris asked.

"Mandy Covington, our neighbor," Adam replied.

Iris smiled. "Your dad said you both liked each other. I think she'll love the necklace."

"I hope so," Adam said. "We really aren't allowed to date, but I'm hoping that will change soon."

"I'm sure it will," Iris said. "You seem like a great young man, just like your dad."

They both walked out of the store with their purchases and met Russell at the jeep. They drove to the Indigo Coastal Shanty and parked. It was busy, but there was a table inside. Today was hot and it felt good to be indoors. They all ordered the fried mahi fish sandwich and agreed it was the best they had ever had, especially with their homemade slaw and tartar sauce. The atmosphere was charming and the staff were so friendly. They had outdoor seating, but that would be better for another season, not summer.

On the drive back towards the island, they passed a bakery that Adam remembered. He asked his dad to stop and they went in to get a cake. Adam explained that this is where mom had always gotten the best cakes. Russell bought a chocolate cake for later. Adam apologized to Iris for bringing up his mom, he wasn't thinking.

"It's fine," Iris said. "In fact, I love the fact that you feel so comfortable around me that you can talk about anything, even your mother."

Russell looked at Iris and smiled. She was rare, indeed. At home, Iris came inside and agreed to a piece of cake. She joked that she wouldn't dream of missing out on the famous chocolate cake. They sat around the island and had cake and coffee. Russell wrapped a piece for her to take to Fern. Iris thanked Russell and kissed him. Adam smirked and Iris came around and hugged him. She said it was a pleasure meeting him and then she left.

They cleaned up the dishes and Adam said he was going surfing. Russell would try to join him later, but he really needed to check his emails and probably make some calls. Adam had already checked to see if Mandy was home, but she said they were all out. They would be back later tonight.

Adam took his board to the ocean and paddled out. There were only a few big waves, so he sat and waited. Adam had a feeling his dad would have to leave soon. Just as long as he didn't have to go with him, yet. Carter and Nathan had been texting asking if he was still coming to football camp next week. He hated that this summer was being cut so short. He would have had a couple more weeks here if it wasn't for football.

But then what? He would still have to go home eventually. That was the problem with summer, it always came to an end. But it wasn't over, yet. Adam decided to give the shark book to Mandy now and the necklace when he was ready to leave. He had it all planned out.

He was able to catch a few more waves then he came in and just laid on the beach. Adam welcomed the warm sun on his skin. Talking to Carter and Nathan had him wondering about football. Would he be captain? It was senior year and so much was changing. He knew he was expected to apply to colleges this fall. Every time he thought about it, it made his head hurt. He knew one place he would be applying for sure, College of Coastal Georgia.

Adam was feeling restless and went and grabbed his bike. He was going to ride up to the lighthouse and back. He enjoyed the physical strain of his muscles. He pushed himself to go faster. He had on his swim trunks and a button down short sleeved shirt that he left unbuttoned. With the wind in his hair and on his body, he closed his eyes.

It was only for the briefest moment that his eyes were closed, but a car came up from behind him and passed him too closely. Adam had to swerve to the right to avoid getting hit. However, the sand was loose and he lost traction. He and his bike skidded along the asphalt as he watched the car keep on driving.

Adam laid there, hurt. He saw his phone next to him, cracked but serviceable. He slowly lifted the bike off of him and stood up. His left leg was bleeding where his skin scraped along the street. He leaned on his bike and limped down the nearest trail. Adam leaned his bike against a tree and saw that he was near Driftwood Beach. He limped to the nearest log and sat down. He had a water bottle with him and poured some on his wound. The road rash ran from his knee to his ankle but once he washed it, he realized it wasn't as bad as it felt. Adam sat on the log and looked out at the beach.

Driftwood Beach had to be the most beautiful beach on the planet. The way the old, abandoned trees were gray and now part of the beach. These trees that were once majestic and standing strong were now laying on their sides, roots exposed and being swallowed by the sand. It continued for as far as the eye could see. It was eerie and breathtaking at the same time. He wished he was here with Mandy.

Adam knew he couldn't ride home without being in too much pain. He decided to call his dad. He explained he was hurt from falling off his bike. Russell said he would be right there, but might have trouble finding the exact place. He turned on his location on his phone to help. Adam watched the waves come up on the beach. If he wasn't in such pain, he would explore the trees and branches more.

Russell honked the horn when he thought he was near. He parked and walked to his son. Russell had found a first aid kit in the kitchen the day they arrived and always wondered which one of them would require the use of it first. He took the antiseptic wipes and gently patted the scratches. Adam made wincing noises as the alcohol touched the wound. Russell wrapped it in sterile gauze and taped it secure.

Russell had never been to this beach before. Adam told him to go walk around, it was too beautiful to not see it from the beach. His father did as he was told. He could see the trees, only half exposed. They were like ship wrecks that were just blown apart into a million pieces. Adam put his arm around his dad and limped back to the jeep. After making sure he son was buckled in, Russell went back for the bike.

"Well, I see you had nothing better to do than get hurt," Russell teased.

"You know me, always an overachiever," Adam replied.

They drove back home and Adam went straight to his room. He took some Tylenol and tried to rest. He heard his dad still working downstairs. Adam turned on tv and started flipping through channels. Eventually, he decided to watch baseball and then drifted off to sleep.

Russell came up to check on Adam when he didn't come down for dinner. He saw that he was sleeping and left him alone. Russell would leave his dinner in the fridge, he could eat it later. A text came in from Iris asking how his day was. He explained that work was getting more difficult and then Adam got hurt. Her day was spent moving her mother's bed to downstairs, temporarily to see how that worked. It was just a single bed from a spare room, so not too difficult.

There was a knock on the back door that made Russell cut the call short. It was Mandy. She explained that she had been trying to text and call Adam but he wasn't answering. She was worried. Russell assured her that he was home. He was probably still sleeping because he had an accident today. Mandy was immediately worried and Russell realized the only way she would be reassured was if she could see him for herself.

"Would you like to go up and see him?"

"Oh, yes, please!" Mandy replied. "I won't stay long."

Russell let her in and she ran upstairs. She knew which room was his but hesitated at the door. He was asleep and she could see his wrapped up leg. She went to sit on the edge of his bed and touched his hand. This made Adam flinch and wake up. When he saw it was Mandy, he tried to sit up and then winced in pain. She saw the pain relievers on his bed side table and offered him two capsules along with some water. He took them. Mandy helped him sit up and propped pillows behind him.

They both looked at his left leg. Blood had seeped through the bandages and Mandy offered to help replace them.

"No, it's fine. I have to shower soon anyway," Adam said.

Mandy looked from his leg to his face. "I have something for you," Mandy said. "I made it."

Curious, Adam looked at Mandy's hands as she pulled a friendship bracelet out of her pocket. It was made of multicolored beads and said, 'Mandy' on it. Adam watched her put it on his wrist. He turned it so he could read her name. He was very impressed.

"Thank you," he said. "I have something for you, too." Mandy's eyes got big at this statement. "I can't reach it. It's behind you on my shelf."

Mandy turned around and saw a book about sharks on top of his shelf. "This?" She asked.

Adam nodded. She flipped through the pages just as she did in the store. She remembered the book and was so touched that he bought it for her, her eyes started to water. She wiped at them with her sleeve and looked up at Adam who was watching her.

"You remembered."

"I wrote something inside,"Adam said.

Mandy turned to the inside of the front cover. There she saw, in his handwriting, 'To Mandy, I love you, Adam.' Mandy leaned down and kissed him. She was careful not to lean on his bad leg. He put his arms around her and she did the same to him. They kissed softly at first. Then they would stop to look in each other's eyes. They had a connection, they both could feel it.

Their next kisses were more passionate. Adam wished she could stay here, but they pulled away. Mandy's heart was beating so fast, she had never had feelings like this before about a boy. It was overwhelming.

Mandy stood up and thanked Adam for the shark book. He thanked her for the bracelet she made him. She smiled and then exited his bedroom. He wished she hadn't left so abruptly. His room felt empty without her there.

Chapter 19

Russell woke up today to a series of missed calls and text messages. Something was wrong. It was sunrise, normally he and Adam went for their run. Today was different. Russell didn't want any bad news without coffee first. He showered and went downstairs.

His first call was to Stanley, his boss. Stanley explained that two of Russell's clients had called him wanting to be reassigned. He was just about to give away his clients to Walter if he hadn't gotten back to him.

"You need to come here, now!" Stanley said.

"I'll be there in four hours," Russell replied.

Russell made some quick calls to Iris and Bob explaining that Adam would be home alone, please check on him. He had to go to Atlanta now and would probably be gone several days. He would keep them posted. Next, he went into Adam's room.

"Adam, I'm sorry but I have to drive to Atlanta now," his dad explained. "I've got to take care of some work in person. I'll be back in a few days. I'll call you."

They hugged and Russell left. He dreaded the four hour drive home, but he also knew this was coming. He even prepared himself for getting fired. He had no way of measuring Stanley's fury without seeing him face to face. This was going to be a very long drive.

Adam sat up and looked at his leg. He supposed it would look worse until it looked better. No dad or car, what was he going to do until he returned? He couldn't even run. The salt water might sting if he went swimming, but he could handle that. He limped downstairs to get something to eat.

He was eating cereal when he heard his phone ringing. He hoped it was Mandy. It was Carter.

"Hey man, when are you coming home?" Carter asked.

"Not yet, my dad just drove back to Atlanta today for work. He's got the only car," Adam explained. "So, I'm here by myself for a few days."

"Oh man, that sucks!" Carter said. "Want some company?"

"What do you mean?"

"Me and my boys can come down and keep you company," Carter replied.

"Sure, if you don't mind the four hour drive?"

"No problem, see you soon!" Carter said.

Adam knew he was joking. There was no way he was going to come all the way out here for a couple of days. All he wanted was sympathy, not company. Adam limped to the living room and turned on tv. He found a movie to watch and then texted Mandy.

It was a new experience for him to be so controlled by a girl. He dated before, but nothing serious. Even Sherry wasn't someone he really loved. This was different. His mood changed depending on whether Mandy texted back or not.

Adam was getting tired of waiting. He turned off tv and went outside. He walked down to the beach and saw Trey skipping stones on the water.

"Hey," Adam said. "What's up?"

Trey pointed up towards the house. He saw Mandy with her parents under the big oak tree in their backyard. "Mandy's hamster died. They're having a funeral," Trey said and scoffed. "So lame."

"Can I come?" Adam was talking to Trey but looking up at Mandy.

"Seriously?" Trey asked. "Do you and Mandy have a thing or something?"

Adam looked at Trey and wanted to deny it. "She's cool," Adam said.

Trey stared at him as Adam walked past him and towards the small funeral for the hamster. Mandy did not see Adam approach but her parents did. They simply smiled. When Mandy saw him join their little circle she beamed. There were tears in her eyes, but she lit up when Adam was near. She started saying a sweet little prayer for her hamster, Snickers. They all replied with 'Amen'.

Mandy's parents returned inside. Adam sat with Mandy on their back porch. They watched Trey skipping stones and secretly held hands.

"I was reading my book last night," Mandy said. "I love it."

"I'm glad," Adam replied. "I love my bracelet." He paused before asking, "When do you think you parents will accept me?"

"I don't know. I keep telling them how nice and responsible you are."

They both heard the door open and they released their hands. It was Julie telling Mandy it was time for lunch. Adam was not invited, so he left. He walked out to talk to Trey. He explained that his dad was gone for a few days, maybe they could play video games or something.

"Sure man, just tell me when and where," Trey said.

Adam walked slowly back home. His leg was hurting and he wanted to lay down. He wasn't laying very long when he heard honking out front. Then his door bell started ringing. Adam almost fell over when he saw Carter and Nathan standing in front of him.

"What? You guys actually came?" Adam asked.

"Of course, we said we would," Carter said.

"You got any food? I'm starving. Carter wouldn't stop anywhere," Nathan said.

Adam watched in disbelief as his two high school friends raided his fridge. He sat with them as they filled him in on all the gossip from home. Who was dating whom, who was sleeping with whom and who was fighting with whom. There were even names mentioned that Adam didn't know.

He quickly realized that he didn't care about any of the gossip from home. He didn't care about home. All he cared about was here. His friends represented his past and Adam wasn't a big fan of his past. He actually dreaded the idea of going back there soon.

"So how long are you guys staying?" Adam asked.

"Until after the party," Nathan said, looking at Carter and smiling.

"What party?" Adam had a bad feeling in his stomach.

"The one you're throwing tomorrow!" Carter said. "I brought everything I could from my dad's liquor cabinet. He won't even notice it."

"I'm not throwing a party here," Adam said.

"Too late," Carter said. "As soon as you said your dad was away, it went out on social media. Tomorrow this place will be hopping."

Adam felt sick. It was like a tsunami you saw coming but could do nothing to stop. That was what Carter and Nathan were. Carter brought a bottle of tequila out of his bag and Nathan grabbed chips from the kitchen and they walked to the back porch.

"Wow, this is nice!" Carter said. "A little pre-party before the party."

He offered the bottle to Adam but he declined. Instead, he grabbed a soda. Carter and Nathan sat on the porch swing and drank tequila and ate chips. It was surreal, he still couldn't believe they were here. Adam pulled out his phone and ordered pizza.

Trey stopped skipping stones, saw kids on Adam's porch and decided to come over. Trey had never seen these kids before. Adam introduced them as friends from school. Trey raised his eyebrows when he put two and two together.

Adam jumped off the porch and grabbed Trey's arm. He pulled him away from the porch and explained that this wasn't planned. They called and he happened to mention his dad was away. They just showed up. Trey couldn't believe it. He would be in serious trouble if it happened to him.

"That's not all," Adam said. "They are planning a party here tomorrow. It's already posted on social media."

"Dude, how are you gonna get out of it?" Trey asked.

Adam just ran his hands through his hair. "I don't know." Adam was starting to panic.

They each brainstormed ideas. Trey offered to tell his parents. Adam said, 'no' because secretly that would ruin everything for him. Adam suggested they call the police, but there was nothing to report. Plus, he had to go back to school with these guys soon. Whatever happens will determine his fate for the rest of senior year.

In the end, they decided to let it play out. Maybe it wouldn't be so bad. Trey said he would help comment on the invite on social media saying it was cancelled. They went back to Carter and Nathan. The pizza arrived and they were all eating. They mentioned wanting to go in the water. Both Trey and Adam told them it wasn't a good idea. They were drunk. The last thing they needed were two bodies floating in the ocean.

Finally they gave up and went inside. Adam turned on tv. They watched a movie until Carter and Nathan passed out. He left them sleeping on the couch. Adam went back outside with Trey.

"I saw the book you gave my sister," Trey said.

Adam waited. He didn't know what he wanted him to say. He assumed he also meant that he saw the inscription he wrote inside the front cover.

"You love her?" Trey asked.

"I do."

Trey looked up and rolled his eyes. "I knew there was something."

"I would never do anything to hurt her," Adam said. "You have to believe me."

"I love you like a brother, man," Trey replied. "It's just weird."

"I don't want it to be. It doesn't have to be. But your parents won't let us hang out together, so it's hard." Adam was sincere in his answers. Trey had to believe him.

Trey thought about it. This was one of his best friends and his sister. "If you break her heart, I'll break your neck. Understand?"

"Yes." Trey and Adam did their silly hand shake. "I'll talk to my parents and see where their heads are at. No promises. You're leaving soon anyway."

Adam hated to be reminded of leaving Jekyll Island. Especially with those knuckle heads sleeping on his couch. Trey left and said he'd be back to help with the party.

Adam called his dad to see how he was doing. He was fine. Meetings were taking all day. His dad asked how things were at the beach house. He said things were good. Technically, it wasn't a lie. He just didn't know how they were going to be tomorrow. He said he would come back as soon as he could. Adam told him to take his time.

What a mess! Adam needed to clear his head. He was still holding off going in the water. He was afraid the salt water would still hurt too much. Instead, he sat on the adirondack chairs. All he could do was look out into the water and pray. Mandy sat down beside him. He didn't even hear her approach.

At first, they sat in silence. Then she reached her hand over and he took it. It was like a life preserver during the tsunami. He knew that no matter how hard he held on to that life preserver, the tsunami was still going to wash him away forever.

"I probably shouldn't be here," Mandy said. "Especially since your dad's not home."

Adam nodded. They would both be in big trouble.

"But I don't think I can stay away from you, Adam." Mandy was watching him.

Adam looked over at Mandy. "Tomorrow you had better stay away. Bad things are going to happen and I don't want you involved." He could not explain any more than that.

"What bad things?" Mandy asked.

Adam was too ashamed to say. He couldn't even look at her.

"You're scaring me," Mandy replied.

"Trey knows. Listen to him. I don't want anything to happen to you," Adam said. He released her hand and went inside his house.

Mandy was scared for Adam. She didn't know what was happening or why but she went to find Trey. At first Trey didn't want to tell her. He didn't believe Adam told her about the party, but then how else would she have found out. All Trey knew was that they had to do anything they could to prevent the party from getting out of hand.

It was all over social media. Trey tried saying it was cancelled, but not everyone believed him. It was a nightmare. He wasn't able to sleep and he knew Adam couldn't either. It wasn't until Mandy came into Trey's room crying that he realized she had strong feelings for Adam. She was scared for him and couldn't sleep. Trey held his sister and said he would do whatever he could to help his friend. To help Adam.

Chapter 20

Russell was in his office early. Vonn brought him coffee and also let him know that Stanley was here. Perfect, just the person he wanted to see. He was nervous but also ready. Yesterday's meetings with his clients went better than expected. It took a lot of sweet talking to get them to see his side. Russell needed confirmation that Stanley wasn't still going to give his clients over to Walter. Not after all the work he had put into this these last few weeks.

Stanley was just sitting down when Russell walked in and sat opposite him. Russell gave him the updates on the blueprints and how they have reached a tentative agreement with both clients. They were pleased to speak to Russell in person and that alone nearly put them at ease. He was not going to sit silently by while his clients were given away to Walter. That was not an option.

Stanley assured him that he wasn't thinking to do that anymore. He spoke with the clients personally and they assured him that plans were back on track. However, time was running out at the building site, so they needed to be signed off on today. Russell leaned back and ran his hand through his hair. This was going to be a long day.

Russell didn't know how he would pull it off, but he would. His job at this company depended on it. He went back into his office and called Vonn. Russell had her set up meetings at the nearby restaurant for each client. Nothing made men happier than food and drinks. If this didn't work today, then he may as well come back and clean out his desk.

Today was the day Russell would find out if he still had a job or not.

TODAY WAS THE DAY ADAM would find out if his dad would kill him or not.

Adam had a text from Trey. He wondered if he should come over now. Adam told him to wait. He didn't want his parents to get suspicious if he was out all day. He would definitely need him later. He heard talking downstairs and went down to see what they were getting into. Adam wanted to get this day over with.

Carson and Nathan were awake, but they didn't look so good. They were hungover and hungry. Adam made some pancakes and bacon. He asked when they were leaving and they just laughed. Apparently the party was still on. Everything he said to them to try to cancel the party just made them laugh more. He really didn't like them very much anymore.

Adam didn't know what to do while waiting for strangers to show up at his house. He took Carter and Nathan swimming. His leg was healing and the salt water didn't sting so much anymore. Adam even let them use his surf board, even though they had a hard time staying up. They all laughed as each one tried and each one fell. It was late afternoon. Adam kept looking at the house. Even though no one was here yet, he wanted to make sure the house was still standing.

They all went in to change and eat. Carter had carried in all of the alcohol he brought in his car. It looked like a full bar set up in Adam's kitchen. When he heard cars honking and the door bell ringing, it was like deja vu. Only this time, strangers were coming in his house. From no where, music was blaring through speakers and pizzas were arriving, and even more guests.

Adam had secretly moved things he knew his dad would freak out about, but he couldn't bubble wrap the whole house. The best he could do was be on alert. He texted Trey and said it was happening. As more people arrived, it was harder to keep watch. He tried to contain everyone inside by locking the back door and closing the curtains. He knew this wouldn't work forever, he just needed it to work long enough so that people would leave.

Adam tried to do a quick head count. It wasn't as bad as he imagined. He didn't know if more were on their way, but he tried to relax a little. Trey tried to keep everyone eating and Adam tried to keep everyone downstairs. Maybe if people didn't get so drunk, they could just drive away later. Just when he thought it was going okay, more people arrived.

Carter and Nathan were in their element. This is what they did during the school year. They partied every chance they could get. Adam remembered the party they had even before finals. Adam didn't drink and probably never would. This was what happened. He secretly sabotaged the bar. He would dump some bottles and fill them with water. He put out paper plates, cups and plastic ware so that dishes wouldn't get broken. Well, at least he tried. Adam swept up what was left of a coffee mug.

Some of the kids were going out the back door. So much for thinking they wouldn't figure it out. Adam asked them to stay on the porch. The nice, new porch he and his dad had just refinished. Adam thought he was starting to have a panic attack. He never had one before, but was pretty sure this was it or a heart attack.

Adam went back inside and into the kitchen. That's when he saw Mandy. Why was Mandy here? Adam quickly went over to her and grabbed her arm.

"What are you doing here?" Adam asked.

"Helping you," Mandy answered.

"Helping me? How?" He didn't wait for an answer. He took Mandy and was heading towards the back door. Just then a drunk Carter grabbed her.

"She's a pretty one, isn't she?" Carter grabbed her butt and was going to kiss her until Adam punched him in the jaw. Mandy screamed.

"Get out of here!" Adam yelled at Mandy. She ran out the door.

When Carter got up he couldn't stand very steady, but knew it was Adam who punched him. Adam pleaded with him to stop, he didn't want to hurt him. Carter laughed and lunged at Adam but he was taller, stronger and sober. Adam simply moved out of the way and Carter fell onto the floor. Nathan carried him to the couch and that's where he stayed.

The night was wearing on long enough. Adam wanted everyone to leave. He did not know these people and they should not be here. Strangers were walking around the beach and he was afraid they would wonder into his neighbor's yards. Trey was on beach duty to try to keep everyone in Adam's backyard. It was impossible.

It was when someone had wondered into Iris's yard that she got curious. She grabbed her flashlight and walked towards Russell's house. As she got closer, she heard the loud music and could see a lot more people sitting all over the place. Iris walked up the beach, through the backyard and onto the porch. There were girls and guys of different ages, colors and sizes. Iris continued in the house and walked through the downstairs. Iris and Adam locked eyes and Adam froze. Iris made a gesture that he should follower her and he did.

"What's going on?" Iris demanded. "And you have exactly five seconds to explain before I call the police."

"I can explain," Adam started. "I talked to some buddies from home and mentioned dad was out for a few days. They said they planned to come and have a party but I didn't believe them until they showed up with a party. You have to believe me, I didn't plan this!"

Iris looked at Adam who was nearly ready to have a nervous breakdown. "Okay, but I'm calling your father now. Just be thankful

I'm not calling the cops." Before Iris made the dreaded phone call to Russell, she pulled the plug on the speaker and yelled at the top of her lungs, "GET OUT NOW!" It worked.

Those that could still walk, did leave. The rest that needed help were removed by friends. Adam was walking around the downstairs, cleaning up when Iris heard the most chilling cry she had ever heard. She ran to the living room and saw Adam kneeling on the floor. He was cradling the broken urn of his mother. He was sobbing uncontrollably and rocking back and forth. He cradled the urn like a newborn baby.

Iris could only touch his shoulder for comfort. She wanted to offer more to Adam, but it was not her place and he probably wouldn't accept it. Her first priority was to get Russell home. She didn't care if he was signing the damn peace treaty, he needed to get home now. She didn't know how to explain it or if it was better left unsaid, but she needed to make it urgent enough that he left now.

Iris did her best to convince Russell to come home. She made it sound urgent enough, but that no one was hurt. She saw Trey standing in the doorway, unsure of what to do. Iris talked to him about what needed to be done first. They needed trash bags. Iris and Trey went through every room in the house and bagged up the trash. There were six bags of garbage that she instructed Trey to take to her trash can only.

Next, they cleaned up the kitchen, mopped and vacuumed floors and wiped down tables. Altogether it took them almost two hours. Adam remained crying in the same place. It was heartbreaking because Adam was a good kid. She believed his story and she hoped his father wouldn't be hard on him. The place looked almost like normal, except for the broken urn.

There was nothing she could do about that now. It was broken. Maybe they could glue it back together. Luckily the bag that contained the actual ashes wasn't punctured in the fall. This was something Adam had to get through. Grief couldn't be denied, it had to be dealt with.

When Russell finally pulled up in front of the house, only a few forgotten remnants of a party were found in the bushes. Russell walked past these and into his house. It looked relatively unscathed. He was surprised, however, to see Iris sleeping on his couch and Adam curled up in the fetal position holding Lynn's urn. He was pretty sure that what he suspected happened here, actually did happen.

It looked like a party had taken place. He couldn't believe that Adam would have been the mastermind behind it. Someone was behind it, but who? Certainly not Trey, he wouldn't have done something like this at his house. He felt hurt, betrayed and tired. There was nothing he could do now about any of this.

It was dark and he didn't want to turn on any lights and disturb anyone. He wanted to walk around and inspect every piece of furniture and every room but he resisted. This wasn't the place or time for that. Russell decided to leave everyone sleeping where they were and deal with it in the morning. He couldn't even imagine what the explanation was but he was glad Iris had called him. He went upstairs, showered and climbed in bed. Hopefully things would look better in the daylight.

Chapter 21

Adam held his mother's urn most of the night. He had let her down. He had let everyone down. Adam had woken up sometime in the middle of the night. He saw Iris still asleep on the couch and the memories of what happened here came back to him. He was ashamed and angry at himself for letting it happen.

He gently set the broken urn down on the floor, thankful that none of the ashes had escaped. He put a blanket on Iris and then went upstairs. He saw his dad's shoes and knew he had come back. Adam supposed he should be grateful that he didn't make a big scene in the middle of the night. Let everyone have a good night's sleep first.

He went into his bedroom and laid down on the bed. He didn't remember sleeping, instead he remembered crying. Crying downstairs and crying upstairs, that was what he remembered. He thought about Mandy being groped and almost kissed by Carter. Adam was so disappointed in himself. There wasn't anything his dad or Iris could say that he didn't already say to himself.

Russell woke up and went downstairs to make coffee. He saw that both Iris and Adam were gone. He had done a lot of thinking while he drove the four hours last night. His first thought was that it was time to go home. They had stayed too long at the beach house and all the good it did for them has now been ruined in one night. How was that possible?

He took his coffee outside to the back porch. A few plastic cups reminded him of why he had to come back here. Luckily he had a successful dinner with his clients. Stanley had given him a deadline of last evening and he got both clients to sign off. He had wanted to celebrate, but the phone call changed all of that. Russell heard the urgency in Iris's voice and jumped in the car immediately.

He would have to call Iris later and both apologize and thank her for everything she had done. Russell heard someone coming down the stairs and poured another cup of coffee. Adam entered the kitchen and sat down at the island. He smiled at his father as he passed him the cup of coffee. Adam was waiting for the lecture. It didn't come.

"We're packing up today and leaving tomorrow," Russell said.

Adam simply nodded his head. He knew this was coming. It was the only logical conclusion. It was really only a few days earlier than they originally planned.

"But first," Russell continued. "We are going to do something that we should have done when we first came here. We're going to spread mom's ashes."

Again, Adam knew this was coming. He pushed his cup away and ran his hands through his hair. Russell could hear the quiet sobs as he came to terms with the inevitable. Russell came around and hugged his son. They both stood in the kitchen and clung to each other as if the tighter they held on, the less it would hurt.

Russell released Adam and went to get the urn. They carried it out to the ocean and stood on the edge of the water. They watched the slight ripple of the water and for a moment everything felt right. Russell set the broken urn on the sand and picked up the bag of Lynn's ashes. With one hand he reached into his pocked and pulled out his pocket knife.

"I think we should say something before we do this," Russell said.

Adam couldn't talk. He was too emotional to say anything.

Russell spoke. "God, thank you for the twenty years we had with Lynn. She was the light of our lives and we loved her very much. She is no longer in pain and has come home to the beach house and to You. Amen"

With one swift motion, Russell cut the top of the bag and the ashes started flying out. They swirled and danced as the wind caught them and carried them off. Adam could just stand and watch as the last of the ashes were strewn into the ocean. It was a release and a relief to have finally done it. He knew his mom didn't want to stay trapped in the urn, she wanted to be in the ocean.

They were standing there, watching the waves when Iris cautiously approached. She didn't see the urn on the ground until she got closer. "I'm sorry, I don't want to intrude," Iris said. "But I wanted to just see how everyone was today."

Russell turned around and gave her a hug. He let her know she wasn't intruding. They just released Lynn's ashes and were planning to return home tomorrow. Russell thanked her for everything she did yesterday. Even Adam gave Iris a hug before he turned and went back inside.

"It's time," Russ said. "We need to get back to our lives. But, I want to still keep in touch with you."

Iris nodded and said she would like that. They kissed. It was too bad that their relationship was still so young. He really hoped that it would last. So did Iris. They agreed to get together later that day so that he could say a proper good bye to Fern, too.

Russell came back into the house and sat next to Adam on the couch. The house felt different without that urn on the mantel. It felt empty and full at the same time. Adam knew his mom would always be with him, but now it felt even stronger, even though the house felt emptier.

"We'll always have our memories of mom, this place and the new ones we've made," Russell said. He was looking at the fireplace and remembering his memories with Lynn. "Come on, I'll make us some breakfast."

It was a somber day and Adam felt lost. Later he went over to the Covingtons and asked to see Trey. He let them know their plan to leave the next day. Trey came outside and they walked to the beach. Trey had been fighting back the urge to call Adam and find out what happened when his dad came home last night. Adam explained how he really didn't say anything. Adam already felt horrible and his dad could tell. Now Trey felt horrible. He didn't want his friend to leave, not like this.

"Where's Mandy?" Adam asked.

"Inside," Trey said. "She's so upset about the whole thing, but especially about your leaving." Trey turned to his friend. "I think my parents were starting to warm up to you, but then they heard the party. They were going to call the police but I begged them not to."

Adam didn't think it was possible to feel any worse, but he did. They promised to keep in touch and text everyday. This was probably the second hardest goodbye he had to say. He needed to see Mandy. Adam and his friend did their silly hand shake that they've been doing for as long as they could remember. They laughed and hugged before Trey went home.

Adam took his shirt and shoes off and went into the water. Now more than ever he needed to feel the warm embrace of the ocean. He would miss this most of all. He was tired of being sad, lonely and alone. He wanted Mandy by his side but that wasn't going to happen.

He dove to the bottom when he stepped on another seashell. This one was larger than the other but still a perfect spiral shell. He put it in his pocket and kept swimming. He never wanted to get out. It wasn't until his father called his name that he reluctantly returned to the house.

Russell had dinner ready and they needed to pack up. They each wrestled with their own thoughts in silence. It was time to lock up the house again for another year. After they cleaned up, Russell went next door to say good bye to Iris and Fern. Adam went upstairs to pack.

He stopped when he got a text from Mandy asking if she could come over. Sure, he texted back. He told her to come up to his room. Adam combed his hair and put on a shirt. Mandy quietly knocked on his door and then entered. Adam could tell she had been crying and she ran right into his arms.

He held her until she pulled away. They sat beside each other on his bed and held hands. Adam apologized for everything, it was all his fault. She was sorry for even coming over last night. She knew he said to stay away but she couldn't. There was so much Adam wanted to say to her but he couldn't get it out. He wanted her to have a great year at school.

Mandy wished he could stay, transfer to a school here. He knew his dad would never let him do that even though it was his friends back home who were the bad influence. He was going to have to see Carter and Nathan again and he was ready. Those jerks ruined the end of his summer and they would pay for it.

Mandy said she wished she had something to give him so she took off the scarf she wore to keep her hair up today. She folded it up and handed it to Adam. He took it and brought it to his nose. It smelled of her perfume and he thanked her. He stood up and went to his dresser. He opened the top drawer and took out a small blue velvet bag. He sat back down next to Mandy and let the contents drop into her open palm.

She touched the small image of a hammerhead shark and then looked up at Adam. They looked into each other's eyes as if the secret to life was held within them. It was Adam that spoke first by offering to put it on her. They both stood up and Mandy held up her curly, shoulder length hair. Adam took the necklace and attached the clip that held it on her delicate neck.

Adam couldn't resist to bend down and kiss Mandy's neck where the necklace now resided. Mandy turned and they kissed with longing. They were always feeling like they never had enough time together, just the two of them. Adam knew his dad could be home at any minute, but he didn't care. This moment was about him and Mandy.

They moved to his bed and laid down. They laid next to each other and just stayed that way. It was nice feeling Mandy's head resting on his chest. This was the intimacy Adam craved and it was nice just to be near her. He meant to touch her arm but instead touched her breast.

"I'm sorry," Adam said.

Mandy sat up. "No, it's just that I haven't.." Mandy didn't know how to say it. She had never been like this with a boy, let alone gone any further than kissing.

"No, it's okay," Adam replied. "It's my fault. I'm sorry."

They both stood up and Adam hugged her. They promised each other that they would stay in touch and tell each other about their days. They would video chat and it would be just like they were in the same room. It was a lie they both desperately wanted to believe.

When they finally kissed goodbye and Mandy left, he went about packing up his stuff. He was still wearing the bracelet Mandy had made him and now he tucked the scarf she gave him in his backpack. Adam was glad they had come to the beach house. It was still magic.

Adam walked over to his shelf where the first spiral shell he found this summer was sitting. He reached in his pocket and took out the one he found today and set them side by side.

"Thanks, mom," Adam said softly.

Chapter 22

As Russell turned the key to lock the beach house for the final time that summer, it was bitter sweet. The jeep was already loaded up and Adam was sitting in the passenger seat. He watched his father put the spare key under the ceramic turtle in the front garden and they drove away.

Just as they had arrived seven weeks earlier, they were returning in a silent car. Russell was mostly thinking about work. He didn't have much time to check his emails and wondered what surprises were waiting for him. He called his clients and they still seemed satisfied, so he shouldn't have much cause for concern.

Adam could only think of Mandy. Even after getting a text from Coach Booker about football camp starting on Monday, he couldn't concentrate on football. He had stayed in shape, he wasn't worried about that. School started in two weeks, that's what really had him down. Senior year was a lot of pressure. He had a pretty easy schedule, could even leave before lunch, so how hard could it really be.

Pulling into their driveway back home was surreal. Adam couldn't stop looking at the house as if it had changed in the last couple of months. Maybe it had. Or maybe it was just him who changed. Adam grabbed all of his things and went straight to his bedroom. He texted Mandy that they had made it and she sent a heart emoji.

His room at home was very different from his room at the beach house. Here he had trophies, pictures of him and his friends and it was three hundred miles from Jekyll Island. Adam unpacked and tried his best to focus on the coming days of football camp and then school.

Football was a great distraction. Adam was able to have a talk before practice with Carter and Nathan. He couldn't help it if he tackled them a little too hard during practice, though. Adam was quarterback and team captain. Sometimes revenge was sweeter when they weren't expecting it. Adam was in top form and was sure he would have scholarship offers this fall.

Cheerleaders kept flirting with Adam. He was polite but firm. He had let Sherry know he met someone last summer, so she tried to calm the squad down when the games started. Sherry was the captain of the cheerleaders and still Adam's friend. They still hung out, mostly in groups after games, getting burgers or ice cream. Sherry met a guy over the summer, too, so their friendship was easy to come back to.

Unlike junior year, Adam was easily passing his classes. Senior year was everything he hoped it would be. The younger kids looked up to him and he caught everyone's attention while walking down the hallways. He was able to leave the building after his last class at noon. Adam usually just drove home and ate lunch. He even thought about getting a part time job. All the while he was counting down until next summer.

RUSSELL HAD A HARD time adjusting to going back to work in his office each day. He missed the relaxed nature of working from the beach house. He didn't think it affected his productivity, but Stanley did. Stanley gave Russell a new client that had a reputation of being difficult. Russell believed this client was offered to Walter and he turned him down. No problem, Russell would work with this client and they would be eating out of the palm of his hand in no time.

Russell was glad that Adam seemed to be making a seamless transition back to home life. His grades were good, his team was winning and no parties were being thrown at home. It was all positive. He knew that he and Mandy still kept in touch, so did he and Iris. If he didn't sell the beach house, maybe they could drive down during winter break or something.

He was thinking of selling the beach house. It was Lynn's so it was never brought up to sell it while she was alive. But Lynn wasn't here anymore. It was an expensive place to keep going all year with the bills, taxes and insurance. He had some inquiries out to various realtors to see what the market value was now. He wasn't going to say anything to Adam until he was sure what his decision would be.

Russell knew that selling it would not be a popular opinion. He even wondered what Iris would say if he told her he was considering selling the beach house. That was their strongest connection. It was only a thought, something he didn't really have time for at work. Russell tried to focus on his blueprints, but just couldn't.

If Russell left work now, he might just get through traffic early enough to catch Adam's game tonight. He turned off the lights and headed home. He changed clothes and drove to the high school. Russell tried to remember the last time he went to one of Adam's games and didn't even know if it was high school or middle school. His workaholic lifestyle meant a number of things had suffered in the past.

Adam saw his dad sit down in the stands while he was warming up on the field. He smiled and waved and he was surprised when he felt happy to see him there. Adam played his hardest but the team just made too many mistakes. They lost. Russell patted his son on the back and said he would meet him at home.

Russell grabbed some tacos on the way home and ate while waiting for Adam. He called Iris and told her about making it to Adam's game. She was glad they were still doing well. Iris wanted to come up to visit, but now that she was her mother's caregiver, it was more difficult. Fern was doing well, but getting weaker. Her leg was out of the cast, but she was unsteady.

Russell understood. It would be harder for them to get together unless they came down there. That was going to be hard to do, but he would try his best. It wouldn't be so impossible if they lived closer. Now he sounded like Adam.

Adam came home a little bit after his dad. He ate while he video chatted with Mandy. She had stayed up to hear all about his game. She said she was sorry they lost but knew they would win their next one. He could see the shark necklace she wore and thought back to the night he gave it to her. He thought about her often and wanted to see her so badly.

Mandy said school was going good. She didn't go to Trey's games, so she didn't know if he was winning or losing. Adam laughed. He asked her about the waves, he was always interested in how big they were. He left his surfboard there and couldn't wait to get back on it. She was trying to convince Trey to drive up to see him. At least then she could come along, but he wasn't interested, not now that school started.

Adam dreamed of when they were older and could go and do whatever they liked. Mandy said she was tired and said good night. He went upstairs, showered and went to bed still wearing Mandy's bracelet.

THE NEXT FEW WEEKS were busy and that's exactly how Adam liked it. He had a meeting with the school counselor, only this time it was about college applications. Coach Booker made tapes of his football plays and sent them to recruiters. Things were starting to feel real and moving fast. He even had appointments set up for SATs and ACTs in the coming months.

The air was cooler and felt better during practice and training. They weren't killing themselves in the heat. Adam tried to get his father to drive down to Jekyll Island for Labor Day weekend, but Russell said he had a work function and couldn't get away. They had been home over two months and it was so hard getting through each day. Mandy would send texts, pictures and voicemails so that helped.

Russell was actually coming home around five each day. Sometimes even earlier. It was different having time in the evening to actually cook or go out and do something while it was still light out. He and Adam could still sit around the kitchen island and talk at dinner like they used to at the beach house.

October brought even cooler weather and the homecoming game. Adam knew everyone expected him to go to the homecoming dance, too, but he wasn't. He didn't tell everyone about Mandy, she was private and he wanted to keep it that way. All the girls at school kept leaving him notes in his locker or on his car. Some just gave a phone number, others were more descriptive about what they wanted.

Adam wasn't interested. He kept his nose down, worked hard and kept up his long distance relationship. Carter and Nathan eventually made up with Adam and even apologized to his dad. Just for fun, Russell made them wash their cars one weekend. They swore they wouldn't plan any more parties at anyone's house but their own. Adam still didn't trust them, but he only had to deal with them until the end of the school year.

Adam and his friends were excited for Halloween coming up. Carter said he'd have a party this year, again. Every year Carter threw the biggest and best Halloween party. His parents were always traveling, so it was never a big deal with their family. He had the blow up characters in the front yard, strobe lights, streamers and scary music. Neighbors never complained because everyone's house was doing almost the same thing on Halloween, just maybe on a smaller scale.

Adam tried to describe it to Mandy. She said it sounded like fun. Some places decorated like that on the island, but because most houses are only used during the summer, it wasn't necessary to decorate so much. They both thought about being vampires for Halloween.

"Would it be weird to coordinate our costumes from three hundred miles away?" Adam asked.

"No," Mandy replied, "because we would know."

Mandy knew there was a lot of pressure on him at school. Trey talked about how it was being a senior and Mandy wondered how either of them did it. There were so many people to please like parents, teachers, counselors, coaches and teammates. Adam was trying his best.

Russell was glad he was able to go to Adam's homecoming game. They won and it was good to witness the team coming together in victory. Russell was still getting information from realtors about selling the beach house. Adam still didn't know.

He was mostly unsure if it was a good financial move right now. The comparable sales in the area showed that it had great value right now but he wondered if it was a good time to sell. With winter and the holidays coming, people weren't typically inclined to purchase real estate. Russell decided to put it all on the back burner for now.

Today was Halloween. Adam told his dad that he was going to Carter's to help set up after school. He was going to be a vampire, just as he and Mandy discussed. He was just going to wear his black jeans and some black fabric for a cape. He wasn't so much worried about being authentic, just comfortable. The only thing he didn't have was a white dress shirt. He decided to look in his dad's closet, he wouldn't mind if he borrowed one.

Adam didn't go into his dad's room much for the same reason he wouldn't want his dad in his room. He was walking out of the closet when some brochures caught his eye. They were from The Coastal Realtors, The Jekyll Group and Island Real Estate. Then he saw the beach house address along with prices and comparisons.

Vampire costume forgotten, Adam grabbed his keys and ran to his jeep.

Chapter 23

Adam thought about calling his dad but didn't want to hear any lies or excuses. How could he want to sell the beach house, mom's beach house? Adam had one destination in his mind and no one was going to talk him out of it. As he looked up the directions on his phone, he also turned off his location.

Russell wouldn't be expecting him home until very late, it was Halloween and he was supposed to be at Carter's all night. He didn't even have a plan. His goal was to be at the beach house and remember how magical it was. How could they ever sell it, it was mom's final resting place?

Adam didn't talk to or call anyone. This was all about the house. He thought about Mandy and then realized that if his dad sold the beach house then he would never see her again. No more summers on Jekyll Island. He didn't think he could live in a world were they didn't own that house anymore.

Why was his dad doing all of this behind his back? He thought they had a stronger relationship now. One that allowed them to talk about all of these major decisions. Right now nothing else mattered to him except getting to the house.

Hours and miles flew by. He stopped to get gas and wondered if he should let his father know he was almost there. No, he wouldn't let him talk him out of going. Adam got back on the road and drove the remaining miles. As he got closer, the anger turned to urgency. He was so close to the house and Mandy. He crossed over the causeway bridge and was nearly there.

Adam pulled into the driveway and stood looking at the house. The same hesitancy he felt back in May was there, again. This time he was alone. He had never entered the house without a parent with him. He expected to see a 'for sale' sign in the from yard. He lifted the ceramic turtle and unlocked the door.

Inside was cold and dark. In summer, the house is bright and welcoming. In the fall, it is eerie and very different. It was evening and Adam wasn't quite sure what he wanted to do. He had bought some food at the gas station and sat at the kitchen island. It was the same kitchen island that held so many happy memories only four months ago.

It was a strange feeling knowing that no one knew he was here. He would wait to text Mandy. It would be easier for her to get away when it was trick or treating hours. Right now he had the house to himself. He ate the chicken sandwich wrapped in foil and the chips. He didn't turn any lights on in case someone was looking and called the police.

Adam laid on the couch, suddenly needing a nap. He woke up an hour later and it was dark. Adam lit a few candles and placed them around the room. He decided to text Mandy and let her know he was here. At first she didn't know what he meant.

"I'm here! Next door. Come," Adam texted, again.

Mandy was quietly tapping on the back door within minutes. Adam walked over and let her in. There was an awkwardness at first. They hadn't been near each other in nearly four months and the familiarity was gone.

"Where is your costume?" Adam asked.

"I only got as far as the black skirt and white shirt. I'm a female vampire and we wear skirts," Mandy replied. "What about your costume?"

"I have my black jeans and white shirt, well it's my dad's shirt. I was in his room to get it and that's when I saw that my dad is selling the beach house," Adam said.

Mandy didn't want to believe it. Adam told her all about the various brochures from a bunch of local real estate offices here. Then he saw the listing prices and comparison prices, it was too much. He just got in his car and drove here.

Mandy didn't know what to do. Part of her felt so bad for this boy who was trying so hard to be an adult but really just wanted to be protected by his parents. The other part was screaming that the love of her life was within touching distance. She wasn't sure what the right way to help him was.

"So your dad doesn't know you're here?" Mandy asked.

"No, and I'm not going to tell him," Adam replied.

Mandy was pretty sure his dad would figure it out, but she wouldn't be the one to tell him. Instead, she slowly approached him and gave him a hug. Adam hugged her back. It was just like the hug they gave when he left. They were hanging on for dear life.

Adam brought Mandy into the living room, the only room that was lit by candles. He explained that he didn't want to be found out, yet, so he wasn't turning on any lights. She was okay with that. Adam sat with his arm around her. It was getting cold and he grabbed the blanket hanging off the back of the couch.

They sat like that for a few minutes. Adam's heart was racing and he couldn't believe he was really here holding Mandy. Neither one of them knew when the next time would be when they could actually see each other again. Now they were here together. The realization was sinking in for both of them.

Mandy sat up and took Adam's hand. She put in over her heart and looked into his eyes. Adam, startled by what she was doing, searched her face for an explanation. She asked him to feel how fast her heart was beating. He took hers and did the same. She felt his heart racing, too. They smiled and continued to stare in each other's eyes. The candlelight offered a dim glow in their eyes but it was enough light to see their expressions.

Adam lowered his head so that they were nose to nose. He leaned in and kissed her lightly on the lips. He pulled back and watched her face. She smiled and then reached up for his face. Her hand caressed his jaw and she pulled him down to kiss her again. This time it was stronger and with a freedom they hadn't had before. They were in a house alone and no one knew it.

Adam's hand moved to her breast but Mandy didn't make any sound this time. She let out a low moan and Adam froze. He straightened up and pulled his hand back.

"Why did you stop?" She asked.

"I'm sorry," he replied. "I got carried away. We don't have to do anything."

"I want to," Mandy said.

Adam looked at her. "I want you to know that this isn't the reason I asked you to come over. You have to know that. We don't have to do anything you aren't ready to do. It's okay."

Mandy didn't say anything. She slowly removed her shirt and sat there in just her bra. Then she took Adam's hand and put it back where it was. Mandy watched Adam's face as he looked down at her bra and removed it. He could see Mandy's breathing get quicker and shallower.

"We don't have to do this," Adam said quietly.

"I want to," Mandy said. "I want you to be my first."

This was not Adam's first time, but he was certainly no expert. It still felt awkward but this was someone he loved. It felt different, it felt right.

Adam removed his shirt and Mandy touched his chest. It was lean and muscular, just like she had seen it all summer. They were both nervous and their movements seemed hesitant. Mandy was feeling self conscious but she was with Adam, the one person she trusted.

Adam put the blanket on the floor and brought Mandy to lay on it. He came down beside her and kissed her starting at her neck. He said he would be gentle and he was. Mandy never knew pleasure like she experienced with Adam.

Adam held her and they cuddled by the candlelight. She was so happy she could cry. Even Adam hadn't been this happy in a very long time. He wished they could have lit the fireplace, but the candles would have to do for now.

It was too cold to sleep on the floor, so Adam and Mandy grabbed the candles and went up to his room. They slept together in his bed just like he had imagined. Mandy texted her parents that she was staying at a friend's house. She would rather stay here and be punished then go home and know he was in his room alone.

They stayed together all night and it was better then Mandy could ever imagine. She couldn't think of being with anyone else. They were in love and wanted to be together. Adam would make sure he never sold this house. He didn't know how, yet, but he would think about it.

The next morning, Mandy got up, showered and wore one of Adam shirts. Adam followed her downstairs and they foraged for something to eat. There were still crackers and peanut butter in the pantry, plus juice he had bought at the gas station yesterday. It was a feast to them. They ate and giggled. It was nice just being happy in this moment.

Mandy had an alibi and Adam was sure his dad would just assume he stayed at Carter's. It was a Saturday, so no one would be calling from school, either. It was the perfect day. They stood side by side and finished their breakfast. Just being near her made it hard to focus on anything else.

Adam went into the living room and turned on tv. He flipped through the channels and noticed that all the local ones were talking about a storm. Mandy came and sat beside him and his attention was immediately drawn to her. They started kissing again but Adam was still half listening to the news reports on the tv.

Adam realized it was much darker than it should be at noon. He decided to turn the volume up on the news. Just then they saw lightning and then jumped when it was followed by a loud thunder clap. Mandy was getting scared now. They got dressed and looked out the windows.

There was a storm coming over the water and it was big. There was continuous lightning and thunder as the sky darkened. There was a loud crack as they suspected lightning struck a nearby tree. More lightning strikes and thunder. The wind was blowing everything in sight and Adam thought about taking the swing down off the hooks. They forgot to do that when they left in July. They tried to look around for anything else that could be blown away and were satisfied that just the swing needed their attention.

Adam and Mandy were being blown around as they managed to take the swing down and lay it on the porch. Just then another lightning came close and it hit Fern's house. Adam went out into the wind and rain to make sure he saw it correctly. Fern's roof looked like it had a hole in it and was on fire.

No longer concerned with being found out, Adam told Mandy to call 911 and give Fern's address, their attic was on fire. Adam was going to go over and get them out. Mandy nodded as she went onto the porch to call the fire department. Adam ran next door to make sure everyone got out safely.

Chapter 24

Adam was banging on Fern's doors and windows from the back porch. The wind and rain mixed with the thunder and lightning was making it hard for him to hear his own voice. Adam was yelling for them to get out. Most likely, they knew the storm was coming and closed all of the window and shutters and were hunkered down for the storm.

Adam was not giving up. He could see the flames in the attic windows and didn't know how long it would take to reach the upstairs. He was sure there was smoke inside by now. Why weren't they coming out? He ran to the front door and rang the door bell. He saw a face peek from behind a curtain and then the front door open.

He was sure that the shock of seeing Adam made Iris hesitate longer than usual. But she eventually opened the door to see what the matter was. Adam had been saying the same word for the past twenty minutes.

"FIRE!"

Still unable to comprehend what Adam was doing here and why he was yelling fire at her, she invited him inside.

"No! Your house is on fire! Get out now!" Adam yelled.

Iris's eyes widened and she came outside. She saw with her own eyes the flames coming from the attic.

"We've got to get you and Mrs. Fern out now! Come to my house," Adam instructed.

Adam followed her inside and told her calmly that the fire department is on their way. Iris was to get all the valuables she could carry and he would go and carry Mrs. Fern outside. Iris nodded and went from room to room. She threw purses, computers, paperwork, jewelry boxes, photo albums and pictures into bags and carrying them out the back door.

As soon as Adam emerged with Fern, they heard the fire engine at the front of the house. Adam told Mandy to help Iris and Fern into his house, he would talk to the firemen. In the wind and rain, Mandy managed to help the women into Russell's house. They sat in the living room and waited on word from Adam.

The sound of the fire engine brought all the neighbors out to see what was going on. The Covingtons froze when they saw Adam talking to and directing the firemen at Fern's house. They watched in disbelief as he went from back door to front door to make sure no one went inside. He was covered in soot and was completely calm.

Bob sent Julie and Trey back home. Bob came up behind Adam and asked if everyone got out okay.

"Yes, they are at my house," Adam replied.

"Okay, I'll go check on them," Bob answered.

Adam knew, at that moment, they would be forbidden to see each other again. They didn't have to be told what happened between them, they would know. Bob would know Mandy lied about her whereabouts and it would be Adam's fault. He didn't want to face anyone yet. He stayed with the fire fighters and communicated back to Iris. After they were sure that the fire was contained, they left. Adam sat on Fern's back porch and thought about the day. How did he get into this situation?

He was covered in soot from head to toe sitting on his neighbor's back porch. His dad didn't even know he was here and he spent the night with his girlfriend, whose parents are at his house right now. He knew the day could and would get worse. When their parents figured out that they were lied to so that they could have one night alone, he may not survive.

Confident that the house was still empty, he decided to bite the bullet and call his dad.

"Dad, I'm at the beach house. Mrs. Fern's house was struck by lightning and caught fire. They are okay and at our house."

Russell tried to break down the information Adam just gave him into pieces he could comprehend. None of it made sense, not one word. He had just gotten a call from Iris that was just as far fetched as the one Adam was telling him. Russell couldn't believe this was happening again.

"I'll be right there."

Adam decided to return home. The only ones he saw were Iris and Fern. Iris explained that Bob took Mandy home. She tried to explain the she was helping you when the storm started, but she wasn't sure he was buying it. Adam just ran his hands through his hair. Why did things like this keep happening to him?

Iris explained that she had already called her insurance company and Russell. She apologized because she didn't realize he didn't know about Adam's being here. He shook his head. Fern was asleep on the couch. Iris invited Adam into the kitchen to talk.

"Look, I don't know what's going on between you and your dad," Iris said. "But I can't believe you drove out here without telling him."

"I know."

"But, on the other hand, if you weren't here at that very moment, we may not have survived."

Adam looked at her. He had come to that very same conclusion. It was a double edged sword. He was wrong to come, but in the right place at the right time. He couldn't wrap his head around it. He started crying.

Iris, unsure why he was so emotional, hugged him.

"Dad wants to sell the house. I just couldn't let him and I was so upset that I just drove here. I can't let this house go, ever."

It was starting to get clearer to Iris. Russell had mentioned to her that he was thinking about selling. She had actually helped with getting various realtors and comparisons to him. She was not aware that he told Adam about it, though. He said he was only thinking about it.

Iris didn't know what else to say, it was a mess, quite literally. It was still storming outside, but not as bad. Adam went upstairs to shower and change. No longer worried about turning on lights, he sat on his bed and waited for his dad to come.

Adam must have dozed off because when he woke up he heard his dad's voice downstairs. He was hoping that seeing Iris would warm him up a bit. Adam didn't want to be confronted in his bedroom, so he went down to see his father.

Russell came over and gave his son a hug. "What you did was reckless and stupid and reminds me of when I had to come here because of a party, but you saved these women's lives. I think that makes up for some of your stupid behavior."

"Thank you," Adam said.

Russell let him know that they were not done on the subject, but right now he needed to make everyone comfortable. He invited Iris and Fern to stay at their house as long as they needed. The insurance adjuster would be out tomorrow and they should know better how to proceed. The fire fighters had attached a tarp for now.

"Dad, I need to go see the Covingtons," Adam said.

"Why? What happened over there?" Russell asked.

"Nothing, I just need to talk to them," he replied.

Adam went out the back door and over to the Covington's house. Bob answered the door and let him in. Adam tried to think about what he would say and decided to just be truthful. He explained that he found out his father was going to sell their beach house.

"The house that had been in my mother's family since before she was born. Before we left in July, we threw her ashes in the ocean. It is her final resting place," Adam explained. "As soon as I figured out what his plan was, I had to come. I didn't tell anyone, not my dad, Trey or Mandy. I just walked in my door and was scared that my life was falling apart."

Adam took a deep breath. "I love your daughter, sir, and would never do anything to hurt her."

Bob looked at Adam, "So you think spending the night together is okay?"

"No, sir, it just happened. I'm sorry," Adam said. He surrendered to whatever Bob might do or say to him. He was tired of hiding and the secrets.

"Well, Adam, I appreciate your coming here and talking to me. I still have things to discuss with my daughter, so I want you to please go back home," Bob said calmly.

"Thank you, sir," Adam replied. He looked at Mandy and smiled. She smiled back. It was done, the secret was out. Let the chips fall where they may.

Adam walked back home and his father met him on the adirondack chairs. The storm had passed and Russell had more to say to him.

"Iris told me you saw the real estate brochures," Russell said. "Why didn't you come and talk to me about them instead of driving all the way out here?"

"I freaked out, dad. All I could think about was mom. This is her house, her final resting place. No one else can own this house," Adam replied.

"Son, I was only getting information. I never decided to sell it for sure."

"But how could you even consider it, especially without talking to me first?"

They were both at a standstill. They were both right and wrong.

"I thought we agreed to talk things out with each other," Adam said.

"We can," Russell replied. "I want us to feel like we can discuss anything. I won't sell the house."

"I slept with Mandy," Adam said.

Russell turned to look at this son, then looked back at the ocean. "Okay."

"We love each other, dad," Adam continued. "I went and told that to Mr. Covington, too."

Again, Russell looked at his son. "Okay." He waited for more confessions, but there were none. He loved his son very much and knew there was a lot of pressure on his shoulders this past year. But he has changed, he became a man in these last few months. He decided to treat him like a man.

"Okay, I understand why you did the things you did, but you've got to stop acting on impulse. If I did that at work, I'd be fired on the spot."

"I know."

"For now, we have to figure how everyone is sleeping in this house tonight," Russell said.

Both men walked back to the house. It was such a mix of emotions to be back at the beach house in the fall. Adam went upstairs and made up the two spare bedrooms, even though Iris said her mother would probably be more comfortable on the couch.

Russell went over to Fern's house to take a look. Water had come through the ceiling but it wasn't too bad on the first floor. He grabbed some more things he thought they would like and then brought some things from the fridge. It was nice being here with Iris, again.

Iris and Russ found themselves alone in the kitchen. They really hadn't had a private moment to talk since he arrived. She explained how Adam was so calm when he took control of the situation today.

"He was just like his father," Iris commented.

"I am proud of him for doing that," Russ said.

"You should be," Iris replied. "And try not to be too hard on him. This house means so much to him. You should have told him what you were planning."

"I didn't even know what I was going to do," Russ defended himself.

"And he and Mandy are in love."

"I know," Russell said. "He's not the only one." Russell turned to Iris. "I love you."

Iris blinked back tears. "I love you, too."

Iris and Russell were kissing when Adam walked in the kitchen. He put his hand over his eyes like he was ten years old. Iris and Russ laughed.

"What is it?" Russell asked.

"I made up all the beds," Adam said.

"Thank you, son," Russell said to Adam as he turned and went. Russ turned back to Iris, "Shall we?" They both smiled as they went upstairs.

Chapter 25

Russell was nervous. He wasn't sure Iris would come up to his bedroom. They both stood there like awkward teenagers.

"I love you, Iris."

"I love you, too, Russ."

They kissed. They both had such an adrenaline rush today and the fact that neither one of them expected to see each other for a very long time, was still exciting. They laughed nervously as Russell removed his shirt and pants. Iris removed hers. They were standing in just their underwear.

Russell took Iris's hands and brought her to the bed. They got under the covers and continued kissing. Russell hadn't been with anyone since Lynn. For Iris, it had been several years, but this was different. They both proclaimed their love for each other.

Their kissing turned from sweet and friendly to passionate and wanting. They had each thought about making love to each other over the summer. The first time Russell saw Iris in a two piece bathing suit he thought about taking her to bed. He would never have suggested it at the time, but the thought did cross his mind.

Iris remembered seeing Russell shirtless in the water and wanted to touch him very badly. She, also, had wild thoughts about him in bed but knew he wasn't ready for that at the time. She was glad he was now. Their hands moved around each others bodies that night without inhibition. When they finally made love, it felt new and familiar at the same time.

Later, sitting up in bed, they talked about what this meant for them. Russell was still unsure about the house. He didn't really want to sell it. He would hold off any and all decisions at least until Iris's house was ready to move back into. There was a lot to think about.

Downstairs, Adam made sure Fern was settled and that she had everything she needed. He said he would go back over to her place in the morning and see what else he could salvage. This made Fern happy and she was so glad he was around.

"Not everyone feels that way right now, Mrs. Fern," Adam replied.

"Adam, you were sent by an angel," Fern said and went to sleep.

Adam was very tired himself. He went up to his room and got in bed. He thought about what Fern said, an angel. He knew this house was magic and that his mother was still here. It made his head hurt to think that she had something to do with bringing him here at the right time. Adam didn't believe in ghosts but he believed in spirits. He always believed he could feel his mom's spirit here.

He decided to try and text Mandy before he actually slept. When she finally responded he asked how things were at home. He was so scared and nervous after confessing his love for her to Mr. Covington that he was sure he would never be allowed to see Mandy again. He almost resolved himself to going back home and not seeing her any more. The thought of doing that was crushing him.

Mandy said that she sat everyone down and explained the whole situation. She promised her parents that it wasn't planned, even showed them the text messages. That Adam was there half a day before he even told her. She admitted that it was wrong for them to be alone, but they loved each other.

Then the storm came and Adam was the first one to discover the lightning strike. She explained how Fern and Iris had no idea that lightning even struck their house until Adam started banging on the door and got them out.

Mandy told her parents that it was like he was sent there to do this. Adam pulled the phone away from his ear. He couldn't believe what he just heard. Mandy was still talking and when he put the phone back up, he heard that she was allowed to see him tomorrow.

Adam felt his whole body slump from the release of tension. He was holding in all the stress from the day and with one sentence from Mandy, it was gone. He could almost weep with joy, but held it in.

"Just come over whenever you can," Adam said. "I'll be waiting."

"Okay," Mandy replied. "I love you."

"I love you, too."

Adam was smiling as he touched the bracelet Mandy had made him. He never took it off. His future was still up in the air. For the time being, the beach house was safe. His dad would never kick Iris and Fern out after saying they could stay here. He figured it would take months to repair their house, so that means they would be back here next summer.

The reality of what happened yesterday was hitting everyone today. Fern was sitting on their back porch just as she did on hers. She remembered it all, remembered that if they had been stuck in that house with the smoke getting thicker, they would have died.

Russell and Iris were making breakfast in the kitchen when Adam entered. They kept their gazes down but couldn't keep from smiling. Adam just smiled, too, knowing what they did and he was happy for them. He and his dad met each others eyes and Adam nodded. Russell smiled and handed him a dish of eggs and bacon.

They each had plans for the day. Russell would go over with Iris and talk to the insurance adjuster about the house. It might take awhile, but there was a lot of damage throughout the whole house. Fern was to stay here and not see the house if possible. Plus, they didn't need her to fall again.

Adam said he wanted to search the attic for more blankets. He was sure there must be some around but they never needed them in the summer. He thought his mom stored a bunch of stuff in the attic that she wasn't ready to get rid of. Adam let his father know, in full disclosure, that Mandy was allowed to come over. She could help him look in the attic. Russell was okay with that.

After breakfast, they all went their separate ways. Adam waited for Mandy and then they went up into the attic. They had to access it from a pull down staircase in the hallway of the second floor. It was dirty and creepy as it made noises when it was fully extended. Mandy acted like she wasn't sure she wanted to go up there, but Adam assured her nothing would happen to her as long as he was there.

Adam went first. Each wooden step creaked as he put weight on it. He made it half way up and then looked for a light switch. When he turned it on, he went up the rest of the steps. Adam looked around and told Mandy to come up. There was so much stuff up there that he knew nothing about.

He wondered if his dad even knew everything that was up here. It was dark and dusty but he and Mandy were going through totes and bags that were along the far wall. They weren't finding blankets, yet. There wasn't a lot of lighting in the attic so they stayed in the main space with the vaulted ceiling. They split up to cover more space.

Mandy hollered when she found a box market 'blankets'. She opened them and sure enough there were plenty of blankets for all the beds. Adam didn't immediately answer because a box marked 'Lynn's things' caught his attention.

He was sitting on the dusty floor now with the mysterious box on his lap. He opened it with such care, not knowing what treasures might be inside. He knew the words were in his dad's handwriting, so he must have put this up here after she died. Inside were some medical papers, hospital files and old bills marked paid.

Adam almost put the box down when he spotted a leather book at the bottom. He reached in and dug it out of all the other paperwork. He moved the box so that the leather bound journal was on his lap. He knew this was his mom's journal. Adam knew she kept journals but didn't write in them everyday, just when she was moved to write something down. She wrote for special occasions, birthdays and holidays.

Mandy, curious that he wasn't excited to find the blankets they came up there to find, came and sat next to him. He hadn't opened it, just touched the still soft leather of the cover. Adam stayed looking at the journal without moving.

"Are you going to open it?" Mandy asked.

Adam simply nodded his head and opened the cover. He started tearing up when he realized the first entry was the day she found out she was having a boy. His mother's handwriting, he hadn't seen that in a year and a half. Adam wiped away the tears and read his mother's words. Words that dated back over eighteen years.

Dear Journal,

Today I just found out that I am having a boy. My baby boy. I've always loved the name Adam. It is a strong name that fits my first born. Hopefully, first of many kids.

Adam, if I could write to you personally and if I could picture you reading this right now, I would say that I will spend every second of my life to make sure you have a happy one. Things will happen that will make you sad and angry, that is life, but happiness should be your way out. Find your happiness, wherever it is. I found mine in your dad. He makes me so happy, as you do. I can't wait to meet you and show you the world. It's so big with so many interesting people and places.

I met your dad while traveling in Florida. I know, not very exotic, but he eventually took me to Paris. We will have to wait a bit now to travel again, but I have a list of places I want to see.

Maybe you can go with me someday. Berlin, Dublin, Budapest, Sydney, Hong Kong, Phuket, Cairo and Rio, just to name a few. The world is open to you. Be kind and people will be kind to you.

Love Always,

Mom

Adam was crying. He closed the journal. He couldn't read anymore right now. Mandy hugged him and let him cry. They both sat on the dirty floor and held each other. Everything else around them melted away. The flood of emotions that flowed through Adam took him by surprise. He never thought he would find something like this here.

She never had any more kids. The cancer and her many years of treatment took that away from her. Adam knew growing up that she always wanted more, he just never fulling understood why she didn't until he was much older.

Mandy suggested they go back downstairs. She carried the blankets and Adam brought the journal. He turned off the light and closed the stairway. Adam didn't need to show the journal to his father, he was the one who put it in the attic in the first place. Instead, he took it to his room and placed it carefully in his bedside table's drawer.

"Do you want to read more?" Mandy asked.

"Not now," Adam replied. "I still need to process what she said and the fact that it exists."

Adam was still lost in his own mind. They laid down on his bed. It was not romantic, it was for comfort. Adam laid on his back staring at the ceiling. Mandy curled up next to him. They didn't say anything for a long while, just being together was enough.

"Do you want me to stay?" Mandy asked.

"Always," replied Adam.

Chapter 26

Fern's house needed a lot of work. The insurance adjuster walked Russell and Iris through it all. Russell helped her pack up what she could from the house. It was sad, not everything survived the fire. This was Fern's whole life wrapped up in that house. Iris's things were there, too. She broke down a few times trying to find several items. Russell just held her.

"Iris, it will be okay. I'm here."

"I know," Iris replied. "Thank you for that."

They relied on each other more than they wanted to admit to each other. Iris didn't know how she would have gotten through this if he wasn't there. They filled bags and boxes and took them to Russell's garage. It would take months to get Fern's house finished but at least they had somewhere to stay.

Bob came over to see Russell. The two men walked out onto the beach to talk. Bob had a few topics he wanted to discuss with Russell, but he would start with Fern's house. He had a great contractor that worked on their house a few years ago. He gave the information he had written down to Russell. Russ said he would call them first thing in the morning. Bob said he had walked over earlier and looked at the place. They were lucky they got out when they did.

This brought Bob to a second topic he wanted to discuss, Adam. Russell was ready to defend him if things went too far. First, Bob said Adam was a good kid, he always like him when they came for summers. But when he professed his love for his daughter and then found out they spent a night together, his feelings were changing.

Russell stood up straighter, but Bob put out his hand. "Hear me out," Bob said. He went on to explain that they had a long talk with Mandy, they all did. She sat them down and explained everything. Bob understood that none of this was planned, it was a misunderstanding about Russell wanting to sell the house. Then there was a domino effect that ended with Adam saving the lives of two women.

Bob had to admit that his feelings had come full circle. He was back to thinking that Adam was a good kid. He still didn't like that they spent the night together, but it's done. He just wanted assurances that it wouldn't happen again. Russell couldn't promise him anything other than he wasn't selling the house now. He was impressed with Bob and how he worked through all of this.

Russell let Bob know that he and Iris were a couple and Bob just nodded his head. He knew it was just a matter of time. They actually laughed together on the beach and it felt like an olive branch was offered. Bob was a good friend and Russell hoped it could continue. They both returned to Russell's house and Bob let the ladies know that if there was anything they needed, please come and tell him.

Mandy heard her father's voice downstairs and listened. He wasn't yelling or angry. He was actually talking to everyone and offering to help. She had hoped that her talk to her family explained everything about the situation. She would not stop seeing Adam, but knew they made a mistake. Mandy told Adam that she wasn't sorry it happened. He wasn't either.

Adam knew his dad probably wanted to get back home tomorrow. He asked Mandy if she thought she could get away later tonight. She wasn't sure, but she would try. She decided to go downstairs and see her dad so that he didn't worry about where she was. Adam stayed in his room. He was tired of dealing with people right now.

Alone now, Adam opened up the journal again. He touched the pages that were slightly indented from the pressure of his mom's pen onto the paper. He read another entry.

Dear Journal,

Maybe from now on I should simply write, Dear Adam,

We are at the beach house and I am the happiest I've ever been. You are alive and kicking as I'm sitting on the chairs near the water. I watch the waves come in and out and it is rhythmic, soothing, and predictable.

When my parents bought this house, I came here as a child. The neighbors were older. One side was Mrs. Fern and Mr. Gene. The other side was and even older couple. Mrs. Fern had kids, but they didn't love it here like I did. My friend was the ocean. I couldn't wait to get up to see the sunrise and hated to leave it at night. I can't wait to take you in the ocean.

It's the same feeling I get when I travel, you are one of billions of people. In the ocean you are a tiny drop of water. The ocean needs us just like we need it. Enjoy it, protect it and love it. And please always love this house. It will be yours someday and that feels right. I grew up here, you will grow up here and your kids will grow up here. This makes me happy.

Thank you.

Love always,

Mom

"You're welcome, mom," Adam answered quietly. He closed the journal and decided to join the group downstairs. He saw that Bob and Mandy had left. Fern was sitting on the back porch and his dad and Iris were in the kitchen. Adam put on his jacket and decided to walk on the beach.

Adam wished he could go grab his surf board and head out into the water. He could, but he would probably freeze. He made a mental note to get a wetsuit. The second best was walking on the beach. He needed to think and clear his head. So many things were happening at once that he needed to process everything.

He was pretty sure his dad wasn't going to sell the beach house. Fern and Iris were living in it until next summer and they would be back. So if that was still a threat, he had until next fall to deal with it. As for Mandy, he thinks they are free to be a couple although he, technically, never asked her to be his girlfriend.

Another thing that he couldn't get past was that his dad and Iris were a couple. Would they get married? Would she be his step mother? He shook his head to help comprehend how so many things have changed in his life. He didn't tell his father he applied at colleges near here along with ones back home. He would wait for acceptance letters to come in before he brought it up with his dad.

A thought that kept creeping into Adam's head was why his dad needed to sell the beach house. Why couldn't he sell the Atlanta house? Adam would be away at college next fall, he already proved he could work remotely with occasional trips to the city. Why sell the beach house?

Adam didn't even realize he had started running. He had run further than he had all summer. There weren't any houses up this way. It was mostly sand dunes. Adam took off his shoes and socks and stood with his feet in the water. He started moving his feet around looking for seashells and spotted something triangular and dark. He reached down before it washed away and held it in his palm. It was a shark tooth. It was the size of his fingernail.

Adam tried looking for more but didn't find any. He put it in his pocket to give to Mandy. He hoped she could come over tonight. The house was pretty packed so he thought they could go somewhere in his jeep. He didn't want to waste a single moment with her. It may be months before they saw each other again.

Adam started walking back towards home, holding his shoes and socks. His feet were cold, but he loved the feeling of the water on his bare feet. The sun was low and ready to set. He hated how short the days were at this time of year. It would be dark by the time he got home. Adam called his dad to let him know he was on his way. Russell said his dinner would be waiting for him on the kitchen counter.

Russell and Iris were sitting on the couch watching a movie. Iris picked a romantic comedy, not his normal type of movie. They had fixed Fern a proper bed in the dining room so that she could be more comfortable. Russell and Iris had been able to bring over much of their things on the first floor of their house.

When Adam got home, he ate his dinner and went upstairs. He wasn't ready to read any more of his mother's journal, so he showered and changed in anticipation of Mandy coming over later. When Mandy finally called, Adam told her to come around front, they were going out. He told his dad they were going to get ice cream and grabbed his keys.

Mandy climbed in the passenger seat and they went into town. It was just like the summer, only they couldn't put the top down. He didn't even know if there were ice cream shops open in the winter here. Instead, Adam saw a coffee shop and they went in. Mandy ordered a fancy coffee with lots of names. Adam just got his black.

They found a table in the corner and talked. Mandy said she wanted to come to his graduation. Adam said she didn't have to because the minute he graduated, he was driving down here to see her. They both laughed at the image. It was true, though. He would spend every second between high school and college here at the beach house.

"I applied at colleges around here, too," Adam said.

"That's nice, but I don't want you to give up on your dreams of playing football," Mandy replied.

"I'm not," Adam said. "I actually was thinking I might become a teacher."

"You'd be a great teacher."

They enjoyed talking about their futures because they included each other. They held hands as they talked. It was something so special and intimate. Adam never wanted this moment to end because he knew as soon as they went home it was back to reality.

Adam suggested that they go for a ride. They went back in his jeep and drove to the lighthouse. The beam of light from the top made everything around them glow. They were still holding hands. Mandy leaned over and kissed Adam. When the gears between the two seats made kissing awkward, Mandy suggested the back seat.

"Mandy," Adam started, "I love you, but I think we should wait."

"You regret what we did, don't you?" Mandy asked.

"No," Adam replied. "I don't, but I was selfish and I'm sorry."

"I'm not." Mandy leaned over and kissed Adam.

Adam loved Mandy too much to take advantage of her or the situation. He knew they both wanted to give in to their emotions, but this was not the time or place. He decided it was time to head home.

Adam put the car in drive and Mandy started crying. She was going to miss him so much. How was she going to get through another six months without him? He didn't have an answer because he didn't know either. He knew if he pulled another stunt like he did, just driving down, his dad wouldn't be so understanding. He would have to follow the rules, for now.

They would have to rely on texting, calling and video chat. Holding and touching would have to wait. Adam squeezed her hand and she looked over at him. She knew in her heart, had known since she was old enough to ride a bike, that she would marry Adam one day. She didn't know if Adam knew it yet, but it was enough that she did.

Chapter 27

When everyone arrived in the kitchen for breakfast the next morning, Russell wanted to discuss their future plans. He confirmed what Adam suspected, that he would not be selling the beach house, which put Adam's thoughts at ease. He wanted Iris and Fern to feel welcome here and told them not to worry about anything.

Russell was making a lot of promises that even he was questioning his ability to fulfill. He told Adam they would have to go back home very soon. This, Adam already knew. When they finally had time alone, he showed his father the journal he had found in the attic. Russell nodded.

"Have you read it?" Adam asked.

"Yes," his father replied. "Have you?"

Adam shook his head. "I have only read a few entries. It's too hard."

"Most of it was written directly to you," Russell said. "When she died I just put it away with all the other things that were too hard to deal with. I would have eventually given it to you, but last summer we were so happy, it was too soon."

Adam wasn't mad. He knew it was all just as difficult for his dad as it was for him. Maybe even more so. He just knew that now that he had the journal, it was proof that his mom would never let them sell the beach house.

Adam took the journal and sat on the beach. It was still early and the sun was just coming over the ocean. He opened to the next page and read his mother's words.

My Dear Adam,

We are at the beach house again. Just got in yesterday. You are seven now and I can't believe how fast the time has gone by. You love dinosaurs and brought your favorites with you. In fact, we weren't allowed to leave until you could.

You ran straight to Trey when we got here. You two are inseparable. Little Mandy tries to keep up with you boys but you don't usually let her play. I hope that as you grow up you will have time for Amanda. She adores you so. I may not live to see that day, but know that I am always with you.

I have just been diagnosed with cancer. Your dad and I have talked and cried, but I will fight it. But just in case Cancer wins, I want you to rely on dad and your friends when you feel sad. This isn't the kind of disease that many survive, so we are keeping it from you just in case. Your childhood should be carefree. Full of sun, sand, ocean, Trey and Amanda.

Love Always,

Mom

Adam looked out at the ocean. He was tearing up at the fact that she knew even ten years ago that she may not win. She fought this disease ten long years. He could never have siblings because of the disease and treatment, so much loss.

Mandy came over and sat beside Adam. She had seen him walk to the water and wasn't sure if he wanted privacy or not. She took his hand and asked if he wanted her to leave.

"Never," Adam replied. Actually, they both knew their time here together was limited. He and his dad would leave soon. She would have to stay strong until next Memorial Day party.

"Will you be my girlfriend?" Adam asked.

Finally! Mandy thought. "Yes!"

They kissed, it was official. Despite what their fathers might say, they were even more committed to each other than before.

Inside, Russell and Iris were making plans of their own. Iris was glad she moved up to Jekyll Island. Even with the obstacles that they were facing right now, she didn't want to be anywhere else. In fact, she was glad she was with Fern when this happened. She didn't think she would have survived the fire, especially if Adam hadn't been home.

Iris wanted Russell to stay longer. She understood his life was near Atlanta, but she moved to the beach, why couldn't he? She mentioned that he could freelance or work remotely again. There were options if they were going to try and make this work. She wanted their relationship to work. Iris could feel that Russell was the one.

Russell said he would consider everything. He had a lot of things to think about when he went back home. He wasn't satisfied at work anymore, he could admit that. But that was also nothing new. He had been dealing with an unfair boss and a devious coworker for years. He was constantly trying to prove himself at work.

Those decisions and more would just have to wait. He needed to get him and Adam back home. This detour was unexpected and yet incredibly necessary. Russell told Adam to get ready and they would be leaving. Iris assured him they would be fine and she could handle the insurance adjuster and the contractor. If she needed his help, she would call.

Adam and Mandy had already said their goodbyes. Their relationship was in a good place. He just wished they could stay longer, like five months longer. Adam made sure he packed his mom's journal.

The ride home was quiet as usual. They occasionally talked about what was going to happen in the next week or two, but really they both wanted to just turn around and forget it all. Adam knew it would be stupid to leave in the middle of senior year. They would stay until graduation and then have another summer together.

Adam was starting to get college acceptance letters. They were great offers. He was getting scholarship offers from Division 1 schools, even. He would think about them but his heart was set on a school near Mandy. He knew that was not a way to choose a college with a fantastic football program, but it would wait until he saw all of his options.

THE HOLIDAYS AT HOME were the worst. Thanksgiving dragged on and Russell actually cooked ribs this year for dinner. The old traditions didn't seem right. They needed to make their own normal and they were figuring it all out as they went. Things at work were getting hectic again and Russell was thankful to have a few days off for the holidays.

Russell convinced his younger brother, Ted, to come up for Christmas. It would be nice to see him again, too. Ted agreed to come for a week and everyone was looking forward to it. Adam loved his Uncle Teddy. He wished they didn't live so far apart so that they could see each other more often.

Uncle Teddy was fun, and always talked to Adam like an adult, not a child. His parents didn't tell him until he was nearly a teenager that Uncle Teddy was gay. It wasn't something he was hiding, they just didn't know how to explain it to Adam until he knew about liking a boy or a girl.

It never changed anything for Adam, he always loved Uncle Teddy. His signature gift was a teddy bear. Adam had several and still slept with them. Adam really wished Mandy could come up for Christmas. She asked her parents if she could drive, even asked if Trey could come, too, but they said, 'no'.

Adam wasn't exactly sure why they were against it, maybe they were secretly hoping their romance would fizzle out. Not if they could help it. Adam and Mandy were video chatting when Uncle Teddy came through their front door. Mandy was able to say, 'hi' before she let Adam go spend time with his uncle.

Ted had been to their house many times, but had to admit it was very different without Lynn around. She was the warmth. The guys were doing their best. Adam, now eighteen, was focusing on graduating and then moving out. Ted was proud of his hard work and dedication, especially under such hard circumstances.

It was late one night, Russ and Ted where drinking whiskey by the fireplace when Russell expressed his desire to quit. He had explained the situation many times to his brother, who understood the dynamics at Russ's work. Ted thought that his brother was depressed.

"A change might be good for you, Russ," Ted said. "I mean a big change. Sell this house, quit your job and move to the beach house."

"Don't think it hasn't crossed my mind," Russ replied.

"Well, I'm telling you to put more thought into it than a casual one. You have enough clout and seniority that you could walk into any architectural firm and demand a position. Or take a more relaxed approach and be your own boss. Start your own company or freelance work."

Russ looked at his brother. He never really put much serious thought into it. It was a passing dream, not a reality.

"If you sold this house, which is much bigger than you need, especially once Adam goes to college in a few months, you would be buying yourself time to get settled," Ted said.

Russ sipped his whiskey and stared into the fire. "I really do need to consolidate into one house."

"Exactly," Ted said. "And when you are old and alone, where do you want to be living?"

The question hung in the air until it hit Russ on the head. Ted was right. Where did he really want to be? He was nearly middle aged and needed to really think about his future.

"You really have a great point, Ted."

Ted sat back, sipped his whiskey and gloated. "I know!"

This is what he missed. He missed being near people that he loved and loved him back. This big city had turned cold and it wasn't welcoming anymore. Not like Jekyll Island and running on the beach at sunrise. Waking up with Iris next to him. Ted helped him come to a decision.

It was on Christmas morning that Russell announced to Adam that they were selling the house. He waited until Adam got good and mad about selling the beach house until he smiled and said, "This house!" Adam couldn't believe his ears. He hugged his dad and uncle. It was the best Christmas gift he could have gotten!

Adam went up to his room to tell Mandy. She was thrilled even though she knew he wouldn't be there full time. If he found a college close enough, he could maybe come home every weekend. It was still the best news she had heard in a very long time.

Russ and Ted called their parents to let them know Russ's decision. They were happy for him. Russell invited them to the beach house when it was their permanent home. He felt lighter somehow. His next call was to Iris. Everyone was having a good Christmas but the next ones would be even better.

Adam couldn't believe it was really going to happen. He never thought his dad would agree to sell their house. He as grateful for Uncle Teddy's visit. His dad had finally listened to someone about what he should do with his future. Everyone knew he hated where he worked. Now he was taking matters in to his own hands.

If Russell truly wanted to build a future with Iris then he had to go where she was. He was the one able to move. He would think about the details later. Right now he was glad he made a decision. It would be rewarding to quit at work. He couldn't wait to see the look on Stanley and Walter's faces when he handed in his resignation.

"Hello, New Year," Russell said quietly to himself.

Chapter 28

Russell walked into his building on Peachtree Street with a smile on his face. He greeted everyone with a cheery, 'Hello'. Vonn was especially suspicious. Russell had entered with his blueprints and laid them on Stanley's desk. He loved the look of confusion on his face when he also handed him his resignation.

"I had decided to be adult about this and simply say, 'thank you' and walk out," Russell said. "But then I remembered how you treated me over the years and just wanted to add that you are a terrible boss. You play favorites and then pit them against each other. That's no way to build a team."

Stanley looked at Russell's resignation letter and shook his head. "Please don't do this, Russell. I was actually going to fire Walter this week. He screwed up a clients blueprints and they went with someone else. He doesn't have the finesse that you do."

"Well, I would advise against firing Walter," Russell said with a smirk. "You're going to need someone to boss around. I'm cleaning out my desk now."

Russell walked to his office and started taking things off the walls. Vonn came in with a confused look. Russell explained to her that he's moving and that he just quit. He offered her anything she wanted in his office and she hesitantly took a gold colored clock that had sat on his desk for as long as he worked there. Vonn hugged and thanked him and said things wouldn't be the same around here without him. Russell, unfortunately, knew this and felt sorry for her. She would now be Walter's assistant and that sounded horrible.

Russell went to see Walter. Walter didn't know anything about the resignation, yet, and thought Russell just wanted something. Russ went to say what a greedy, slimy and back stabbing person he was. He even went on to say how he hoped he never saw him again.

Walter's face went red with rage and he banged on his desk. "Wait until I tell Stanley what you just said! You will be fired."

Russell laughed. "Then you'd better hurry up and get in there before he sends my resignation to HR."

Russell went back to his office, picked up his box of things and walked out. He felt nothing. After so many years at one company, he should feel something, right? He carried his box down the elevator, out to his car and drove south down the highway towards home.

It was April. Spring brought everything to life, along with his own excitement to move out of the big city. Plans were set in place ever since his brother, Ted, visited over Christmas. A realtor was lined up, movers were scheduled and he and Adam were packing. It was exciting for both of them.

Russell kept up with the repairs at Iris's house, too. They would be completely done in a couple of weeks and be moved in before Russell and Adam arrived. Iris said that Fern was doing well, but missed her house. She was well enough to keep walking on the beach but Iris kept an eye on her.

Every time Russell spoke to Iris, he longed to be by her side. He was grateful to be in a relationship with someone who understood the complexities of his world. Russell even thought about proposing, how crazy was that? Last summer really did change their lives for the better.

Adam was ready for senior year to be over. His friends were talking about prom, but he had no interest in that without Mandy. She wasn't able to make the drive, she had enough to do with school back home. It wouldn't be long until summer, then they would be reunited.

Adam had received many scholarship offers and was ready to commit to Georgia Southern University. They had a great football program and they offered him a scholarship to play. The only thing is that he didn't tell his dad. His dad had wanted Adam to go to a bigger school with a bigger reputation, but he knew he wasn't going into the NFL. Football would give him an education, and that's what mattered the most.

The fact that Georgia Southern was only an hour and a half from Mandy, was not just a plus, it was a deciding factor. Adam wouldn't tell his father that, but he knew he would guess. It didn't matter, it was Adam's future and Adam's decision. It still didn't make it any easier to tell his father what his decision was.

Graduation was around the corner and Uncle Ted and his grandparents were coming. Adam couldn't believe this was finally happening. He had been ready for graduation since sophomore year, ever since his mom got sick for the last time. Guests would be staying in hotels since the house was nearly empty except for essentials. The plan was that after graduation, everyone was heading to the beach house.

Russell had most things packed up in his bedroom. There was a stack of books that were Lynn's that he wasn't really sure what to do with. He went over again to read the titles. One stuck out to him as a book he had bought for her. It was a book of poetry, her favorite poet. He picked it up and thumbed through the pages, not really looking at the words, more for the memory of it. Russell stepped back when something fell out of it. He bent down to pick up a folded piece of paper.

'Russell,' it said on the outside in Lynn's handwriting. He never suspected anything was in the book and realized that she must have written it right before she passed. She had this book with her everyday near the end. The words brought her comfort. Now he had to see what her words were to him.

My Dear Russ,

Life sure didn't turn out how we planned. That night at the beach house, in front of the fireplace, I will always remember that time with you. I won't make this a long letter, I know how you don't like sappy sentiments. Just know that you made me so happy. I hope I made you happy, too. Adam is perfect. Please don't be so hard on him, but make sure he is a good kid. I know he will be kind, gentle and loving, just like his father.

My last wish for you is to be happy. Find love. Get married. Live.

Love always,

Lynn

Russell didn't realize he was crying until a drop fell on the paper. Lynn planned this, he thought. Russ even smiled as he thought of her, in heaven, looking down and telling him to find the book with the letter now. Just as he was moving on with his life, Lynn gave her blessing. Russell returned the letter to the book and packed it in his backpack.

Adam enjoyed having everyone in town for his graduation. He saw his Uncle Teddy and grandparents a couple times a year, but now it was even more special. Just as his family was feeling smaller, there were reminders like these that he knew he had plenty of family that loved him.

Uncle Teddy gave Adam a laptop and gadgets for college. His grandparents gave him money. He appreciated everything he received and especially that they came all the way out to Georgia. It was fun seeing Atlanta as a tourist through their eyes. They especially love the World of Coke.

Adam was able to spend some quality time with his grandparents, too. They took him out to dinner and talked about this future. He mentioned that he'd like to be a teacher. What he never realized was that his grandmother was a teacher until Russell was born. She had taught kindergarten and loved it. Actually, she missed it, even thought through the years how she would have liked to have returned to the classroom.

Adam loved math and science. He was thinking to be more of a middle or high school teacher, but he would see where life took him. Adam hoped they would come visit more often, but knew as they got older, it would be harder. He promised them and himself that he would visit them often.

It was funny, Adam thought, how something you have wanted to happen for years was now actually happening and you wanted it to slow down. He knew in his mind that this was it, this was the last time he would be with these high school friends in these hall and at this school. This was the last time that he would drive down this street and turn into this driveway.

It was all becoming real and it was scary. Even though he dreamed about the day he would go back to the beach house, sell their home and he would go off to college, it was happening and it was frightening. It was the beginning of the end but it would be okay. Adam would be okay.

When Adam told his dad where he was going to go to college, he admitted he was disappointed but he also acknowledged that it wasn't about him. If this was what Adam wanted, then why should it matter that Russell wanted something else? It didn't. Adam wanted to be closer to family, not a thousand miles away.

Adam called Mandy. He longed to hear her voice.

"Congratulations!" Mandy said. "I can't believe I'm dating a college boy now."

Adam laughed. "I wish you were here."

"I know, me too," Mandy replied. "But you'll be here tomorrow. It will be worth it. We have all summer."

It was true. They had all summer and there shouldn't be any more reason for sneaking around. Mandy assured him that his parents came around and would accept Adam as her boyfriend. Adam thought that they secretly wished that a long distance romance wouldn't have worked and that they would have broken up by now. So when they didn't, her parents had no choice but to accept him.

That was okay with Adam and Mandy. They proved they could handle being apart, so now they could be together. Adam walked around the house one last time. It was empty and would soon belong to a new family. He was happy about that. He knew that they would make lots of memories of their own through the years.

The moving truck had just left. It was just Russell and Adam left to follow in their own vehicles. It was bittersweet to leave this house and neighborhood, but they were going to a house they loved more. That was the consolation prize, the beach house.

The drive to Jekyll Island felt different this time. For Russell, it was his second chance. It would be a new job, new house and new relationship all at once. He had a lot riding on this but was also sure that he couldn't lose. For Adam, it was a new world of possibilities. His life was just starting and this was only the first step. New house, college, career and relationship. They were just steps to his future.

Russell and Adam had both arrived at the beach house before the moving van. They each parked and stepped out onto the driveway facing the front of the house. It was just like last summer. The hesitation of stepping inside was still there, but unwarranted.

Standing at the front door was symbolic. They were entering Lynn's favorite place. It was her house and her world. It was now theirs to live and grow in. Russell would move on in life and love. Adam would start a life that could go in any direction.

Father and son looked at each other and smiled. This was where they were supposed to be. It took them a while to figure it out and make it work but it felt right. They each put an arm around each other and stepped into their home on the beach. It felt warm. It was home.

Chapter 29

Arriving at the beach was emotional for Adam. The last time he was here, he was uninvited and it turned into chaos. It worked out eventually, but it was still a memory he would rather not have. The house was dark, quiet and empty. Adam felt like he needed to tip toe as he walked from room to room, as if ghosts were lurking around every corner.

Russell carried groceries into the kitchen and brushed right past Adam. Not as concerned about the quiet or any lurking ghosts, Russell was ready to be settled. He had applications submitted and interviews lined up. He wasn't sure if he would work for another firm, start his own or simply freelance, his options were wide open.

Russell had let Iris take what furniture she wanted. They needed it and Russell was coming with a house full of furniture from their other house. It seemed like everyone was giving them time and space to get settled. The cars were both unloaded and Russell laid out the food that they brought from their refrigerator that needed to be eaten.

Bits of leftovers may not have been their first choice of a meal, but it tasted good. It was their first dinner in the beach house as their year round house. It was a momentous occasion and Russell opened a bottle of wine.

The moving van arrived and they watched everything get unloaded, set up and arranged. It would take days or even weeks to get their things exactly how they wanted them, but it was fine. They weren't going anywhere.

Russell and Adam went to sit on the back porch swing. All their hard work from last summer still looked great. They looked out at the ocean, each in their own thoughts. The sun was setting behind them and it cast a warm glow on the water. What a difference a year made!

Last summer they had come to Jekyll Island unsure of their futures and unsure if they could handle coming back here. They soon learned that not only could they handle it, they craved it. The beach house was what healed them.

"We made it," Russell said.

"Yes, we did," Adam replied. "And I'm glad we did it."

"Me too."

Russell went in to watch a movie. "For old time's sake?" He asked his son.

"Only if it's an action movie," Adam said.

Father and son sat on the couch in the living room eating popcorn. This was what bonded them. Adam knew he could always count on his dad. His dad was his constant. Adam was going to need that anchor the next few years as he goes through life.

Adam had texted with Mandy. She knew he made it there safely but would give him time to settle in. It was not easy staying home, but she had all summer with him. Russell also texted with Iris to let her know they got in okay. He asked about Fern and she was doing good. She was back to walking to the water to talk with Gene.

After the movie, Adam went up to his room. Nothing much changed there, except he got rid of all the clothes that didn't fit him. Now it was truly his room. His shelves were now overflowing with school books, football gear and seashells. All the parts of his life were coming together here. He was starting to feel whole again.

Russell relaxed with another glass of wine on the back porch. It was calming to be here and he was hoping it would be good for his health, too. At his last doctor appointment, he was borderline for high blood pressure and Russell attributed that to his job. He was also developing a cough, that they were treating like asthma. He didn't smoke, but perhaps from second-hand smoke or even pollution. He was sure that the ocean air would improve that, too.

Russell was confident that moving to Jekyll Island was going to be great for his family. He was also secretly glad that Adam wouldn't be very far away at college. And then there was Iris. He hoped he had a future with Iris.

The next morning was the beginning of their summer vacation. Russell and Adam were awake at sunrise and went for their run. It was wonderful to be back into that routine. The mornings were still a bit cool and when they got back, they went for a swim. As everyone else was just waking up, they came out to see the new year round residents.

First was Trey and Mandy who came to say that they were so excited for them to be living next door. Trey was actually going to the same college as Adam and they were trying to sign up to be roommates. Mandy would be a junior and was happy just to be one year closer to graduation.

Russell went inside so that the teenagers could hang out in the water. He had other neighbors to visit. He went up to Fern's back porch and saw her alone. Russell joined her to catch up. She was getting around just like before her fall. He was so grateful for that because Fern was very independent.

She complained that Iris hovered too much and just wanted to be left alone. Russell laughed and asked if he could go inside and see the house since the fire. He knew that ceilings, floors and walls had to be redone. The roof and some of the attic had to be rebuilt. To look at the house now, one would never know that such devastation happened here. It was amazing.

Russell found Iris in the kitchen and came up behind her and hugged her. She turned to kiss him and put her arms around his neck. Finally, she was back in his arms, Russell thought. It had been a long time since they saw each other and spent the night together, but it was worth it now. Now they could see each other as often as they wanted to. Iris has just made some muffins and offered one to Russ.

He sat at the kitchen island, ate his muffin and drank his coffee. This was what he was missing in his life, having a companion that he wanted to wake up to every day. Iris was just glad to have Russell around for a distraction from her mother. It was definitely an adjustment for two people who lived independently to now live together.

Fern liked doing things a certain way and so did Iris. Fern liked leaving dishes pile up and then doing them all at one time. Iris was the type of person who washed a dish when it was placed in the sink. This clash also happened when they did laundry, grocery shopping and cleaning up. Iris had to remind herself that it was her mother's house, her rules.

Outside, Trey and Mandy were both glad to see Adam. They said their family was doing another Memorial Day party in a couple of days and it was going to be a blast. Adam remembered last year's party being awkward. It was the first time he had seen Mandy in two years and was instantly caught off guard.

Last year Russell was uncomfortable being at the party because he was being forced to mingle with everyone while falling apart inside. He was no longer falling apart, he was being put back together. This year's party would, indeed, be one to remember.

The three teenagers were on their surfboards just enjoying being kids for the summer. No more pressures of school, family or coaches. They could all breath a sigh of relief at the simple pleasure of sitting on their boards waiting for a wave.

Adam couldn't keep his eyes off of Mandy. He hadn't seen her since he drove to the house unannounced on Halloween night. The last seven months were so hard to get through without seeing her.

They talked on the phone but that was not the same. He missed her touch, the smell of her hair and her kiss. Even now it was all he could do not to go over and kiss her. He just kept telling himself there would be time for that later.

Mandy's heart was racing when she saw that Adam was in the ocean, it was her idea to get their boards and join him. Trey wanted to, but Mandy needed to. She had to be within reach of him. Her breathing got fast and her face was flushed but hopefully no one noticed. She managed to come and give him a hug when they got to the water without making much of a scene.

Touching him sent a shock wave through her system. She was afraid to stare at him the entire time they were on the water, but they had moments of uninterrupted gazes. Adam was even more fit and muscular than before. He mentioned that it was because of football training and wanting to be ready for college ball.

Trey, too had been working out for football, but he didn't look anything like Adam. He had more hair on his chest then she remembered. He had even let his hair grow out so that it was falling down the front of his face. With one hand, Adam pushed his hair out of his eyes and then looked directly at Mandy. She missed watching those simple movements of Adam running his hands through his hair.

Mandy was in a bikini and was looking good to Adam, too. Her hair was to the middle of her back and she looked beautiful. Her smile was so bright and easy, Adam couldn't help but return the smile. They managed to catch some waves and have fun on the water.

When Trey went home, Adam took Mandy to his back yard and kissed her. He drew her close to him and could feel the warmth of her body on his. He tasted the salt water as he kissed her cheeks, neck and forehead, too. Mandy was breathing fast, shallow breaths and she held on to his strong arms while he kissed her. She returned the kisses to his face, neck and chest.

It was too much all at once and she broke away, holding him at arms length. She felt dizzy and lightheaded as if being near him was a drug that she had too much of. He watched her as she slowed her breathing and then looked up at him.

"I've missed you so much," Adam said.

"I've missed you more," Mandy replied.

They sat on the steps to Adam's back porch and held hands. This was as much as she could handle after that. Adam kissed her hand in his and asked if they could hang out tonight. She agreed. He still needed to help unpack and get things put away, so maybe after dinner. She would be looking forward to it.

Russell asked Iris if they could hang out later today. She said her mother usually went to sleep around eight. Fern's bedroom had officially been moved back upstairs since she was fully recovered. Fern was feeling more independent and back to normal with the house finished and things back where they were.

Iris liked that her mother could do more for herself, again. Fern was still quiet. She didn't talk to everyone as much as she talked to Gene. She kept up her walks to the water and would talk to her husband for an hour each night. It was comforting for her to always have him there to talk to, whether he was really there or not.

Fern was feeling more melancholy than usual. She supposed it was because with Iris here, it reminded her of when the kids were little. She wished her son, Forrest, would come visit, but he was busy. She was glad to be back in her house, although grateful to Russell for giving them a place to stay. This beach was special.

Fern didn't care how many people told her to move and find a nice little retirement home where she can mingle with people her own age and would be less dangerous with the storms, hurricanes and all. Fern loved her ocean and it was where Gene was. She would never leave.

Chapter 30

Plans for the big Memorial Day party were underway. The Covingtons were hosting and there was a lot to be done. Bob and Julie always handled the grilled items. The rest of the neighbors divided up the side item, drinks and desserts. Since Russell and Adam weren't the best of cooks, they said they would bring drinks. Iris would make macaroni salad and cupcakes.

It was Russell and Adam's first full weekend back at the beach house and they were ready to relax. The party was tomorrow, so today was preparations, shopping and swimming. Adam went with his dad to get the sodas and the beer for the party. It was energizing to have the party to look forward to. They even picked up some fireworks for tomorrow night.

Russell went over to see Iris and helped with getting the food ready. He didn't know how to make anything, but could handle frosting some cupcakes. It would also give them a chance to spend more time together and talk. He wanted her opinion about his new work opportunities and he was even considering getting his own realtor's license.

Adam texted Mandy and asked if she wanted to get out of here and go for a ride. She came over immediately and they drove into the city of Brunswick. Mandy knew this town well. There was a mall, the college, lots of cute shops and restaurants and a marina. It's where they kept their boat.

They went to get some Japanese food at Fancy Q's and then coffee at The Gathering Place. It had a cute little thrift shop attached that she always wanted to browse. It was a great afternoon of talking and holding hands. Adam missed her so much. She was still wearing the shark necklace he gave her and he touched it with his finger.

"I'm glad you're still wearing it,"Adam said.

"I never take it off," Mandy replied. She looked down at his own wrist and saw the 'Mandy' bracelet he still wore.

The both smiled and kissed. It was soft and gentle. They were in no hurry and just enjoyed being in each other's company. They continued to walk around town and go inside little shops around the historic downtown area. It felt so familiar and natural to be walking on the tree lined streets and holding hands with Mandy.

Mandy enjoyed the time with Adam, too. She had waited too long to hold him. She would put an arm around his waist and he would look down at her. It was the most wonderful feeling in the world to be able to do. She knew Adam would leave in August for college, but she would make the most of the summer while he was all hers.

When it got too hot to just walk around, they got back in Adam's jeep and returned to Jekyll Island. He didn't drive straight home, though. He went to the lighthouse. There were parks and plenty of trees to sit under and have privacy.

Adam parked and they were hesitant to get out. They held hands and just stared at each other as if trying to memorize the smallest details and changes. There were subtle changes, but nothing drastic. They were still the Mandy and Adam that they remembered.

Adam was the first to lean over and kiss her. That kiss opened the flood gates of emotions for both of them. They started out kissing which led to touching. When it got to be too much for them, they stopped. It was not the right time or place and they pulled themselves apart. Now that they were back together, Adam wanted their time together to be special.

He put the jeep into reverse and they returned home. Adam's house was empty and they sat on the couch. Mandy said the place looked different with the furniture they brought from their other house. It was more modern and had a cozy feel to it. Mandy laid down on the couch with Adam and they actually fell asleep in each other's arms.

Russell came home later to find them still asleep on the couch. He touched Adam's arm and said he had better let her go home. Not realizing she had been gone so long, Mandy checked her watch, kissed Adam and walked home. Adam sat up and asked where he had been. Russell explained that he was making food for tomorrow and Adam laughed, not believing him.

They smiled and both changed to go surfing. It was such a clear sunny afternoon and the waves were just right. They managed to catch a few waves and then waited for more. Adam talked about his morning with Mandy and Russell was glad things were working out for him. It was good to see him smiling so much.

Adam even commented on how happy his dad looked. Russell admitted that he was finally finding the joy in life, again. He was never sure he could find that kind of love again, but he thinks he might have come close. The fact that there was the possibility of a future with another woman made it worth while to Russell.

Father and son enjoyed their time in the ocean. Whether they actually got to surf as much as they wanted to wasn't really the point. They just liked catching up and spending time together. As the evening wore on, Russell said he would go in and put a pizza in the oven. Adam said he would be in soon.

Adam watched as Mrs. Fern walked to the water and talked. She used hand gestures and even laughed at something she said. She looked happy when she talked to her husband. It was their nightly rendezvous. Adam wondered what her life was like when she was younger. He decided he would sit down with her this summer and ask.

Baseball season started tonight and Adam called Trey to come over and watch the game. The three of them sat, ate pizza and watched the Braves play. It was good hanging out with the guys and getting together with Trey. They would be roommates, so they needed to know how to live with each other.

Trey and Adam loved each other like brothers, so it was still a bit awkward to be dating Trey's little sister. He tried not to do much kissing or hugging in front of Trey, but he couldn't always promise that would be the case. Tonight was all about the guys, though, no girls.

Julie and Bob tried setting ground rules with Mandy this summer. Mandy just couldn't promise that she would never be alone with Adam. That was impossible to promise. They basically said they just wanted to know where she was. Her parents admitted they liked Adam, even trusted him, but he was still a boy.

Mandy spent the evening with her mom in the kitchen making jello salad, cookies and hamburger patties. The Covingtons had invited all the surrounding neighbors so it was bound to be a big gathering, again. There was a slight chance of rain tomorrow night, but everyone kept their fingers crossed that it wouldn't rain on the party.

Mandy sensed that her mother was always secretly on her side, even though she openly sided with her dad. Julie remembered Lynn in her prime and always loved little Adam hanging out with her kids. Julie and Lynn would hang out on the beach and watch them play all day in the sand. They were built-in best friends.

When Lynn started getting sick, she always worried about Adam. Lynn had asked Julie to promise to look after Adam, especially after she was gone. Julie promised she would and held a soft spot in her heart for the sad little boy who had to watch his mother slowly die. Julie had to admit she was worried that Russell would up and move him and Adam away from Jekyll Island.

Even though the beach house was a reminder of Lynn's death, it was also a testament to her life. Julie loved this place almost as much as her family. Sometimes Julie wondered if they weren't even on the same level. She had lost a best friend and Bob didn't always recognize that his wife was hurting, too.

Bob was a man's man, he and Russell could go out fishing and not say one word about their feelings, but just being together was enough. For Julie, that wasn't the case. She felt the loss of Lynn and had no one to tell. Mandy was too young to take on that much sorrow. So, Julie kept it in and looked after Adam.

"Mom," Mandy started, "there's something I want to give to Adam but I need your help."

Intrigued, Julie replied, "Sure."

Mandy did not elaborate and Julie did not push. She knew her daughter enough to let her come to her about it when she was ready. Julie knew they exchanged little gifts through the years, but she was never invited to help before. She tried looking at Mandy as a stranger might see her. She was tall, pretty and very kind. She looked older than seventeen and that's what worried her.

Julie knew Adam liked and respected her, but he was eighteen, soon to be nineteen and Mandy has been head over heals in love with Adam for as long as she could remember. What would happen when Adam goes off to college and finds girls he liked better? Julie felt justified in worrying about her daughter's heart.

They managed the long distance relationship pretty well last year, so maybe they are strong enough to get through the coming years, too. Julie knew he was going to Georgia Southern and it wasn't too far away. That was comforting and concerning all at the same time for a mother.

Julie released Mandy from kitchen duty and Mandy went upstairs to shower and get ready for bed. She was excited about the Memorial Day party tomorrow and called Adam when she was sitting in bed watching tv. Mandy always felt calmer talking to Adam. Conversations with Adam would often include their future.

Adam would say that being a teacher was good, because when Mandy became a marine biologist he could follow her anywhere and be a teacher. Every state had teachers. Or if she wanted to transition into a vet or in a lab, he would support her and move with her. It was dreamy and wishful thinking, but why couldn't it turn out that way?

Being with Adam made Mandy feel like she could be or do anything. It was a heady and wonderful feeling. They asked about each other's day. Adam missed hanging out with Trey and thought it will be fun being roommates. Mandy warned him that he is only pretending to be neat and clean. The real Trey is dirty and disgusting. They both laughed.

After they hung up, Adam thought about something Trey said tonight. He said he invited the group of kids from his school, like last year. He made it sound all innocent when he said he wouldn't be responsible if some girls showed up, too. Adam had to think if he was secretly trying to sabotage his relationship. Perhaps Trey wasn't very happy with his sister dating his friend.

Adam just hoped this plan didn't actually work and get Mandy mad thinking the girls were his idea, too. He hoped their relationship was strong enough to withstand one party on Memorial Day. If not, this would ruin their summer and it would be hard to get Mandy's trust back.

Adam would make sure nothing happens. Mandy would have to know that he would never do anything to hurt her. He was tired of thinking about it. There was nothing he could do now. He would just have to wait and see what Trey had planned. All Adam wanted was a great party with his girlfriend. Nothing and no one else mattered.

Chapter 31

The long awaited party was finally here. It was the Covington's official kick off to summer. Russell was glad that Bob had taken over the tradition after Lynn got sick. Russell did not miss the work involved in hosting the annual Memorial Day party for the neighborhood. Bob was doing a great job of making it bigger every year.

The whole day was devoted to grilling, eating and swimming. The volleyball net was set up as well as corn hole and kites. This was the day to kick back and only think about summer and having fun. That's all that was on Adam's mind today when he and his dad did their run at sunrise.

Father and son were in good spirits and excited about today. When they got home, they showered, changed and had breakfast. There was no rush today. Russell took his coffee outside on the porch and Adam joined him. His father had purchased a drone and he was eager to use it later. But right now all he wanted to do was relax.

They waved at people who were going to Bob's house. The great thing about living next door to the party was going home when it became too much. Hosts can't leave. Russell had a few coughing spells but they seemed to be getting better lately. He wasn't stressed out much anymore.

Russell had gone to a few interviews but wasn't satisfied about any of them. He was still leaning towards freelancing as his full time work. There was no hurry, he was taking the summer off. Russell was nervous about something, though. He shifted in his seat and looked at Adam.

"I have something to run by you," Russell said.

"What is it?" Adam asked.

"Well, you know I really like Iris and she likes me."

Adam smiled, thinking it was funny how uncomfortable his dad looked right now. "What are you saying?"

Russell took a deep breath and looked at his son. "I want to marry Iris but I want to know what you think about it first."

Adam sat up straight. He didn't know what he was expecting his father to say, but it certainly wasn't that. "Oh," Adam said.

"You're mom has been gone two years now, I think she would be okay with me finding love again," Russell said, thinking of the letter he found in her poetry book. "I found it, son."

Adam smiled. He knew they were good for each other and that they made each other happy. How could he say no? Why would he deny his father any kind of future happiness?

"Of course, dad," Adam said. "Go for it. She may still say no."

They both laughed and it eased the tension Russell had been feeling. If Adam hadn't liked the idea of a step-mother, he didn't know what he would do.

"Thanks."

"When are you going to ask her? Today?"

"I think so," Russell answered.

Russell had been playing it out in his mind for days. He had bought a ring and was ready. He just didn't know if he could actually ask Iris the question. Adam was encouraging, so that was half the battle. The other half was seeing if Iris would say, 'Yes'.

Adam helped his dad take the coolers of beer and soda next door. Bob was getting the grill ready and warmed up. There were a few clouds, but that just helped keep the heat down a few degrees.

Bob shook hands with Adam and Russell and invited them to help themselves.

There were just pastries and fruit right now. They helped themselves and walked around. Soon they found themselves included in a game of corn hole. As more people arrived, more food was brought out. People were bringing so much food, another table was set up.

Russell sat near Bob and they talked sports. The Braves won and they wondered how the season would turn out. Adam saw Trey and Mandy come outside and went to see them. Trey wanted to go surfing but Mandy was wearing a bright yellow sundress. She looked beautiful and tan. Mandy had something in her hand but waved him off to go play with Trey.

"I'll come find you later," Adam promised.

Mandy and a friend each grabbed a kite and extended the string. Even in the water, Adam watched her every move. He saw Mandy laugh as her kite got higher and higher. The wind caught the colorful image of a butterfly and it looked as if she was taking it for a ride. The wings seemed to flap as the wind pushed and pulled on the plastic frame.

Her friend had a traditional diamond shaped kite with a long tail. Hers floated just as high as the butterfly and nearly tangled until the two laughing girls ran opposite ways on the beach. It was so sweet to watch her having so much fun. Adam almost wished he had decided to stay on the beach and run on the sand with Mandy.

The wave that overcame Adam nearly pushed him to the bottom of the ocean. When he came up his eyes were red and he was coughing and gasping for air. The salt water stung his eyes, nose and throat. He excused himself and paddled back to the shore.

Mandy had brought in her kite and was sitting drinking lemonade on one of the beach chairs. She patted the chair next to her and Adam sat down.

"Are you okay?" She asked.

"I'll be fine," Adam replied. "I've been tumbled many times. I'm going to get some water."

Mandy waited for him to come back and sit next to her. When he did, she handed him a square gift wrapped in red paper. Adam looked at Mandy with a confused look and slowly opened it. "What is this for?"

"You've given me so much. I wanted to give you something, too," Mandy replied.

Inside the pretty wrapping paper that was tied with ribbon was a silver framed picture of them. It was taken last summer at their Memorial Party. Mandy's mother had taken it and they were standing side by side with Mandy looking over at Adam. He remembered that day. He had only just seen Mandy again after two years and he was so conflicted inside. He was attracted to his best friend's sister that he had grown up with.

"Thank you," Adam said. "I'll take it with me to college."

Mandy blushed and they kissed. He really did love it.

"I'm going to go put this in my room and change," Adam said. "You can come keep me company if you want."

Adam had a smirk on his face and Mandy nodded. She followed him into his house and they went upstairs. She sat on his bed as he went into his bathroom to change out of his wet clothes. When he came out she jumped into his arms.

They kissed like they have been wanting to the last several days. As they kissed their hands moved and searched. Adam's hands went to Mandy's hair, the softness he remembered well. Mandy ran her hands up his arms and to his shoulders. They were around his neck when they heard a noise downstairs.

Russell had come home to find another folding chair. Adam and Mandy came running down the stairs and out the door before his father could say anything to them. They ran hand in hand back out onto the beach. There were drops of rain that would fall and then stop. They went to get some food before any more rain came.

Adam had a hamburger and Mandy had some barbecued chicken. They filled their plates and then went to sit on the porch. They were laughing and giggling when Trey came over.

"My friends are here," Trey said pointing at a group of four boys and five girls.

This is what Adam was dreading. "Okay, maybe volleyball later," Adam suggested.

"Most definitely," Trey replied.

The group of friends came over and got plates of food. One girl kept eyeing Adam and he noticed. So did Mandy. Trey offered Adam a beer and he refused.

"Oh that's right Mr. Goody Goody doesn't drink," Trey said.

"Maybe you've had enough," Mandy replied.

"You don't need to fight his battles, little sister," Trey said. "Come on, Adam, let's play."

Adam squeezed Mandy's hand and went to play volleyball with Trey and his friends. It was hard to watch Adam on a team with a bunch of girls, but Mandy wanted to. Trey was competitive and Adam played his game. It was fifteen love and the girl who liked Adam gave him a high five. When they were at thirty love, she patted his behind. At forty love she put her hands on either side of his face and kissed him.

When the game was over, she pushed Adam against the tree and kissed him again, this time it looked like Adam kissed back. She ran her hands down his chest but he stopped her from going any further. Adam turned back to the porch to see Mandy, but she was gone.

It was getting dark partly because clouds were rolling in, but also because it was evening. Russell saw Iris and Fern coming down the beach. He ran out to help Fern by offering his elbow to hold on to. She took it and smiled up at Russell.

"Always the gentleman, Russell," Fern said. "Just like my Gene."

This made Russell smile. She sat Fern on a chair and he and Iris went to fix her a plate.

"How did you get her to come?" Russell asked Iris.

"I just asked. She said she would love to come," Iris replied.

They brought the plate to Fern and they sat beside her. Before she started eating, Fern looked at them. "You two make a cute couple. I want you both to be happy. I had a nice long marriage with Gene and I don't regret a thing," Fern said then started eating.

Russell gave Iris a quick kiss and they started eating, too. The ring was burning a hole in Russell's pants. He wanted to propose but had to find the right moment. Should he do it in front of Fern?

Russell put his plate down on the grass. Then he stood up, pulled out the blue velvet box and kneeled down in front of Iris. At first, Iris thought he dropped something and was about to get up with him. Then she froze.

"Iris, I never thought I would be able to find love again. I wasn't sure I could even recognize it, be strong enough to accept it and courageous enough to allow it. But I found it in you," Russell said. By now, more people noticed what was happening and had gathered. Adam did, too.

"Will you marry me?" Russell asked.

Iris was crying now and put her hand on her mother's knee. She and Fern exchanged a look of love and understanding. She loved Russell for including her mother in the moment and she knew he was the one.

"Yes," Iris answered.

Russell stood up with Iris and they kissed. Russell dipped her backwards and everyone cheered. There was applause, screams and whistles as Iris showed off the ring on her finger. They both hugged Fern and she smiled. It was a moment that everyone would never forget.

Adam slipped away to find Mandy. He spotted her on the porch, obviously curious about all the hollering. When she saw Adam coming towards her she turned to leave. He caught her arm and turned her around.

"What's wrong?" Adam demanded.

"Why don't you go kiss the other girl?" Mandy replied. It was lame and she knew it but she was hurt.

"What? She kissed me. I pushed her away," Adam replied.

"That's not what it looked like from here," she said.

Adam took her hand and they walked around the house to the sand dunes. He pulled her close to him and kissed her. At first she resisted and pulled away.

"I love you, Mandy, you have to know that," Adam pleaded.

She did. She put her hands around his neck and kissed him. They fell onto the sand and kissed with a passion that they had been trying to hide. When they thought they heard someone coming close, they stopped.

"You know I didn't even want to play in the first place," Adam said. "And I certainly didn't know she would start hanging all over me. I'm sorry, I won't let Trey set me up like that again."

"I know."

"You should play with me sometime," Adam said with a smile. They kissed again and then returned to the party.

Chapter 32

Once everyone at the Covington's Memorial Day party found out about Russell proposing to Iris and that she said, 'Yes', there was an atmosphere of celebration. Bob went into his wine collection and brought out a bottle of champagne.

"To the happy couple!" Bob announced.

Champagne was poured into everyone's glasses and toasts were made for happiness, their future and even more children. Russell and Iris laughed at the last one, not sure that would be happening for them. They kissed, hugged and enjoyed the moment. For Iris, she had almost given up on finding a husband. She had let herself settle for just having a date or a boyfriend.

Russell couldn't believe he could be this lucky in one lifetime. He loved Iris and she would be a wonderful life partner. Fern was happy for them. She just nodded with a tear coming down the corner of her eye. For her, it was finally seeing her daughter happy, something a mother always wants for their child, with someone to spend her life with. And Fern knew Russell, that was even better, it wasn't some guy that Iris brought home one day. Russell was the kind of guy who would love and protect her when she was gone, like Gene.

Fern appreciated that Russell let her witness the moment, but she was tired. She didn't want to make a fuss about leaving so she got up and walked along the beach towards home by herself. When Fern got to her house, she stopped at the water's edge and told Gene all about tonight. She laughed and cried and then suddenly felt very tired. She made her way to the house and went to bed. Today was a big day but it was worth it.

As Adam and Mandy returned to the party, they joined in on the celebration. They made their way to Russell and Iris and saw them kissing. Mandy saw the ring and congratulated her. They were both so happy that Russell had the courage to pop the question to Iris.

Mandy helped her mom bring out more food and the desserts. It seemed like the party was just getting started, again. It was dark and the boys were hollering for the fireworks to start. Bob said to wait a little bit longer, then they would start the fireworks. People were eating, talking and still congratulating Russ and Iris. The newly engaged couple were sitting arm in arm on a blanket near the water. They both jumped when the first fireworks went up and lit the sky and water in reds and blues.

More guests gathered on the beach with chairs and blankets to watch the fireworks display. Adam and Mandy were another couple who sat on a blanket arm in arm. Trey and his friends were in the water and hollering with each explosion. The atmosphere was light, happy and relaxed.

The Covingtons had put on another amazing party. No one could deny that. He finally stopped grilling and was cleaning up when some neighbors started saying goodbye and leaving. Russell and Iris helped clean up the food and take it into the kitchen. Adam and Mandy helped clean up the backyard with trash bags. Trey grabbed chairs and put them all away.

"Great party," Russell said.

"Hey, thanks for providing some of the entertainment tonight," Bob replied. "And come over for lunch tomorrow there is still plenty of food."

"Thank you, we will," Iris answered.

Iris looked around and realized that Fern wasn't there. No one had seen Fern leave or where she went. Russell suggested that she probably went home to sleep and that they would go and check on her. They walked across the beach and into Fern's back door. Iris went into her mother's room to say good night and then froze.

Russell, who was right behind her, went up to Fern. She was still, cold and lifeless. Iris immediately started crying and Russell held her. On what was Iris's happiest day, her mother lived her last. For Fern, it had also been one of her happiest days.

After comforting Iris and leading her back downstairs, Russell called 911 and then he called Forrest. These were not calls that Russell thought he would be making tonight, but he didn't mind taking charge while Iris grieved for her mother. Russell's next calls were to Adam and Bob.

Russell met them outside and explained that they found Fern in bed. Adam actually started crying and Mandy held him. It was sad for these long time neighbors who grew up with Fern always being there. Everyone took a moment with Iris and said goodbye to Fern.

When the police and ambulance came, arrangements were made to have Fern removed. Right after Gene died, Fern had all her arrangements made for her own death. Now it was time to put those plans into action. When Forrest called back, Iris said she would talk to him. There were tears, but she did it.

"Forrest and his family will come tomorrow sometime. With the holiday and little kids, he wasn't sure when they could get everyone together," Iris said. She had been so strong and was now starting to break down. "What about the house? When we get married, what do we do with her house?"

"Iris, you don't have to make any of those decisions now. That is something you can discuss with Forrest months from now," Russell replied. "Please don't stress yourself about it now."

"I'm so thankful you're here," Iris said through her tears.

"Always," Russell promised.

Iris did not want to stay in her house tonight so Russell locked up and everyone came to his house. It was now just Russell, Iris and Adam. Adam hugged Iris and offered his condolences. He loved Fern and she knew that. Adam excused himself and went upstairs. It was now after midnight and he was ready to sleep.

Russell offered Iris a glass of wine and she accepted. They sat on the couch and sipped their wine. There was a sitcom on that he let play in the background. Iris just wanted to sit in Russell's arms. She probably would feel better when Forrest arrived, but he hadn't been home in so long and even doubted how much help he would really be.

Iris hoped Forrest and his wife, Ellen, wouldn't just come and look at it as a financial gain. She wanted to keep the house in the family and they needed to discuss how to do that. Right now, Iris wanted to go to sleep. Russell locked up and went upstairs with Iris. He put her in bed and he laid beside her as she wept.

FORREST AND ELLEN DAVIDSON arrived the following afternoon with their twin girls, Sarah and Sophia, who were six. They didn't have a key and without knowing where the spare key was hidden, he called Iris to let him in. Iris came from next door to meet him.

Russell was standing next to Iris when she introduced him to Forrest and his family. Russell was surprised when a golden retriever jumped up on him and nearly pushed him over.

"That's Fish," Sarah said.

Forrest just shrugged his shoulders, "The kids named him."

"Because he likes being in the water," Sophia explained.

There were awkward laughs as they entered Fern's house. The emptiness was noticeable as everyone walked in. Iris hadn't returned since last night so it was eerie walking around when she knew their mother was gone. Iris could picture her sitting on the chair, crocheting in the corner or sitting on the back porch.

Forrest couldn't picture any of those things. He hadn't been back to visit in a couple of years. There was always an excuse. The kids were sick, Ellen couldn't get off work, he can't make the drive. Something always prevented him from visiting his elderly mother. Well, it was too late now.

"Things look different around here," Forrest said.

Iris knew he hadn't been back since the rebuilding. "Remember I told you there was a fire? A fire that your sister and your mother almost didn't escape from?"

Forrest looked at Iris and then simply nodded his head. She was ready for a fight, but it wasn't the time or the place. She should be glad that he came at the very least.

"You guys can stay here," Iris said. "I'm staying with Russell." Iris held out her left hand to show off her engagement ring. In all the commotion, she never even told him they were engaged.

Ellen came over and looked at the ring and hugged Iris and Russell. "Congratulations! This happened last night, too?"

They all suddenly realized that the two events happened on the same night. "Congratulations," Forrest said but continued looking around the house. He let the dog out the back door so he could run on the beach.

The twins didn't remember their grandmother's house or much of their grandmother. That was something Forrest would have to deal with. It's when you think you have all the time in the world that you find out that you don't. The kids explored the house, Iris set some food out in the kitchen and Russell went out back to give them space.

Russell would miss having Fern next door. He knew she was lonely but she also loved living on the beach. He supposed the engagement was enough for her to finally have peace. He pictured

Fern and Gene together again. It didn't make him sad like it did Iris, he would help her through it.

Russell saw Adam in the water with Trey and Mandy. He walked in their direction and stopped at the water's edge.

"How's Iris?" Adam asked.

"She's strong, but this is a lot happening at once," his dad replied.

"Who's dog?" Trey asked as the golden retriever came swimming out to them.

"His name is Fish. He belongs to Forrest's family," Adam explained.

The kids swam and played with Fish. They found out he loved to play fetch. Russell didn't know what else he could do. The funeral would be in a couple days, then Forrest would probably leave. Russell felt terrible that Iris had to go from a funeral to a wedding, but maybe it was good to have something wonderful to be looking forward to.

Russell wished he could jump in the water, too, but knew he should go back and check on Iris. Russell coughed a bit more on his way back. Adam heard it and decided to ask more about it later. The Memorial Day party seemed so long ago but it was actually yesterday. How could days feel so long?

Iris decided to give her brother space and left their mother's house. She went out onto the beach and saw Russell approaching. She explained that there's nothing more they can do now. It was just waiting until the funeral and then deciding on what to do with the house. Russell put his arm around her and they walked back to his house.

Russell cooked some pasta and shrimp and they all had shrimp scampi for dinner. Adam came in and went to change. They sat around the kitchen table, each in their own thoughts. Not much was spoken, but they were now a family and that was enough right now.

Chapter 33

After the funeral, everyone came back to Russell's house. It was neutral ground and gave everybody an opportunity to relax. The service was short, there would be no burial. Fern wanted to be cremated and Iris had the ashes in a wooden box. Russell and Adam both had memories of ashes in an urn that used to sit on their own mantel.

Today was the second anniversary of Lynn's passing. It only meant something to Russell and Adam. It wasn't as bad as last year, so they were able to move past today's date. Today was about Iris, Forrest and his family. Julie and Bob had prepared some sandwiches and a few sides for a lunch after the funeral.

It was times like these that their beach family pulled together. They did it when Lynn died and now for Fern. He was glad to be here among friends. Iris would soon learn how this support would get her through anything. Iris wasn't expecting a lot of help from Forrest. He wasn't sentimental enough to want to save the house. Iris did.

Iris and Forrest went for a walk on the beach. They brought up childhood memories and their favorite times on the beach. It was a unique way of being brought up and Iris understood it now, the pull of the ocean. They sat on chairs and continued to look out at the waves.

"I don't want to sell it," Iris said.

"I know, you made that clear," Forrest replied.

Iris felt like they were at a standstill. "Maybe we could rent it out until we really deal with the house," Iris offered. It was a compromise.

Forrest shrugged his shoulders. "I do love it here, that was never the issue. It lacked a city with enough jobs to support a family."

"Forrest, you're in IT now, you could work from home if you had to," Iris said. "Ellen is a nurse. When she decides to go back to work, she could get a job easily."

"What are you saying, Iris?"

"Move here. Let the kids grow up here," Iris replied. "Sell your house, you have one here."

Forrest simply shook his head. He never considered moving back to Jekyll Island. This was something he would have to think about and discuss with Ellen. It was definitely a possibility, but was it practical?

They both stood up and returned to Russell's house. Iris was holding up pretty good emotionally. In fact, she had a thought that she wanted to bring up to Russell. She found him in the living room playing with the girls.

"Russ, can I talk to you for a minute?"

Russell followed her outside to the yard. "I want to get married at the end of summer, maybe August, before the boys go off the college," Iris said. "We aren't getting any younger and I don't want to wait. Life is too short to wait for happiness."

Russell looked at her, smiled and then kissed her. "Sounds perfect!"

Iris felt relief when he agreed to her idea. She would plan everything. It would be here on the beach with all their family and friends around them. She would tell Forrest and Ellen now so they could make plans. She knew her mom would approve.

Inside, Iris let everyone know about their plan to marry on the beach at the end of summer. Julie was thrilled and wanted to help. Bob slapped Russell on the back and smiled. Adam was glad it would be before he left for college. He wanted to be best man.

Iris was happy with how this day ended. What could have left her crying in the corner, turned out to be preparing for her future. She was still sad and walking into her house will always be hard, but they spent a lot of time talking this past year. Iris felt like she knew her mother better and that she was now at peace.

After everyone went back to their own homes, Forrest and Ellen talked on the back porch. The same back porch that his mother spent most of her day. They rocked on the swing and talked. He told his wife everything Iris had said about living there full time. It really wouldn't be that much of a stretch to make it work.

Ellen thought the kids were still too young. There were too many concerns with the ocean that she would prefer to give it a try when they are a little older. Forrest smiled, his own memories of growing up here were happy. They tentatively agreed that they would help with the upkeep of the house for the next two years and then revisit the idea of moving down.

In the meantime, they could come more often. Let the kids get to know the beach and the neighborhood. His biggest regret will always be that they didn't get to know their grandma. Forrest knew she was getting old. Even when Iris said she fell and broke her leg, he didn't come. He will make it up to her by letting his kids grow up on the beach like he did.

Adam went outside and put his feet in the water. Mandy was already sitting in one of the chairs. She joined him as he walked by. He admitted that the swing of sad to happy and then sad and happy again was messing with his head. Mandy said she would always be there when he needed to talk.

The wind was swirling around them and kept pushing Mandy's hair in her face. Adam reached over and tucked it behind her ear. Adam's hair was also flying in many different directions and kept falling in his eyes. Tonight they just allowed the intimacy of being close to each other to be enough.

They simply held hands and walked along the edge of the water, just as they did as kids. Adam needed the physical reminder that even though people die, get married or move away, some things stay the same. Like the feeling of holding a girl's hand and feeling the ocean between your toes.

Adam needed to know that the feeling he had right now would never change. The house, the ocean and Mandy would always be there. He looked up at the moon and stars. If he could wish on the stars he would want everything to stay the same. He kissed Mandy and they both went to their separate houses. It had been another long day.

FORREST AND HIS FAMILY left after a couple of days at the beach. There was nothing more they could do. He promised they would be back for the wedding in a couple of months. Russell had called his brother, Ted, and told him all about their plans. Ted was excited that he had found someone and couldn't wait to meet his new sister-in-law.

Russell thought about their honeymoon. Iris said she didn't care where they went. It could be Disney World and she would be thrilled. Russell had his sights set on a bigger destination. He and Lynn had gone to Paris, so he would take Iris to Rome. He would call his travel agent in the morning and plan the whole thing.

Time was moving but it felt like slow motion. July fourth was quickly approaching and that usually meant another party. Maybe this year Russell would suggest their own bonfire. He remembers having bonfires in the past, but the Covingtons never did one. He would call it their bachelor and bachelorette bonfire.

Russell spread the word and everyone loved the idea. Bob suggested that there be a line drawn in the sand, one side was for the boys the other was for the girls. He laughed at this own idea and everyone followed along. The fun would be put back in summer. Adam made sure Trey didn't invite any extra girls this time. He agreed.

Iris called Forrest to let him know their July fourth plans, just in case he wanted to stop by. He said they would think about it. They usually went to Florida for the long weekend. Iris insisted they would love for him and his family to change their plans and come. It was about time she got to spend more time with her nieces.

News of the bonfire spread and everyone thought it was great idea, not only for the holiday but for their pre-wedding celebration. For days leading up to July fourth, wood was brought to the Reed's backyard. The pile kept getting taller and Russell believed it could burn for days. Bob was in charge of fireworks and he would not disappoint.

It was July third, Russell and Adam finished their sunrise run and were back at their house. They were catching their breath and taking off their shoes so they could jump in the water.

"So how does it feel to be getting married next month?" Adam asked.

Russell smiled. "It feels really good. I love her and it just feels right."

"I like her, too, which is the most important part." They both laughed and started swimming.

"I think mom would approve," Adam added.

Russell and Adam enjoyed their time together in the mornings. Russell would miss this when Adam went off to college. He was going to live in the moment until that day came.

"I want you to know that even when Iris officially moves in, I don't want it to feel awkward or that this isn't your home still," Russell said.

"I know," Adam replied. "It may feel even more like home. The house missed a female touch, I think."

Russell put his arm around his son as they walked back towards the house. "So, what are your plans today?"

"I'm meeting Mandy and we're going shopping."

"Shopping for what?" Russell asked.

"Just stuff for the party," Adam answered vaguely.

Inside, the guys showered and changed. Iris had woken up and was in the kitchen when they came back downstairs. She had made eggs and pancakes and they smelled amazing. After eating, they talked about their plans for the day. Iris was going to make a casserole and a cake for tomorrow. Russ had some last minute things to pick up but it could wait until later.

Adam texted Mandy and they met at his jeep. They both were smiling and laughing. They were proud of themselves for being able to pull off such a big surprise. No one suspected their real agenda and it made them feel giddy with excitement. The drive to the airport was only about fifteen minutes. Adam pulled up to the arrivals area and waved when he saw his Uncle Ted.

There were quick introductions in the jeep on the way back home. Uncle Ted was just as giddy when Adam confirmed that his dad knew nothing about his arrival. He was wearing an aloha shirt with royal blue shorts and couldn't wait to surprise his brother and new nearly sister-in-law.

When they arrived at the house, Adam and Mandy walked in first saying to Russell they needed help unloading the jeep. As Russell appeared at the doorway, Ted was standing in full view and yelled, 'Surprise'. It was a moment that could possibly go down in history as the best surprise ever.

Russell started crying when he saw his little brother in his aloha outfit. It was typical Ted and he missed him so much. They hugged and then looked at each other. Russell was speechless. He turned and pointed a finger at Adam and then at Mandy. They laughed with joy that they secretly reached out to Uncle Ted and told him all about the bachelor party.

Ted said the party couldn't start until he arrived. Adam was happy to oblige and was so happy to have his Uncle Ted around. It was important for all of their family to be here for this. Uncle Ted came over to Adam and gave him a hug.

"Thank you for including me in this," Ted said.

Chapter 34

It had been many years since Ted walked into the Jekyll Island beach house. It was familiar but yet new. He brought his bag inside and entered the kitchen. Russell was still getting used to the fact that his brother was standing in his house.

"I have an announcement to make," Ted said while smiling from ear to ear. "I'm officiating your wedding. I got ordained last night!"

The looks of surprise quickly turned to joy as the announcement that Ted just made seemed right. Ted was proud of himself for pulling off yet another grand surprise. There was never a dull moment with Ted and Iris was learning this first hand. Ted pulled two teddy bears out of his bag. One was dressed as a bride, the other was the groom.

"Husband and wife teddies for the happy couple," Ted said. "I was going to bring them next month for the actual wedding, but I thought I might have too much to bring on that trip, what with a tuxedo and all."

Russell and Iris both thanked and hugged Ted. He was the fresh air that everyone was waiting for. Adam showed him to one of the guest rooms so he could settle in. As they walked by Adam's room, Uncle Ted spotted the teddy bear on top of Adam's bed and stopped. Uncle Ted gave a quick look to Adam and went in to hold it.

"You still have it," Uncle Ted said. It was not a question, but it made him think back to an older memory. "I gave you this when your mom first got sick."

They both stood there in silence for moment, Ted holding the bear.

"It helped me then and helps me now," Adam replied.

No more words were needed. Ted laid the bear back on Adam's bed and turned and went to the guest room. Adam stood in his door way a few seconds longer, looking at the teddy bear that has been there for him through the years.

Adam returned back downstairs and looked around. "Where's Iris?"

"Well," Russell started with a smile on his face, "apparently today is the day for surprises! Iris just got a call from Forrest that they are next door and wondered where they should put the food for tomorrow."

Adam smiled. This was more than he ever expected and he couldn't even take credit for Forrest and his family arriving. That was all him. He couldn't wait to show the twins how fun it was to live on the beach. He knew they were only here for the weekend, but since last time they were here was so sad, this trip would be all about fun.

Were Sarah and Sophia his cousins? Step-cousins? It didn't matter to Adam, they were family now and it felt good to have a growing family around him. This party would be epic and he suddenly wondered if they had enough fireworks.

Adam went next door to the Covingtons. Trey was outside setting up the volleyball net. Trey confirmed they had plenty of fireworks, even more than they did for Memorial Day. Adam helped with the tension lines that held up the net. They talked about college and moving away.

"I'm going to miss this," Adam said.

"Me, too." Trey replied. "I've never lived anywhere else but here."

"Well, we definitely need to come home on weekends," Adam said. "You know they are going to miss us much more, plus it will show them we are still alive after we don't answer every text they send every minute of the day and night."

Both boys laughed as they finished putting up the net. It would be nice to have someone they knew at college. Although, Adam heard from Carter that he also got a scholarship to Georgia Southern University. He didn't tell anyone else, especially not his father. It was a big enough college that he hoped he would not see him too much, but the football field was another story.

They each discussed what they were bringing into the dorm so they didn't end up with two of everything. There would be one gaming system, one tv, one mini fridge and one microwave. They didn't think they would be in their rooms much anyway.

Mandy came out when she saw that the boys were done putting up the net. She asked Adam if they could go for a walk. They strolled up the beach hand in hand. He would miss this the most. At first they just walked together without saying anything. Adam wondered if there was something on her mind.

"How are you doing today?" Adam asked.

"Good," Mandy replied. She was nervous and didn't know how to bring it up with Adam, so she was just going to blurt it out. "Iris asked me to be her maid of honor."

Adam looked at her, "That's great."

"You really think so?" Mandy asked. Unsure if he meant it or if he was just being nice.

"Yeah, why?"

"Well, I just wasn't sure how you'd feel about me being on Iris's side during the ceremony and well, she's marrying your dad." Mandy spoke nervously and choppy. "I didn't want you to think I was actually choosing sides or anything."

Adam let out a small laugh. "It's fine. I know she's not my mother and I know you aren't choosing her over me and my dad. Really, I'm glad she asked you because that means we will walk down the aisle together and be in front of everyone with them."

Mandy gave Adam's hand a squeeze. He was so understanding. It was going to be so hard being away from him. She still had junior year to get through before she could have another whole summer with him.

They stopped walking and kissed. They had walked quite a ways from home and no one would notice them out here. They were surrounded by sand dunes. Adam placed his hands on either side of Mandy's face and kissed again. Mandy simply wrapped her arms around him. There was no pressure to go further than kissing and when they stopped they walked back towards home.

RUSSELL WAS HOLDING the torch that would ceremonially light the bonfire. He held it high as everyone watched and were ready to party. First, Russell wanted to say something to everyone before it got too late.

"Thank you everyone for coming to our bachelor and bachelorette bonfire. It means so much that family came from miles away to be here and celebrate with us tonight. And to all of our family and friends that are here tonight, thank you for helping to plan, set up and make this the best summer blow out Jekyll Island will ever see!"

There were cheers, whistles and applause as Russell brought the torch to the bonfire and brought it to life. It roared and crackled and everyone moved closer to experience the moment. Bob had tried to draw a line of demarkation for the two sides so that the bachelor could have his party and the bachelorette could have hers but it didn't last. This group of family and friends could not be contained by a simple line in the sand.

Fish was running around and barking as the two little girls followed. Adam had taken them out on his board earlier today. Ellen had little life jackets for them, so they felt free and fearless on the water. They were naturals. Adam predicted that they would be living here full time by next summer.

Uncle Ted had another aloha shirt on today with fire engine red shorts. He also must have brought a lei because he was in full Hawaiian gear. The fourth of July will never feel the same again after tonight. There was plenty of food, even more than their last party because Ellen was a great cook and brought over enough dishes to feed the whole island.

Ellen and Iris were getting closer and that was such a welcome change. She had never felt that connected to Forrest's family before and she was welcoming the chance to get closer to them, too. Somehow Ted had started a limbo line and it was the best thing ever. Everyone joined in.

Trey was in charge of music and explained that he didn't have much 'old people' music. Russell laughed and assured him that anything would do. Confirming that if it was once played on the radio, then they probably knew it. The music did get everyone dancing. The alcohol helped, too.

Julie was blending margaritas and that was the drink of the night for the girls. The guys preferred beer and whiskey. It was a fun evening of laughter and family. Earlier in the day, Iris and Forrest had discussed spreading their mother's ashes tonight. They both thought it was a great time to say goodbye and move forward with their futures.

Iris went into her house and took the decorative box off of the mantle. She carried it to the water. No one noticed what Iris had until she turned to the crowd and made a little speech.

"Tonight is about new beginnings. Well, it only seemed fitting to release mom's ashes into the ocean that she loved so much. She can finally be with our dad physically as well."

The talking and music had hushed while Iris spoke. Forrest had joined her at the water and together they cut open the bag of Fern's ashes and let them blow into the water. It was emotional for brother and sister but it was also healing. She was there the night Russell proposed and Iris knew she was looking down now and was happy.

Russell came and gave Iris a hug. He knew how hard it really was to release the ashes of a loved one. He allowed her a moment to be sad and then she wanted to rejoin the party. Tonight was a happy occasion. She walked to the porch with Russell to get some cake.

The cake was red, white and blue but also decorated with 'Best Wishes Russ and Iris'. They cut a couple pieces and went to sit on their adirondack chairs. They sipped their drinks and ate cake while waiting for the fireworks to start.

"I think I'm going to write a book," Iris said.

Russell looked at her. "Really, about what?"

"Grief."

"Well, that sounds like a subject we all know a bit about," Russell said.

"Exactly, it will be about all sorts of grief and I would like to have you contribute a chapter," Iris replied. "In fact, everyone should."

Iris stayed in her own thoughts for a while thinking about her idea for a book. Who better to write it than everyone who has gone through it? They all had experienced grief and loss. Maybe writing it down and sharing it would also be cathartic.

"Well, I think I have my first client," Russell said.

"What?"

"Yes, I've been posting on several sites who might be interested in using an architect for drawing up plans and a couple people reached out to me," Russell replied. "I'm meeting one client next week."

The boom of the first fireworks startled them both. They were each deep in their own thoughts about their futures. They were at a point in their lives when they could literally do anything they wanted. Iris dreamed of writing a book, so the chance to actually write one that was close to her heart was too important to pass up.

Russell would always love architecture and even though he was no longer with a well known firm didn't mean he couldn't still catch some big clients. It all depended on how much work they were willing to put into their dreams.

Investing in oneself was something Russell was learning. His family, his son and his future. He knew it was up to him to search for his own happiness and he was glad he did.

Chapter 35

Iris found herself digging around in her mother's attic after Forrest left. She was looking for anything she could use as decorations for the wedding. There was only a week to go and she felt a bit overwhelmed. She didn't even find a dress she liked, yet. Iris thought she might find her mother's good crystal vase and champagne glasses up in the attic. She had been up there all morning and was not finding anything.

She was about to go back down stairs when she spotted a box in the far corner. It looked like it might be marked 'wedding' but couldn't make it out from here. She moved an old rocking chair, a lamp that was missing a shade and a box of books to get to it. The large box was lightweight and dusty.

As she eased the lid off, she realized exactly what this was. It was secured in paper and plastic to preserve it, but she recognized it immediately. It was her mom's wedding dress. Iris wouldn't be able to get a good look at it up in the dingy attic, so she closed the box and carried it down to the living room.

The dress had to be nearly fifty years old. Iris was as delicate as she could be when she lifted it out of the box and let it fall to its full length. It was the perfect balance of lace and satin. It had a boat neckline and long sleeves made of lace. The dress had a partially open back and gathered at the waist. The skirt was satin and went to the floor.

Iris's hands were shaking as she tried it on. She twirled in the full length mirror and started tearing up when she saw how wonderful the dress looked and fit. She would soak it overnight in a delicate detergent, just to clean it up. She would not tell Russell, either.

Iris was still shaking as she held the dress and laid it in the sink to soak. What a wonderful find! She would still have to go back up in the attic and look for the crystal. That could wait until tomorrow. Today was for being thankful for the gift from her mother.

Mandy was stressing out about her dress. Actually, the fact that she didn't have one was stressing her out. Iris told her that she really didn't care what she wore. It could even be the beautiful yellow sun dress she wore last summer. It was so striking on her, it stuck in Iris's memory.

They would collect wildflowers the morning of the wedding for their bouquets and their hair. It was the guys who had to be sure they had their clothes ready on time. Iris did not want suits. It was an authentic beach wedding in their own backyards. They didn't even need shoes. Khaki pants and a white shirt was the only thing Iris required. If they wanted ties, suspenders or even hats, that was purely up to them.

Iris returned to Russell's house and there was a commotion of his own going on. The boys were moving into their dorms tomorrow. They would drive back for the wedding, but they must bring all of their things now. Adam said he had everything and Russell double checked to be sure he was right.

Adam and Trey were ready and excited. It was their first taste of freedom and it would be even more fun to be experiencing it with a best friend. Their dads kept reminding them that football and grades were the priority. 'Can't have one without the other,' Russell would say. Parties can wait until they come back home. The two boys were so different, Adam hoped Trey would follow their advice.

The boys played in the ocean all afternoon. It was their last chance and they wanted the memory to carry them through the beginning days of school. They had their surfboards and were waiting for a wave, just like they've done for a dozen summers before. Adam enjoyed just hanging out with Trey, but he was going to miss Mandy the most.

Mandy came out to the water crying. At first Adam thought something happened and paddled back to shore. It didn't take long to realize that she was already crying because Adam was leaving. He hugged her but it would never be enough to change what would be happening tomorrow.

"It's only for a little while, I'll be back before you know it," Adam promise. "It's not like the end of summer when we didn't see each other for six months or longer. I'll come as often as I can."

"It will be so lonely here without you," Mandy replied. Mandy continued hugging Adam. She planned to go with the two families when they took the boys tomorrow. She wanted to see where they would live so she could picture it when they talked.

"I will see you tomorrow," Adam said. They kissed before they went to their own houses. Russell had suggested that since it was their last night as a family, they would not have one big going away party. Tonight was all about the Covingtons and the Reeds.

Russell cooked steaks while Iris made mashed potatoes and broccoli. There were brownies and ice cream for dessert. The three of them sat around the kitchen table and talked about college, the wedding and the surprise honeymoon.

"Wait, you still don't know where you're going for your honeymoon?" Adam asked.

"Oh your father does but I don't. He won't tell me," Iris replied.

Russell smiled and chewed his steak. It was all planned, two weeks in Italy traveling from the top to the bottom. He had never taken this kind of trip before and even he was excited. Iris would be thrilled when she found out at the airport.

Adam enjoyed watching their interaction. It was kind, happy and loving. Last year at this time he was stressed, angry and a workaholic.

Even Adam could appreciate the change in his dad. Love had a way of making everything else in your life better.

Everyone went to bed early in preparation of move in day. Adam called Mandy before he went to sleep to talk. He told her all about the surprise honeymoon. He said how his mom had a list of places she never got to see and he promised himself he would go to every one on that list. Mandy knew he would.

The next morning, the Covingtons and the Reeds headed to college. They had their cars loaded with dorm necessities and got an early start. There was nervous energy all morning as everyone was trying to remember all the last minute things.

Mandy was allowed to ride in Adam's jeep and they held hands. There were a total of four cars going in the same direction since Adam and Trey each wanted their cars on campus. It allowed them the freedom to come home whenever they wanted.

Move in day at the dorm was chaos. There were parents, students and siblings all unloading cars full of too much stuff. There were rolling containers to help take things to their rooms and in the parking lot were temporary dumpsters for all the trash and cardboard packaging that would be thrown away today.

Trey and Adam's room was on the first floor. The room was a nice size but typical for a dorm room. Two beds, two dressers and two closets along with one bathroom. Julie and Iris got to work making the beds. Bob and Russell helped set up the electronics. Mandy started hanging clothes and stocking the mini fridge with snacks.

After two hours, it looked like a real bedroom. Adam brought the picture Mandy gave him, but there wasn't a lot of room for other personal items. The shelves were for books, shoes and snacks. The dresser was for clothes and under the bed storage was everything else.

Julie hung up their towels and stocked the bathroom with soap, shampoo and cleaning supplies. When the boys were satisfied that the PS5 was hooked up, they really wanted to play. For them it was a new adventure. For the parents, it was losing a member of the family.

After several hints by the boys that everyone could leave now, they did. Iris reminded them that the wedding was this Saturday. They must be home in a few days. They agreed and promised they would be there. With nothing more to do, The Covingtons and the Reeds left minus two boys.

Mandy rode home with her parents and teared up the whole way. She knew it was only for a few days and that she was being ridiculous, but she couldn't help it. Julie was sympathetic and let her be alone when they got home. This would be their new normal for only one child at home.

Russell felt it worse, at least he had Iris. The house would have been unbearably quiet without her there. The memories of loss would have been too much. Iris kept him focused and in the present. Plus, they had a wedding to get ready for.

Iris had started writing her book on grief. She had mentioned to everyone that she wanted a chapter in their own words. That meant Russell, Adam and Forrest. She expected them to finish their assignment by the time they returned from their honeymoon. Russell felt like he could write several chapters and Iris encouraged him to do it.

The next couple of days were filled with the last minute details. Iris's dress was clean, pressed and hanging in Fern's house. The guys had their pants and shirts ironed and they decided on blue bow ties. The food was already planned between Julie, Ellen and Iris. It would be handled just like one of their big summer parties.

Julie made the cake and Iris made her promise it would not be too grand. She just wanted a simple white cake. Julie just smiled and said she would do it. She couldn't help it if a few decorations ended up on the cake. Iris would love it.

Iris had called a friend to be the photographer. Being a realtor, she knew who to call to get great shots taken. The photographer would be there from the morning until sunset. It was starting to feel real. Everyday she would go and sit in front of her mother's wedding dress and just stare at it.

Russell looked at Iris. "How do you feel, the night before your wedding?"

Iris just smiled and said, "Ready."

They sat on the porch swing and watched the ocean covered in the same red and orange as the sunset. It was their last day of being single. Everyone would be arriving tomorrow morning and the ceremony would be at three.

Iris actually felt very relaxed. It was probably the most casual wedding in the history of weddings. If they weren't ready at three then it would be at five. Ted was playing the role of minister, there was no venue, no caterer, no closing time. Just them on the beach.

She never really dreamed of her own wedding. She knew other girls planned where, when and with whom, but not her. She never envisioned a color scheme, a dress or a wedding party. Her wedding would be a reflection of her and Russell's life. It would also represent their future. They would have all their loved ones around them. That was the only important thing about her wedding, that she would be surrounded by the people who meant the most to her.

Chapter 36

Russell and Iris's wedding day started off pretty chaotic. Everyone arrived early that morning, Uncle Ted and then Forrest with his family. Russell had a big breakfast planned for everyone but nerves did not allow most people to eat.

Ted wore a dark purple suit and it looked fantastic on him. Iris insisted that everyone could dress casually, but Ted felt that because he was the officiant of the wedding, that he should be more formal. That was fine, that was Ted.

Forrest and his family did not suffer from nerves and ate breakfast. The twins had pink dresses on and kept twirling around the kitchen. Even Fish wore a special blue bandana around his neck. It was Ellen who looked beautiful in a sage green halter top dress. It showed off her tan perfectly. She wore her blond hair back in a fancy pony tail.

When it was time for Iris and Russell to get ready, the men all went to Russell's house and the women went to Fern's house. Mandy and Julie came with their dresses in hand and started with hair and make up. Iris made sure her photographer went to both houses but kept her mouth shut about her dress.

Ellen kept the girls busy by giving them the extra ribbon to play with. Since she was already dressed, she helped Mandy and Julie. Mandy's long hair was perfect already, she just wanted it pulled up at the sides. Julie wanted hers pulled up all the way to a bun. Make up would be quick and simple. The women only needed a bit of lipstick, mascara and maybe some eye shadow.

Mandy wore the bright yellow sun dress that Iris loved on her. It was such a great color to match with everyone else. Julie wore a paler yellow dress that was sleeveless and to her knees. They complimented each other perfectly. They looked more like a mother and daughter than any other day in the past.

Iris's curly hair was going to be a struggle to keep from looking like a fuzz ball in the wind. The women worked to twist it around to the back and then secure it. It looked beautiful with the headband of flowers that Mandy and Julie worked on. They helped with her make up and then turned towards the dress.

The dress, Iris knew, would be the center of attention and well-deserved. The one thing she found in the attic that she wasn't even looking for. It washed up nicely and hung out of the way for weeks so that no one saw it or ruined it.

Ellen held it open for her as Iris stepped into it. It had only needed minor repairs, a missing button, a rip on the bottom seam and a stain on the front that required extra special attention. It looked like it came right off the store rack yesterday.

Iris stepped into her mother's wedding dress and Ellen helped pull it up and over her shoulders. She gave Iris a minute to adjust the fit and then buttoned up the back. It was made for her, the fit was perfect. When she finally turned around to reveal the dress to the other women, Iris cried.

It was overwhelming to see these friends and family tearing up while looking at her on her wedding day. The dress deserved to be honored in this way. It was hard to imagine that if she didn't go in the attic that day looking for a crystal vase, she never would have discovered this treasure probably ever.

They all came up to hug Iris and wipe away her tears. "Time to open the champagne!" Julie yelled and they all went downstairs to toast to the bride-to-be. Julie even let Mandy have a few sips. This was, indeed, a special occasion.

At Russell's house, since Ted was already dressed, he felt it was his duty to instruct the other men on what to wear. Russell and Adam were given strict instructions to wear khaki pants and white shirt. Beyond those details, Iris really didn't care. They thought about blue bow ties and after Ted stepped back and really looked at the ensemble, he approved.

Bob had dark blue pants and a light blue button down shirt. Julie approved the combination and thought it would look good with her and Mandy's shades of yellow. Forrest had on dark khaki pants with a similar sage green shirt to match Ellen's dress. They would look so fantastic standing with their two girls in their pink dresses when they posed for family portraits later.

Trey technically wasn't part of the wedding party, but wanted to blend in, so he found his only pair of khaki pants and a light blue shirt. Trey also wanted a bow tie, so he took one from the pile and tried to put it on. Russell helped. The men were ready.

"Time for a toast," Bob said. He pulled out a bottle of whiskey and enough shot glasses for everyone. He winked at Trey and Adam and said it was a special occasion, so it didn't count today. Trey smiled but Adam was conflicted. He didn't drink but knew this was important to his dad.

"To Russell and Iris, may they have many happy years together!" Bob shouted. Everyone emptied their glasses except for Adam. He took a sip, made a face and passed it to his dad. Russell knew his son's convictions, winked at him and then finished his son's shot.

At three o'clock, those not in the wedding party took their seat. The seating was made up of various outdoor chairs that everyone had on their porches. To create some sense of uniformity, Julie had tied blue ribbons on every seat, so they fluttered together in the wind.

Ted was up front with the ocean behind him. He held a tablet so that he could read the official words to make the marriage legal. Bob and Julie took a seat up front as did Forrest and Ellen. Trey took a seat in the next row and was in charge of babysitting the twins during the ceremony.

A few more neighbors arrived who knew and loved Russell and Iris. This was a big day for the neighborhood. They didn't often have weddings. The guests filled up about three rows of seats. Small and intimate, exactly what Iris wanted. Trey had the music ready to play as Mandy and Adam stood at the back of the aisle.

Adam stood tall and proud, his hair blowing slightly in the wind and smiling so sincerely. Mandy had her arm in his and was holding her handmade bouquet of wildflowers. Adam looked down at Mandy and whispered, "Ready?"

Mandy smiled back and nodded. They walked slowly down the aisle and then Adam went to stand next to his father and Mandy stood on the other side waiting for Iris.

Iris stood at the back of the aisle alone holding a larger bouquet of hand picked wildflowers. She had flowers in her hair and wore her mother's dress. She looked down at Russell and he put his hands to his face. He teared up as he saw Iris standing there.

The guests all stood as Iris walked slowly down the aisle. She looked like the perfect bride in the boat neckline of lace, lace down her arms and the white satin that gently glided over the sand at her feet.

Iris couldn't believe this day had come. Russell couldn't believe he could get so lucky twice in his life. He had slight recollections of his first marriage to Lynn, but because it had been so completely different, today felt new. It was a fresh beginning for both of them.

Russell wiped at his eyes as Iris came further down the aisle. When she came in front of Ted, she handed her bouquet to Mandy and turned to face Russell. They both smiled and laughed through the tears. Adam looked over at Mandy and she was wiping away a tear, too.

Iris and Russell held hands as Ted started his speech. They improvised their vows. They each expressed how this unexpected love found them when they both needed it the most. Now they were vowing their love in front of all their friends and family.

Adam handed his dad the rings when it was time to place them on each other's fingers. A symbol of their love and commitment to each other for the rest of their lives. Adam was so happy for his dad. He had the courage to come to the beach house after his wife died and opened his heart to love again. It was truly inspirational.

"You may now kiss the bride!" Ted announced.

Cheers and applause as Russell kissed Iris. Mandy gave her back the bouquet and the newlyweds walked back down the aisle together. Next, Adam put out his arm for Mandy and they followed behind. It was over. Now pictures, party and honeymoon.

The photographer was doing such a great job. She was getting all of the family portraits done and even individual portraits. Mandy asked her if she would do one of just her and Adam and she said she'd be happy to.

The group shot would probably be the most memorable. The Covingtons, the Davidsons and the Reeds were all ready and smiling when Fish decided to join the group photo. The first few shots probably came out great, then Fish decided he wanted to play and jumped up on various members of the first row. The photographer was sure that the following photos included shocked faces as the dog jumped from person to person.

Iris said it didn't matter. It may be one of the latter photos she decides to hang above the mantle. Everyone laughed and enjoyed the party. They ate and danced into the night. When the sunset cast a warm glow on the water, the photographer suggest a few more photos. Bow ties and flowers were left behind, these photos captured the person behind the dress and tie.

The candid photos at sunset represented the individuals and their love for the newlyweds. Russell and Iris after having danced for two hours gazed into each other's eyes and it was caught on camera. The twins playing in the sand was a perfect photo at sunset. The day was wonderful but the night was magical.

Russell and Iris started saying their goodbyes even while guests were still dancing and partying. They had a flight to catch at eleven tonight. Russell still kept it a secret from Iris but all would be revealed when they checked in at the airport.

There were hugs, tears and well wishes from everyone as they made their way back to the house. They both showered and changed. Iris hung her dress up and put on nice looking casual clothes, since she didn't know the destination, only that they would be flying overnight.

Russell took their bags out to the car. Adam would drop them off at the airport because he was the only one sober, besides Mandy came along, too. Russell and Iris sat in the backseat. They looked and acted like newlyweds. Adam laughed as he glanced in the rearview mirror from time to time.

Mandy held Adam's hand the whole way. It felt so romantic to her, coming from a wedding and being all dressed up. She was sitting next to the boy she walked down the aisle with, even though they were only the best man and maid of honor. Mandy closed her eyes and imagined it was them driving to catch a flight for their honeymoon.

"We're here," Adam said since no one else noticed he had pulled up to the drop off point at the airport.

They all got out of the jeep and helped with the luggage. More hugs and more goodbyes. Russell and Iris waved as they entered the airport. Adam and Mandy returned to the jeep and headed back home. Mandy found a song on the radio she liked and started singing. Adam loved listening to her sing, she didn't do it often enough.

He rolled the windows down, joined in and they sang at the top of their lungs. Still holding hands, it would be a memory they both would never forget. They drove straight home and parked. Realizing that no one would be in the house for hours yet, Adam and Mandy ran upstairs to his room.

The romance of the day and night caught them both off guard. Their kisses did not start off soft. These were kisses that were waiting to happen for days. Adam shut the door quietly behind them and they enjoyed the moment.

They could both still remember staring at each other as Ted read the vows. Adam and Mandy couldn't take their eyes off each other during the ceremony. Secretly wishing it could be them at the center, not on the sides. Romance was in the air.

Chapter 37

Adam had heard from his father that they landed in Italy safe and sound. Iris was thrilled when she learned the destination. It was a dream vacation for both of them. They promised they would text with updates and pictures and Adam wished them a great time.

For everyone else not on the honeymoon, it was clean up day. It was also the day that Adam and Trey had to leave to get back to college. Forrest and his family had to get back, too. It was back to school for all the kids the next day. Ted didn't want to be left behind, so he planned his departure for today, too.

Everyone planned the next big get together for Christmas. There were smaller holidays here and there in between, but everyone was going to try and get a couple weeks off for Christmas and New Years.

Uncle Teddy was the first to leave. He had the longer drive back to Orlando and said he was so glad to meet everyone. It was like one big happy family. Ted invited the boys and Mandy to come visit anytime. He had a three bedroom condo with a pool and could get them into any theme park, he had his ways.

The teenagers all agreed they would. For now, the boys had to get back to school. They helped clean up and then packed up their own things. Forrest and his family were packing up, too. Their drive was about three hours, so they were next to leave after Ted.

The twins were sad to leave the beach. The teenagers had shown them how fun the ocean could be and from then on you couldn't get them to come in. They joked that they would need surf boards of their own next summer. They all hugged their new relatives and headed home.

It was just Adam and Trey left. They had both come in Adam's jeep, so along with their own bags, they packed some food and goodies left over from the party into the jeep. Mandy had promised Russell and Iris that she would look in on both houses daily and make sure everything was ok and no critters got in. She would get an extra special souvenir from Italy.

Trey was already in the jeep and waiting on Adam. Adam was still saying goodbye to Mandy. They would be back as soon as possible. He couldn't promise every weekend, but it would be a couple times a month. Mandy frowned but nodded her head. Anything was better than waiting six months.

When Adam finally got in the jeep, they drove off and waved out the window. Trey joked about how they would be back in no time and Adam just agreed. They drove the whole way back listening to their own music and deep in their own thoughts.

Mandy, now left alone with only her parents, put on her bikini and grabbed her surf board. She didn't want to just sit in the house right now. On the water she felt free and relaxed. She could think about Adam and float on the surface of the water in peace.

She thought about last night with Adam. When they had rejoined the party, no one had missed them. They just asked if Russell and Iris made it off okay. What they didn't know was that Trey did suspect that they had been up to something and so did Uncle Ted.

Mandy stayed in the water to surf and swim most of the afternoon. She had school tomorrow, too, and had some things to finish up tonight. She decided to check on the houses before going home for dinner.

She let herself in Adam's house first. Everything was fine, of course. She went upstairs to Adam's room and took a selfie. She sent it to Adam who should be in his dorm by now. She went downstairs, checked the front door and then went over to Fern's house.

Adam texted back a heart emoji that made Mandy smile. She walked around Fern's house and went upstairs. Everything looked fine there, too. She saw a cup on the desk in the corner and decided to wash it. When she got to the desk she realized it was the book Iris was working on.

Mandy knew she shouldn't snoop, but she leafed through some pages and then saw the chapter that Adam wrote. It was sad and from the heart.

"Grief feels like you are drowning. It wasn't your choice but you are now fighting for your life. You know which way it is to the surface but you can't move. You can't see a way out. Grief keeps you trapped in the saddest day of your life. It can take over if you let it. I chose to accept help from my dad and a girl. I was saved by an angel."

Mandy couldn't read anymore. She was already crying trying to read his description of grief. The rest was just too much. She put the papers back how they were and went to wash the cup. She locked up the house and ran back home.

RUSSELL AND IRIS WERE having a wonderful time in Italy. They were reporting back and posting updates on social media. They had gone from Milan to Venice. They would take a train to Florence then on to Bari, Palermo, Naples and Rome. If they wanted to add more destinations, they would. It was more than either had expected.

They were drinking wine and eating cheese, pasta and pizza. They were laid back tourists without a set plan. They chose what to do the day before. Iris wondered if they really had to go home. Unfortunately, Russell said they did. Iris took lots of pictures and videos, she wanted to remember this trip always. She felt like Audrey Hepburn and Katharine Hepburn traveling all over Italy.

As long as Mandy reported back that everything was okay at home, they relaxed even more. They sipped espresso, cappuccino and lattes. Iris was shopping and Russell was eating. This was life at its best, no more sadness.

Mandy visited the houses each day that Russell and Iris were away. Nothing to report. She enjoyed having something to do after school. She missed the boys so much, even her brother. She never thought missing Trey was possible, but getting up by herself and going off to school was quiet and lonely. She even missed his yelling while he played video games.

When Russel and Iris finally returned it was like life was pumped back into the neighborhood. They enjoyed showing pictures to Bob, Julie and Mandy. Iris had souvenirs for everyone. They brought wine and snacks back and had a regular coming home party for themselves with their friends.

Another thing that arrived was the wedding photographer's photos. Because she was a friend, she sent the digital images for Iris but she also included an entire photo album of photos that she had printed. There were tears and laughter as they looked at serious pictures and then the silly candid ones at the end of the evening. They were just missing Fern.

Every single photo brought back wonderful memories of that day. They hoped to see everyone here in the coming months, but they had all agreed to be here for Christmas. Even though it was only September, Iris already wanted to start planning the menu and buying gifts. It would be the best Christmas ever and hopefully the first of many.

Reluctantly, Russell and Iris had to get back to work. Russell added some more clients to his own freelance firm and they were satisfied with his work. He found out he could easily grow if he wanted to get bigger because of all the new development within a hundred mile radius. He didn't want to get big, though.

Iris was also busy selling houses. It was a hot market for buyers and she could also be as busy as she wanted. She didn't want to be busy. She already had the busy work life in the past and decided that it was better to balance work with pleasure. Now that she had someone who was willing to do that with her, her whole perspective on work had changed.

When Iris felt like the manuscript was ready, she found a company that she could use to publish it. She didn't think a book on grief would be a big seller and ultimately found a self publishing company to do it herself. She didn't create the book to be a best seller, it was therapeutic for her. Russell, Forrest and Adam also wrote chapters and each said that they enjoyed the process. It was hard, but cathartic.

Russell was even feeling better. At his last check up, his asthma was gone. His lungs had improved dramatically and the doctor asked him what changed. Russell said his whole life changed. He slowed down, moved to the ocean, worked less, exercised more and fell in love. His doctor laughed and wished he could write that prescription for all of his patients.

It was a whole new life for him. Lynn had given him the permission to be happy that he didn't even give himself. It was all because of the beach house.

Adam and Trey had adapted well to college life. Football kept them busy morning and night. They had to find time to work on school work and sometimes that meant staying on weekends. Adam apologized to Mandy because some months he was only making it back one time.

Mandy understood. It was still better than nothing. When those rare weekends did come, they spent every minute together. He managed to come home for holidays. They spent Labor Day weekend, Halloween and Thanksgiving together when he came home.

The next holiday was Christmas. This would be epic because Ted was coming up and Forrest and his family were coming over. It was getting cooler on the island and fall was turning into winter. The atmosphere changed on the beach in winter.

Russell and Iris had to purchase a Christmas tree. They never needed one before and Fern only had a small one up in the attic. They also needed decorations, ornaments and stockings. They went all out to get the house ready for company that would be arriving soon.

They positioned the tree on the back window faced the ocean. The tree already had lights on it, so they just needed ornaments. Russell had brought some from his other house. Only the few that were sentimental made it to the beach house, though. The ones that Adam made went on first.

When the tree was done, Russell and Iris stepped back and admired the finished product. They sipped wine and welcomed their first Christmas together. It was already memorable, but it would be so great having everyone they loved around them.

Iris remembered Christmases here with her parents and Forrest. It was always cold and lonely because most families didn't stay during the winter and her friends didn't live near her. She liked the beach, but there were always conflicting feelings when she also remembered the loneliness. Now her life on the beach would be different with new happy memories.

Chapter 38

Adam and Trey were the first to arrive at the Jekyll Island beach house. Their classes ended the week before Christmas, so they had more time at home. Their families were happy to see them. It was good to be home, too.

Mandy hugged Trey but ran to Adam's house. She jumped in his arms and they kissed. Mandy hadn't seen their Christmas tree, so she stayed and visited without leaving Adam's side. The whole house had such a wonderful atmosphere of Christmas. The fireplace crackled with a roaring fire.

Iris had lunch ready and Mandy was welcome to join them. Adam filled them in on how college was going and what the new semester would bring. They listened to all his stories of what it was really like having Trey as a roommate and they all laughed. But in all seriousness, Adam liked having Trey as a roommate.

A few days later, Ted arrived. He was able to get ten days off and had been looking forward to this since last summer. Ted put his gifts under the tree along with the ones already there. Russell offered mulled wine and they all sat around the fireplace.

Iris showed him all the pictures from the wedding and also their album from Italy. Ted loved them all. He had so many questions about their trip and admitted he was envious. Russell always wanted Ted to find someone to spend his life with, he deserved it.

Forrest and his family arrived a couple of days before Christmas. The kids had just gotten out of school and they came right to the beach. They took their time settling in Fern's house before going next door to let them know they had arrived. Actually, they think it was Fish's barking that gave them away.

Iris ran over and told them to come whenever they were ready. They had pizza ordered and couldn't wait to catch up. Forrest and Ellen just looked at each other and smiled. They would be over soon, they had news to announce.

When the Davidson family finally walked over to Russell's house, the kids ran right to the pizza. Ellen was too nervous to eat and also couldn't wait to tell their news.

"Excuse me everyone, but Forrest and I have a couple announcements," Ellen said.

Everyone brought their plates to sit in the living room. Mandy was there, too, of course. When all eyes were on Ellen, she suddenly felt overwhelmed and looked at Forrest. He stood up next to her and put his arm around her.

"What we want to announce is," Forrest said. "We are pregnant!"

Cheers and applause burst from their small audience. Ellen looked visibly relieved to have the secret out in the open. "Our baby boy is due in June," Ellen continued.

More shouts of congratulations were heard along with more cheers.

"There's more," Forrest said. "We've decided to move into the beach house. We will put our house on the market after the holidays. Here, she will hopefully have plenty of babysitters to help out with the new baby brother."

Iris couldn't take any more news. She got up and hugged Ellen. She looked at Forrest and said that this was the most wonderful Christmas gift she could have ever gotten. Ellen was in tears, her emotions were not under control anymore and accepted all the hugs she received. Even Ted was tearing up and he lived the furthest away.

Russell shook Forrest's hand and congratulated them both. Next he called Bob and invited the Covingtons over. This was a night to celebrate. Bob, Julie and Trey came over immediately upon hearing the news. They were extended family, too.

Champagne was offered all around. A baby and new neighbors all in the same summer. Next year would be even better than this one, if that was even possible. It was a great ending to a wonderful night. When everyone went back to their own homes, Iris still couldn't believe it was real.

It was all coming full circle. The house Iris and Forrest grew up in was now where they would raise their own children. There was poetry in that. Forrest and Ellen were proud of themselves for keeping it a secret this long. Ellen knew she was already showing, but she hid it well under a sweater. Now, there was no more hiding.

IT WAS CHRISTMAS DAY. It was also a cold forty-five degrees. Sarah and Sophia awoke to find that Santa did, indeed, find them on the beach. Forrest and Ellen watched their girls tear open their Christmas gifts bright and early. Ellen made coffee and tried to stay awake.

Bob and Julie had teenagers and although they had gifts under the tree, probably wouldn't even open them until it was time to go next door for the big gift exchange and party. They enjoyed a quiet house and a simple morning.

Russell and Iris woke up and realized that it wasn't a dream. Ted was in the kitchen already pouring coffee and making toast. If Ted was here, that meant that Forrest was really here, too. It was all real, the moving, the baby and it's a boy.

Adam was still sleeping but he wasn't usually a late sleeper. College couldn't have changed him that much. Iris decided to start the gift giving now. She went under the tree and brought three similar sized boxes to the kitchen. They were marked Ted, Russ and Adam.

Iris slid the ones marked Ted and Russ to each man.

"But I thought the big gift exchange was later?" Ted asked.

"Oh it is," Iris confirmed. "These are souvenirs from Italy. Open."

Ted and Russell did as Iris asked. They unwrapped similar boxes containing similar silver bracelets. They were silver link bracelets and all of them were matching. She picked them out when Russell wasn't looking. She had one for Forrest, too.

"They're beautiful," Ted said admiring both bracelets. Iris helped put them on their wrists. They looked even better on. They were shiny and just chunky enough that you knew they were for a man.

They finished their breakfast and Iris put on Christmas music. She heard foot steps upstairs and knew Adam would be down soon. She felt like a mother of twelve because there were also twelve stockings hanging every which way around the fireplace, one for each of them.

When Adam came down she gave him the silver bracelet. He was surprised and thanked her for thinking of him. Since she and Adam were alone in the kitchen, she took this moment to tell him how she felt about him.

"Adam I want you to know that I think of you as a son," Iris said. "But I don't mean that I feel I am replacing your mom. Never. Just like I tell your father, I'm not trying to replace anyone. I am simply an addition to your family that I hope someday you can accept."

Adam hugged Iris and felt his bottom lip and chin quiver. When he felt he could talk without breaking down he replied, "Thank you, but I already feel like you're part of the family. I see my dad so happy and it's because of you. I love you."

Iris was now almost to tears. "I love you, too." They returned to the living room and waited for everyone else to start arriving. It was already an emotional morning. How was she going to get through this day?

Iris heard Fish barking and knew Forrest and his family were coming. The girls were already carrying a new Barbie doll so she knew that Santa had come. They told their Aunt Iris everything they had gotten while Forrest and Ellen helped themselves to more coffee. They joined the rest of them in the living room.

Iris gave her brother the last of the silver bracelets. He loved it. She gave Ellen a matching bracelet but for a woman. She explained that these were only their Italian souvenirs, not Christmas gifts. Those would come later. The twins were given little coin purses that said, 'Rome' and had little pictures of various sites.

When the Covingtons finally arrived, the party officially began. The music was turned up and Iris took center stage in front of the fireplace.

"Thank you, everyone for spending part of your Christmas with us," Iris said. "As most of you know, I published a book about grief last fall and I asked a few of you to contribute. Well, it is here and I am giving you all a copy. You can read it and share it with whoever you think might need it. It was great therapy to write it."

Iris handed everyone a copy of her book. Everyone knew she planned to write one, only a few knew she did. Adam was embarrassed that everyone would read his words, especially people he knew, but I guess that's why he did it. To help others understand his grief.

Russell nodded to Mandy as a cue to get the gift he had been hiding from Iris. Mandy nodded back and went to the kitchen to retrieve a big box with holes in it. Russell couldn't risk the box being held in his own house, so Mandy was his conspirator and kept it at hers.

Russell took the big box to Iris and said, "Merry Christmas!"

Iris, confused, sat the box down on the floor. It was big but not heavy. She thought she heard something and looked at Russell. Did she really hear a meow? Iris reached inside and pulled out the cutest orange kitten she had ever seen.

"Thank you!" Iris replied. "I'll name her Sandy." Finally out of the box, Sandy walked around the house and smelled everything. Russell, knowing what to expect, had a litter box and food and water bowls already in place.

Iris went over to Russell and kissed him. "You got me a kitten!" She said.

"Yes," Russ replied. "You said you always wanted one but not while living in an apartment. Well, now you have one with thanks to Mandy for hiding her."

Teddy stood up next and grabbed some gift bags behind the tree, one for Mandy, Sarah and Sophia. All three pulled out brand new teddy bears, each with different ribbons around their necks. "From your Uncle Teddy," he said.

Mandy gave Ted a hug and thanked him. Touched by the gesture of including his girlfriend, Adam gave him one, too. The twins ran up to Uncle Teddy and hugged him as well. Iris's rules for the great gift exchange was that it was voluntary and if you did chose to give anything, it had to be under fifteen dollars.

Adam went to the kitchen to get a drink. Mandy followed him holding a gift. Alone, they wanted to exchange theirs in private.

"I got you something, I hope you like it," Mandy said.

"I made yours, if you don't like it I can get something else," Adam replied.

"Don't you dare! I'll love it more because you made it," Mandy said. "You open yours first."

Adam took a moment to appreciate the way she wrapped it. It had ribbon, bows and pretty paper. When he opened the paper he saw a beautiful journal with a tan leather cover. The front was embossed with the letter A. He slowly flipped through the blank lined pages and set it on the kitchen counter.

"Thank you, I love it," Adam said and gave her a hug.

"I know how your mom used to love writing in journals on special days. I thought you might like to do the same thing," Mandy said.

"It's so thoughtful of you to remember that," Adam said and he meant it. He was truly touched.

"I remember how you said she wrote in a journal but she was really writing to you, your future you. And her last wish was for you to be happy, that's my Christmas wish for you, too," Mandy said. "Are you happy?"

"Very happy," Adam said even though the tear coming down the side of his cheek might make her think otherwise. He hugged her so that there was no confusion. "Now open mine."

Mandy unwrapped the fragile gift. It was a large spiral shell with a hole drilled into the top with a red ribbon tied through it. She held it as if it was a bubble that would burst at any moment.

"I love it," Mandy said. "It's like the ones on the shelf in your room."

"Yes," Adam replied. "My mother and I used to find them and collect them. This one I found last summer and it's the biggest one yet."

Mandy gave Adam a hug. She loved this strong, sensitive college boy. This was the best Christmas ever. Adam loved this thoughtful and caring girl. Neither one of them wanted to let go.

That night, after all the festivities ended, Adam sat on his bed. He took out his new leather bound journal and opened it to the first page and wrote his first entry.

Dear Mom,

I'm sitting in the beach house and I've met my future wife.

Acknowledgements

To my husband, Yoshi, for giving me the time and space to write. To my daughter, Alisa, for reading my first draft and loving it.

To my son, Leo, for his constant encouragement.

To my friends and my sister for always being willing to read my first drafts and saying that they were perfect, even when I knew they weren't. Your encouragement has brought me to where I am now.

To Maggie Stiefvater for creating a writing seminar that provided life changing inspiration.

To my parents, who are no longer with us, for their constant love and support.

About the Author

Amy Iketani lives in Stockbridge, Georgia, with her husband and pet cat. Originally from Erie, Pennsylvania, Amy met her husband while working for Club Med and has lived in Florida, Japan and Hawaii. Amy enjoys crocheting, reading, spending time with her two grown children, Alisa and Leo, and traveling with her husband, Yoshi, of thirty two years.

Follow Amy on Instagram @amyiketaniwrites

Don't miss out!

Visit the website below and you can sign up to receive emails whenever Amy Iketani publishes a new book. There's no charge and no obligation.

https://books2read.com/r/B-A-ALFAB-TIDQC

BOOKS 2 READ

Connecting independent readers to independent writers.

Did you love *The Last Wish*? Then you should read *Coming Home*[1] by Amy Iketani!

[2]

Louise Jensen and Jude Weber grew up together on Lake Erie and were high school sweethearts. They are both haunted by a drowning on the lake that happened as children. Louise broke up with Jude after graduation and went away to college. Now a pediatrician in New York City, she has a neurosurgeon boyfriend, Benjamin Brock. The same night that Ben proposes to Louise, she receives a phone call that could change her life. Louise's mother is in a coma and she must return to Erie.

Louise must now face the family and friends she left ten years ago, including Jude. Jude reveals that he still loves her.

---

1. https://books2read.com/u/meqXNE

2. https://books2read.com/u/meqXNE

When Louise returns to New York and accepts Ben's proposal, an unexpected meeting with Jude makes her question her decision. When Louise decides to return to Erie one more time, Ben won't let her go so easily. Does Louise return to her New York life with Ben or does she see a future with Jude in Erie? Louise must now decide where her home truly is.

Coming Home is about the decisions that shape our lives and our happiness. It follows Louise as she both runs away from and returns home to the emotions and friends that she left behind. A book that will take you on an emotional journey with Louise as she discovers herself.

Read more at instagram.com/amyiketaniwrites.

Also by Amy Iketani

Coming Home
The Last Wish

Watch for more at instagram.com/amyiketaniwrites.

About the Author

Amy Iketani lives in Stockbridge, Georgia, with her husband and pet cat. Originally from Erie, Pennsylvania, Amy met her husband while working for Club Med and has lived in Florida, Japan and Hawaii. Amy enjoys crocheting, reading, and spending time with her two grown children, Alisa and Leo, and traveling with her husband, Yoshi, of thirty two years.

Follow Amy on Instagram @amyiketaniwrites

Read more at instagram.com/amyiketaniwrites.